Cover Design by S.E. MacCready

Divided States Logo Illustration by Riley Haring

Upheaval

by AE Faulkner

Book 1 of the Divided States Series

We do not inherit the earth from our ancestors,
we borrow it from our children
- Native American Proverb

Contents

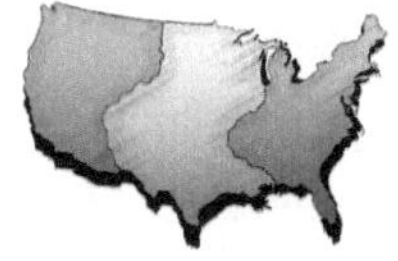

CHAPTER 1

UPPER DIVISION, EASTATES

"Someone's life is about to change." Educator Lynay clasps and unclasps his hands together repeatedly as my classmates and I slide into our seats. *What could make him so enthusiastic on a gloomy Monday?* He makes no attempt to temper his building excitement. "I have a special announcement . . . well, this is really an amazing opportunity."

My best friend, Josli, snaps her head toward me. We share a wide-eyed look of surprise peppered with confusion. Emotion has never spilled so freely from our teacher. While he bustles with unprecedented energy, his perfectly pressed shirt remains unwrinkled, tightly tucked into his blue pants. He's always willing to discuss or explain a concept in great detail, even if his lectures are somewhat monotone. Which makes this morning's animated display unusual and surprising. We all await his next words as a charged buzz slinks through the air.

"Two high-achieving students will be selected from our school to serve as delegates on an inter-Territory delegation." He pauses for a dramatic effect, turning an evaluating eye on the class. "While we've all learned that the Territories adopted the Alliance Agreement decades ago, it seems the time has come for change. Perhaps the terms have become outdated? Perhaps the leaders are relying on the future of the Divided States to lead us all down a new path?" His gaze grows distant, as if possibilities flicker through his mind.

Hushed conversations swell as clusters of students huddle closer and whisper to each other. Random names drift around the room in speculation. Josli leans toward me and whispers, "I bet it's you and me, Everly! Any second now he'll say our names!"

The rising chatter tugs Educator Lynay back to the announcement he was in the middle of giving. He clears his throat, drawing attention back to himself.

"This is history in the making, people. Lessons will be written about this process and the results. And we get to live it." He pauses again, raising a dark eyebrow and standing a bit straighter. "Two of you more so than the rest of us . . . but who knows, maybe the future delegates are sitting in this classroom at this very moment."

A collective gasp sucks the air from the room. Josli stretches her leg across the aisle and taps my foot with hers. Jabbing a pointer finger to her chest, she mouths, "It's me!" I swallow a silent giggle. She has never taken her studies seriously. If they're looking for someone who can rank every guy in school on a hotness scale, she'd be the prime candidate. But somehow I don't think that's what they're looking for.

High achievers. Maybe this is a reward for those who've studied, memorized and tested their way to the top. *An inter-Territory delegation? Nothing like this has ever happened before. Why now?*

Educator Lynay chuckles – an unfamiliar sound that only punctuates what is quickly morphing into the strangest school day ever.

"All of the delegates will learn first-hand more than I could ever teach within these walls. They'll get to see the inner workings of leadership in its highest form. And who knows what kind of inroads this may open not only for them, but for our school. If this . . . opportunity . . . has positive results, the leaders may decide to replicate or expand upon it in other ways."

Excitement flashes through my classmates' eyes as I silently gulp down rising anxiety. I sneak a glance at Josli, but of course she's anticipating it. She's already moved past pretending she'll be selected. Her eyebrows jump toward her auburn bangs as a smile tugs her lips. "Hmmm, high achievers? Now who could that mean, Everly?" she smirks at me. My shoulders rise instinctively as my head drops, hunching in a futile attempt to meld into the desk.

As we near commencement, each student has been ranked by their academic achievements since our first year of schooling. I'm the third top achiever. If I'm lucky, they'll select the top two and completely forget about me.

Exploring the other Territories is stranger than I can even imagine. Everything I need is right here in the Eastates – my family and my friends. The sooner I finish my studies, the sooner I can begin my career path and relieve some of my father's burden.

Learning always gave me a purpose. Like when I'd find my younger brother, Easton, shaking with tears when he was supposed to be peacefully drifting off to sleep. I'd wrap my arms around him and whisper a memorized poem or retell a story I wrote for literature class. Or when dark circles tugged beneath my dad's eyes, I'd stay up late to study by the light of the moon after carving out extra time during the day to pick up our rations or complete an extra household chore so that he didn't have to.

When the darkest memories crept from the corners of my mind, studying provided a welcome distraction, occupying my thoughts with fiction and fractions. I've not missed one assignment. Ever. Not even when Easton and I were excused from school for a week for our allotted grieving period. I still completed the classwork, thanks to Josli, and she turned it in for me so it was never late.

The educators have noticed my scores and persistent dedication. I'm on track to be accepted at my first choice for an occupation – nutritional research. It's an uncommon career path, with extremely limited availability. Researchers aren't needed in our Territory as much as factory workers are. But I know I'd excel in it. I'm eager to learn as much as I can, and I won't stop until I succeed.

I still remember the tantrums Easton would throw during mealtimes. His little face would scrunch in anger. His eyes would pinch closed and his cheeks would blaze crimson. He fussed at every tray of food set in front of him. The best we could hope for was that a meal didn't turn his stomach and make an unwelcome reappearance.

Dad and I would plead and beg for him to eat. When his cheeks grew hollow and his limbs thinned, educators started to notice. The doctor paid us a visit and promptly ordered double rations for Easton until he reached a healthy weight.

With just enough food to go around in our community, it only added to the pressure to make him eat. We couldn't waste rations, and it was clear that others were watching. We had to fix the problem. Luckily, as Easton grew older and more susceptible to reason, he accepted that there was no choice other than the factory-produced sustenance that we all rely on for nutrition.

Still, his outbursts, whether they were exaggerated or self-induced, stayed with me. It was just one more thing I couldn't fix for him. It grew into a motivation to improve the bland blobs I'd just accepted as normal. Farmlands that once nurtured fresh fruits and vegetables were consumed over the years by pollution and environmental degradation. Fresh food is not an option here, but a better way has to exist, and I'm going to be the one to discover it.

Josli nudges my arm, pulling me back into the present, and back to the impending announcement. I don't want to be a delegate. My dad and brother need me, almost as much as I need them.

Educator Lynay launches into the day's history lesson but quickly digresses, interjecting his opinions of how an inter-Territory delegation might best function in various situations. He's just as distracted as the rest of us, and he doesn't seem to notice, or mind, that my peers are consumed with daydreaming about the possibilities.

My thoughts drift to history lessons taught in early school. At the same time we began practicing our ABCs, tidbits about our basic government structure were sprinkled into our studies. At that age, the focus was on numbers. Three Territories – Westates, Centrestates and Eastates. Three Societal Order leaders, one for each Territory. Although each rules independently, times arise when the leaders must agree on decisions that cross the Xones. The odd number ensures there is always a tiebreaker.

I've never been close enough to the border to see one up close, but images of the thick honeycombed Xone walls flash through my mind. Lessons and textbooks I've memorized return, as if summoned by need. The impenetrable sixty-foot walls carve clear barriers between the Territories. They stand tall enough that residents in our neighborhood easily catch a glimpse on their way to work or school. But they no longer warrant a second glance. The Xone wall between us and Centrestates is just a distant giant – an indistinct blur. The walls were built when my parents were kids. Their construction was a major event, but time has faded the novelty and now they just blend into the landscape, a sentinel reminder of our borders. Basically, wherever you're born is where you stay. Citizenship is not granted between Territories. It's not even common to travel within your own Territory, let alone outside of it. We've all been taught that the barriers define and protect us. The only reason to cross them is for trade – and that is limited to those who work as transport overseers. No one else goes near the borders. *So why has that changed now?*

We've been taught that all three Territories function the same way. We share some resources, but only out of necessity. The Eastates is known for textile production. Our factories supply citizens across the whole Divided States with clothing, shoes, towels, sheets and blankets. Centrestates is the powerhouse of the Territories, although we aren't supposed to think like that. They maintain the energy grid that supports us all and grow actual crops. The Westates is known for manufacturing hard goods like tools, machinery and housing structures.

There are rules in place to prevent us from repeating mistakes of the past. All the way back to the country's beginnings, indigenous people cherished the land and animals. Through the years, those values shifted – drastically. Species went extinct. Forests were decimated. Everything we put in our bodies, from air to water to food, was tainted by pollution. The environment basically grew barren from overuse. The repercussions eventually led to societal collapse.

The hour bell rings, jolting me from my wandering thoughts. It signals an official end to Educator Lynay's rambling lesson. As students log out of the classroom's computing devices and push out of their seats, he motions for us to stay in place.

"No need to advance to next period just yet!" His smirk reappears. "I believe we'll all be hearing a special announcement first!"

Temporary annoyance flares into renewed interest. My classmates drop back into their seats, feet tapping and eyebrows raised in anticipation. The silence quickly fades as whispers and gossip flood the air.

Josli leans toward me. "So, what do you think?" I don't bother delaying my answer by asking what she's talking about.

"I think it's strange. Everything works just fine as it is. Why bother bringing in a bunch of kids to talk about it? What do we have to say that's so important? We want less homework and better rations?"

"Maybe someone realizes that things could be better in a bigger sense," she starts. "Like, Ev, what if they actually picked you and me? How much fun would that be?" She wiggles her eyebrows. *Hmmmm. I hadn't considered that.* I know it's not a real possibility, but a trip to Centrestates with my best friend puts a whole different spin on it.

"I'm in!" I say as a giggle tickles my throat. She nods knowingly, as if it's just the two of us about to set out on the adventure of our lives.

A distant buzz grows, quieting the voices within the classroom. The intercom sparks to life, paving anticipatory silence for the principal's announcement. "Good morning, students. As your educators have shared with you by now, the Societal Order leaders have announced the creation of an inter-Territory delegation. This group of delegates will review and make recommendations to revise and update the Alliance Agreement. They will participate in strategy sessions to discuss ways to increase trade and further strengthen relations between the Territories.

"Those who serve in this capacity are the future of the Divided States. And our learning institution has the great honor of having two of our own selected to serve as delegates. Some day they may become our leaders, and they are sitting amongst you right now."

He pauses for emphasis, which only makes my heartbeat quicken as my hands grow slick with sweat. My classmates look just as nervous – some wring their hands together while others shift their eyes around the room, silently evaluating their peers.

"Only two learning institutions in the entire Eastates were chosen to send delegates and we have the honor of being one of them. Two of your peers, those you've known your whole lives, will be leaving us temporarily to represent us in Centrestates."

Along with the rest of the room, Josli practically bounces in her chair even as stillness prevails for just a moment. Too soon, the principal's deep voice cuts through the charged air.

"Please join me in congratulating Hayes Crimshaw and Everly Scott."

CHAPTER 2

UPPER DIVISION, EASTATES

Josli squeals and launches out of her seat, crashing into me in a giddiness-fueled embrace. "I knew it, Ev!" she giggles in my ear. "I knew they'd pick you! I bet you'll be the smartest one there!" My stomach tightens and my vision blurs. It may be the result of my best friend half-tackling, half-hugging me, but more likely my brain is firing panic signals. My classmates' voices blend together in a flurry of conversations – all about me. And Hayes.

My taste buds sour and my heart rate skyrockets. Josli slowly peels herself off me, pressing shaking hands to her nose. A giddy smile peeks out between her fingers. Every cell in her body radiates happiness for me. I can't help but smile back at her. That is, until I notice that the voices surrounding us begin to fade, quickly replaced with eager silence.

I suddenly feel exposed. Bare. Sometimes the way my hair falls, it covers part of my face and I'll just leave it hanging there, blocking me from anyone's direct view. I like that small hint of invisibility. If I could wrap my long brown strands around me and disappear into it right now, I would. *I'm seventeen, what could I possibly have to offer?* Just as quickly, guilt spears through me.

This is an incredible opportunity, and I should defy any disbelief coursing through my classmates right now. *If only I could.* Instead, fear cuts to my core. My breathing grows shallow as I feel the weight of a dozen sets of eyes landing on me, scrutinizing my reaction to the news.

Swallowing the spiking anxiety, I focus on projecting the perfect blend of surprise, happiness and modesty. It's not often that I garner others' attention. In fact, the only other time I can remember is when whispers spread, faster than a wildfire, that my mother had died. I prepare myself for the same range of reactions from neighbors and classmates – from care and concern to ignoring me entirely, choosing the safety of silence rather than tiptoeing around words that they either can't find or fear might come out wrong. Back when it happened, most of them were probably just unsure of what to say, thankful that they couldn't even remotely relate to my situation. Worst of all was those who eyed me with disdain, as if I was a spectacle, or perhaps my loss was contagious and they might suffer just by association.

Educator Lynay maneuvers through the maze of desks while extending an arm toward me as if he's presenting a shiny new object to the class.

"Everly! Congratulations!" His eyes rove the classroom, and he raises his hands dramatically before breaking into a round of applause. When my peers join in, I fight the urge to shrink into myself, as if it's even possible. Heat flushes over my cheeks. As the clapping subsides, he leans down just inches from my ear, his next words meant for only my ears. "You've earned this. Embrace it, Everly. It's well-deserved."

Despite my fears, a smile spreads across my face. He gives me a sharp nod before straightening and sweeping his eyes across the room.

"I believe I speak for all of us, Everly, when I say how incredibly proud I am. You deserve the utmost congratulations. You and Hayes will make excellent delegates."

Thankfully, before he can continue or anyone can add to or detract from his sentiments, the hour bell rings again, signaling it's time to move to the next class. My peers shoot me a few curious glances as they bolt out of their seats, gathering books and bags. Josli slinks up beside me as I slowly stand and shuffle out the door. As much as I'd like to fade into the stream of bodies and the anonymity it offers, an electric buzz seems to follow each step I take.

Muscle memory carries me to my next class. As we walk, Josli launches into a ramble of rhetorical questions – *I wonder how soon you and Hayes leave? How long will you be there? Where will you stay?* She knows I can't answer any of them, but she's powerless to contain the thoughts flooding her mind. It's one of the things I love about her. She's completely free with her thoughts and feelings.

Focusing on avoiding any bodies weaving through the flow of students, the best I can offer is a noncommittal grunt in return. When she falls silent, I glance over to make sure I'm not walking alone. Eyebrows scrunched, she scans me as if I'm a specimen under a microscope.

"Everly, you look a little pale. You know it's all going to be okay, right?" Josli's green eyes reflect concern.

"I know, I know . . . it's all just . . . really overwhelming. And I really wish you were going with me."

"I'll do my best to spawn a curly nest of red hair and find some glasses that magnify my eyes by about a hundred times before you leave. We just have to somehow hide Hayes so I can pretend to be him." She glances to the ceiling as if in deep thought. "Nah, I'm way too cute, no one will believe I'm him!"

I giggle and muster a weak smile. "Distract me?"

She nods quickly and launches into a breathless dissertation about what today's lunch will probably be, how much homework we'll end up with tonight and how her crush still hasn't acknowledged her many attempts to flirt with him. She knows that any topic is safe, other than an inter-Territory delegation. It's exactly what I need right now, and my best friend is an expert at filling silence with nonsense.

Knowing I'm off the hook for reciprocating any sort of response, my mind wanders, tuning Josli out. I try to focus on taking one step at a time, breathing in and breathing out, the here and now. But within a minute, I wish I hadn't tuned in to the voices drifting through the hallway.

Whispered assumptions and accusations reach my ears and flush my cheeks. *She barely talks and she was picked? I bet she won't say two words the whole time she's there. They should have had a test or something to make it fair. Do you think she'll really go? Why was she picked, and not me?*

Just one more class until lunch, but the last thing my churning stomach craves is food. The big announcement, and certain reactions to it, have doused my appetite.

If I could disappear at this moment, I would. Most of the time I walk these halls virtually invisible. It suits me and my peers. The sudden rush of attention fizzles any pride I started to feel from Educator Lynay's encouraging words last period. Yanking me from my thoughts, Josli calls a quick "bye" over her shoulder as she turns down an adjacent hallway, scurrying to her next class. The comfort of having my best friend nearby dissolves like a wispy cloud that's floating away, farther out of reach.

Pushing past the discomfort, I focus on moving forward, forcing one foot in front of the other. Up next is my favorite class, taught by my favorite educator. Maybe today's lesson will distract me from the impending unknown. I slide into my seat in literature just as class begins, which would technically make me tardy. Thankfully Educator Kopitar flashes me a knowing nod but ignores the minor infraction. I guess my new status has one perk at least.

While her lessons typically hold my interest, today I struggle to focus. After a brief review of yesterday's lesson, she instructs us to select a computing device and power it on. We have ten minutes to complete a practice test she's loaded with review questions. While everyone else reads and begins typing, my mind drifts to distant history lessons that have suddenly gained importance, necessitating a deep dig into the corners of my memory.

The three Societal Order leaders meet four times a year. The main purpose is to ensure limited but seamless commerce between Territories. They have no interest in sharing authority or co-leading, but they work together out of necessity.

Eighty years ago, the country was rebuilding after a global pandemic. Millions perished, infrastructure collapsed and the environment faltered after centuries of abuse and overuse. Those who survived struggled to meet their basic needs. And, even with a fraction of the population left, desperation bred violence. Competition for food and shelter ignited small wars in every population pocket. At least among those strong enough to defy the virus.

Supplies of dry and canned provisions eventually depleted. Some were capable of hunting and gathering, but that presented the risk of consuming tainted animals or vegetation. Poisoned land and water didn't exactly yield healthy natural food sources.

As civility deteriorated, leaders rose to establish order throughout the country. They were thrust into power and sent to the then-capital to claim their throne when the single leader of the United States succumbed to the virus. Rather than challenging each other or sharing authority, they came together and drew up a plan – carving the country into three sections with the intent to close borders and function as independently as possible.

They effectively isolated first the country from the rest of the world, and then citizens within the country from each other. They did such a good job all those years ago that it feels like the other Territories are a world away even now.

"Miss Scott? Everly!"

My throat constricts as my eyes land on Educator Kopitar, who towers over me. I guess I've exceeded any goodwill free pass she was willing to grant me when I swept into class late.

"Yes?" I squeak, heat flushing my cheeks.

"Everly, I know this is a very exciting time, but you must still complete your work here, at least until you leave us." She winks and spins on her heel, striding back to the front of the classroom.

I shake my head, clearing out the distractions, and lean closer to my computer screen. *I haven't even started the practice test.* I'm not sure how much time I wasted, but I've got to concentrate. Scanning each question as quickly as possible, my fingers dance over the keys as I attempt to answer each one, even if it's brief. When the ten minutes are up, Educator Kopitar tells us to submit our final responses and shut down the devices.

I spend the rest of class feigning interest as my peers interpret this week's assignments. I grant just enough attention to their answers to formulate an acceptable response when I'm called on. Minutes slither at a snail's pace. When the hour bell rings, I nearly jump out of my seat and sprint through the door.

The cafeteria is inconveniently located on the complete opposite side of the building. My only goal is to avoid talking with anyone between here and there. As I walk, I retreat to the safety of my own thoughts, reprising the history lesson I attempted to conjure in literature.

The three leaders agreed to create three societies that mirrored each other. Each had to accommodate for severely limited resources. Necessities – food, shelter, clothing, electricity – were stretched beyond their limits. They had to be prioritized and rationed. Decisions had to be made and, more importantly, followed unquestioningly.

Centrestates supplies each Territory with energy. When the Territories were mapped out, each one was divided into northern and southern regions, called the divisions. To avoid overburdening the power grid, regions within the Territories were grouped together by their awake status – day dwellers and night dwellers.

The day dwellers, or citizens of the upper divisions, are granted ninety percent of Eastates' power from six a.m. until six p.m. That same source is funneled to the lower divisions from six p.m. to six a.m. Here in the Eastates, Societal Order Leader Tage Ault says this is the most efficient use of resources.

Citizens work, attend school, pick up rations and partake in recreation activities during their designated twelve-hour timeframe. The only difference is whether the sun or the moon brightens the sky. Leader Ault insists that each citizen is equally important, but I wonder if the night dwellers feel that way.

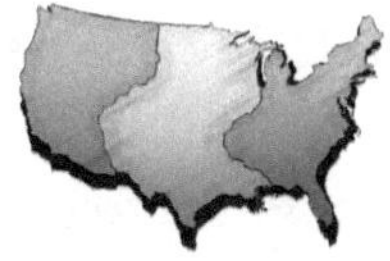

CHAPTER 3

UPPER DIVISION, EASTATES

There's no time for recreational activities during the school and work week, but we get time on the weekends. In the upper division, as day dwellers, Josli and I usually choose wildlife watching for our recreational activity. We have to drag along clipboards and make note of any animals we see, and their condition, but at least we get to explore areas beyond our neighborhood. The more animals we document, the better. It would signal that the land is healing and can support more life. But the numbers we report are pretty low every time – a random squirrel here, a rabbit or two there.

My dad likes to take my younger brother Easton fishing for their leisure time. Anything they catch must be reported to the Nutrition Production Facility and turned in as a donation. Even if they don't get to keep it, my dad says the thrill of the catch is the best part. Besides, Easton probably wouldn't eat whatever they caught anyway.

It makes me wonder what sort of recreational activities the night dwellers have. *I don't think any of ours would be fun or useful in the dark. In that sense, are the divisions truly equal?*

The one thing we all have in common is the need for electricity – the main commodity that necessitated trade across the borders. We all have twelve hours to go to work, school and ration pickups. For the other twelve hours, we remain in our homes because energy allowance is kept to a bare minimum.

Solar-powered devices are allowed during the off-hours but there's not exactly a surplus of them, and they only produce dim funnels of light. Of course, that's if you remember to charge them in direct sunlight. Still, it's better than nothing. I shake away the thoughts and push through the cafeteria doors.

I scan the clusters of swarming bodies in search of Josli. Rising on my tiptoes, I spot her at our usual table, tucked in the far back corner of the room. It's one of the few small tables, with seats we can actually slide around rather than just a long row of stiff stools attached to a never-ending rectangular table.

Catching my eye, she drops her bag and sweeps through the crowd to meet me. We seamlessly slip into the flowing line and wait our turn to collect lunch rations. As mundane as the routine is, it's comforting. *Will I eat in a cafeteria like this in Centrestates?*

"Soooooooooooo . . . how're you doing?" Josli nudges my shoulder as we scan the limited options.

"All right," I admit. She sneaks a side-eye glance my way as I reach for a shallow bowl of noodles in a gloppy white sauce. "I just have no idea what to expect. And I hate that."

"It's like an adventure." Wrinkling her nose, she slides a plate of slightly burnt fish sticks onto her tray. "And you won't be completely alone. Hayes isn't exactly Mr. Excitement, but at least you'll have someone with you. And he won't know anyone either."

"Yeah." I shrug and force a weak smile. She's just trying to make me feel better. *How am I going to do this without her?*

We shuffle through the chute of remaining food options, selecting a few of the less nefarious-looking concoctions. We drop into our seats as if this is any other day, but the feel is all wrong. I pick at my lunch while Josli chatters about how fast my time in Centrestates will go and how I'll probably like it way better than Eastates. I nod and shrug, playing along with her impossible prediction. Mid-bite, her eyes fly open wide and she slams a palm down on the table.

"Ev, I just realized. You're going to meet nocts! Real night dwellers!" I cringe at her use of the slang term for night, or nocturnal, dwellers. She knows we're not supposed to call them "nocts," but it flows from her freely as excitement overtakes my best friend. I wonder if she'd be offended if someone called us "dayds" instead of day dwellers.

She presses her palms together, resting her elbows on the table. It's a useless effort to restrain her mounting anticipation. "Promise me you'll memorize every detail about them! I need to know what they eat, how they dress, what they look like . . ."

That's typical for Josli – craving every drop of gossip I can squeeze out of this trip. Still, my heartbeat surges as her words sink in. I have a feeling I'll find out the answers to all her questions and more.

She pauses momentarily to stab a dry hunk of fish stick and nibble on it. I welcome the break in questioning. But as soon as she chews and swallows, she restarts where she left off.

"Everly, you must be wondering too! Maybe all the nocts are tall, dark and scary!" She twirls an auburn lock of hair around her finger, staring at me expectantly but I shoot her a wary expression.

My eyes dart from side to side, assessing if anyone around us is listening. Luckily they're all caught up in their own conversations, oblivious to our words. They hover over their plates and bowls, pushing food around as they share laughter and gossip. Any buzz over the big announcement is already fizzling, replaced with the latest rumors about who's got a crush on who. Still, paranoia pushes me to exert caution.

"Josli! I don't think we should be talking about all of this." It's not like our conversations are monitored, but this delegation is something directly from the Societal Order leaders. She doesn't even flinch at my warning, but if one of the educators heard us talking like this, they might believe we were making light of it. The least that would happen is we'd be reprimanded for speaking disrespectfully of the Divided States leaders and citizens.

"Oh no one cares! But they will care when you get back! And I'm going to be the first to know every detail about everything you see and do there!" Just as quickly she shifts back to speculating about the night dwellers. "So, what do you think they're like?" Her eyes flash with a curiosity that borders on being prohibited. Sighing inwardly, I resign myself to the topic. She's not going to let it go.

I slump in my seat, eager to end the conversation. Maybe class would be a good distraction right about now. "Night dwellers are probably exactly like us. Who knows if I'll even be able to tell the difference between them and the other day dwellers. Besides, we'll probably just be sitting in classrooms together. We may not even have a chance to talk about anything interesting." My indifference only fuels her curiosity.

"If it's a delegation, you'll have meetings, where you all sit around and talk. And I bet they'll take you to the capitol. At the very least you should get a tour, but maybe you'll even have your meetings there. And . . . since that's in the upper division, you'll function like day dwellers." She folds her arms and leans back in the chair, obviously pleased with the information she's deduced. Never mind that she could be completely wrong. When I respond with a noncommittal smirk, she continues. As she leans forward in her chair, a smile bursts across her cheeks.

"Do you think the nocts will be dozing off?" She yawns and flutters her eyes as if she can't keep them open. "You'll all be in the middle of an intense discussion and one of them will start snoring!" *She's enjoying this way too much.*

"Just because they're used to being inside during the day doesn't mean they sleep every hour that the sun is up. They're not vampires!"

"Well, just in case, keep your neck covered!" she warns, wrapping her palms around her neck protectively in feigned worry.

With that, we both chuckle, remembering the stories about night dwellers from when we were kids. Silly fabrications that made little sense but captured our curiosity and ignited our imaginations. We were all guilty of sharing whispered tales of night dwellers feasting on blood instead of rations. Whether they hunted animals to drain or shared blood with each other, the stories grew more tantalizing as our creativity soared.

When the giggles subside, Josli flashes right back to the interrogation.

"Do you know anything yet?" She twists her hands in the air, as if they're a conduit of her thoughts. "Like, when do you leave? What will you *really* do there?"

I shake my head and blow out a sigh. *I don't know any more about this than anyone else.* It feels like I should, but this was never a question asked of me. I learned about it over a loudspeaker, along with every other person not chosen. *Shouldn't the delegates be asked if they even want to do it?*

Anyone else in my position would probably be excited and proud to have been chosen, but worry shadows my every thought. I doubt Hayes is walking around like a ball of exposed nerve endings, afraid of whatever comes next.

The hour bell rings, signaling it's time to deposit our cups, trays and utensils in labeled dish tubs so they can be washed, ready for the next slew of students.

Filing into the hallway, the crowd absorbs us, two more among dozens of teenagers rushing to their next class. We're carried along in the continuous stream of bodies. I slip out of the flow and into my math class, barely settling into a seat before an announcement turns me right back around.

"Good afternoon, students. I apologize for a second interruption today, but I'd like to request the presence of our inter-Territory delegates, Hayes Crimshaw and Everly Scott, in the main office."

My summons electrifies a renewed buzz in the air. Eager to avoid any sort of dopey grin or encouraging nod, I don't even wait for the educator to dismiss me. I've been called to the office. There's no question that I have permission to go. My peers cast curious glances my way as I rush out the door, their penetrating eyes landing on my back and fueling my steps. I'm eager to leave the unwanted attention behind, even if it's just temporary.

My feet follow the path to the principal's office. I'm grateful it's a mindless effort. Unanswered questions shuffle through my mind, none pausing long enough to truly settle. *What will the other delegates be like? Will I be too shy and self-conscious to share my thoughts? Will we be locked in a classroom together, the door sealed until the Societal Order leaders decide we've met their expectations?*

As I turn the final corner, familiar frizzy red hair and oversized glasses come into view. Hayes Crimshaw waits in the office, practically bouncing on his feet. Of course Hayes is already here. He probably sprinted out of his classroom before the names were even announced. I guess that's why he's the top academic achiever in our class. In the entire school for that matter. *Why don't I feel even a quarter of his enthusiasm?* I was chosen for a reason. I've earned this just as much as he has. But the sinking pit of anxiety in my stomach refuses to let up.

When he catches my movement, he slows the nervous shuffle enough to launch toward me. "They told me I had to wait for you to get here. Come on, let's go!" He turns sharply and marches to the thin wooden barrier separating us from redeeming our big prize.

CHAPTER 4

UPPER DIVISION, EASTATES

Principal DeBrusk settles into his thick leather chair. Resting his elbows on the desk's polished wooden surface, he steeples his hands and leans forward.

"I trust you both understand what an incredible honor this is. Your academic performance has served as a beacon of recognition for this school as well as our community." Genuine pride seeps from his words. "We've caught the attention of the Societal Order leadership and I can't wait to see what you do with it." He smiles as if this is a compliment, but the thought only twists my stomach into tighter knots.

"I think I can speak for both of us when I say we will make you and the entire school proud!" Hayes shoots me a grin. I plaster a smile across my face and nod. He barely knows me, and has no right to speak for me, but in the moment I'm grateful for the excuse to keep my mouth clamped shut. I don't dare speak, fearing what mix of emotions might spill out.

"I'm glad to hear that." Principal DeBrusk nods toward Hayes before eyeing me quizzically as if awaiting verbal confirmation of my agreement. I don't offer it. Instead I force a broader smile across my face.

"I've been told that this council of delegates will be charged with creating a new peace treaty, based on the Alliance Agreement, but updated and improved upon. I guess they're hoping young people will spark new ideas, ones that old-timers like me would never think of." He chuckles to himself, but I sense a hint of regret . . . or is it jealousy? His distracted gaze lands just above our heads. Much like Educator Lynay, speculation seems to consume him. Just for a moment.

"Whatever you all come up with may be adopted across all three Territories. Now I'm sure the leaders will have to approve it first, but there's a good chance something one, or both, of you suggests will become part of our future governing. To do this, twelve delegates will travel to Centrestates. They've chosen two each from the upper and lower divisions of each Territory."

His jaw hanging in awe, Hayes shakes his head. "This is unbelievable. Only twelve chosen and we're among them. I can't wait to get there."

"Well good!" Principal DeBrusk taps his hand on the desk to emphasize his appreciation for Hayes' enthusiasm. When he shoots me a side glance, I sense his disappointment that I'm not echoing the same sentiments.

"I've spoken to your parents to explain the process and they were all agreeable. So basically, you'll both get a two-week vacation to Centrestates, and you'll be excused from your studies during this time."

Two weeks? My stomach clenches and I swallow the bile burning the back of my throat. I'm leaving home for two weeks. I've never spent a night away. Ever. I focus on breathing in through my nose and out through my mouth while holding my facial muscles in an expressionless mask.

"Now don't misunderstand. Your time will be spent purposefully. But you will be excused from all your usual schoolwork and duties while you serve on the delegation. They'll take care of you while you're there. And as soon as you've fulfilled your duty to the Societal Order, you'll be delivered right back here to complete the school year."

Hayes nods enthusiastically. "How soon do we go?" Goose bumps creep along my arms. I don't want to know the answer, but either way it will consume my every thought until the time comes.

"The day after tomorrow," Principal DeBrusk announces, raising his hand in the air and wiggling two stubby fingers for emphasis. *That's it? Two measly days to prepare?* "You'll take that time to pack clothing, finish up any current outstanding assignments and bid your loved ones farewell . . . for now." He slides his chair backward a foot as the wheels squeak in protest.

Flattening his palms atop two small stacks of papers I didn't notice before, he pushes them across the desk's surface toward us. "These are your instructions, where to report and when. Take them home and show your parents. If you have any homework to complete, finish it tonight and deliver it to the school tomorrow morning. Otherwise, we will see you upon your return."

He raises his eyebrows as his eyes volley back and forth between us. I guess we're dismissed. Hayes and I awkwardly turn toward each other and slowly rise.

As we walk toward the door, Principal DeBrusk stands, adding, "Good luck and we can't wait to hear all about it when you return. I'm thinking we'll hold an all-building assembly so you can share your experience with everyone."

My lunch threatens to make an encore appearance while Hayes' shoulders straighten with renewed pride. I mumble a "Yes, sir" in unison with Hayes' enthusiastic rendition before we slip out the door.

How can life change so drastically, so quickly? How am I going to do this?

The rest of the day passes in a haze of jumbled thoughts and anxiety-ridden daydreams. I manage to shuffle through my classes, displaying just enough attention to slide past the educators' notice. If I answer a question early in the lesson, I can safely allow my thoughts to drift as long as I offer a nod or other physical affirmation at a critical point in the discussion.

When the final bell rings, I rush outside to meet Josli. She's already waiting for me. Although she casually leans against a handrail clutching her workbooks, she's clearly ready to pounce.

"Hey!" she calls, waving as if I don't see her. When I draw near, she tilts her chin down and quietly asks, "You doing okay?" She eyes me as if I may bolt rather than answer the simple question.

I release a sigh. "I kind of have to be okay with everything. Don't you think?"

She nods, flashing me a sad smile, and nudges my elbow. "Come on, let's walk home."

***

As we walk, my eyes track every last detail I'll be leaving too soon. Rows of brick homes line the street. The once deep crimson blocks have faded and crumble at the corners, but they serve their purpose. Each house looks the same, weathered by decades of storms, sunlight and a shortage of building materials for upkeep.

Josli tugs me close for a quick hug before we part ways. Somehow my feet carry me the rest of the way home. Left alone with my thoughts, I wish I could give this opportunity to someone else. Not that it would ever be a choice. Still, I bet most of my classmates would eagerly volunteer to go in my place – crossing the Xone walls and visiting another Territory. As exciting as it may turn out to be, I'm perfectly fine staying right here.

I shuffle up the two steps leading to the front door, pressing my palm to its smooth surface. Swirling my fingertips in the dust, I draw a heart. Satisfied with the remnant I'll leave behind, I slip inside our small, unremarkable home.

Pausing just beyond the doorway, I swallow the emotion tugging at my chest. Hesitation plants my feet in place, but I've got to keep moving. I want to analyze every inch of our space, deliberately, committing it to memory. The sagging green couch. The narrow cracks sprouting from the corners and ceiling. The chipped blue vase my parents were gifted on their wedding day. All the imperfections embedded within these rooms, embracing me with tangible comfort.

Our house is just like all the others in the neighborhood – just one among rows upon rows of boxy, brick structures. The only difference is the memories it holds. Immortalized reminders of my mother, random moments that flood my mind. If only they would flee just as quickly, but the flashbacks linger – of her reading to Easton, helping me with homework, unpacking the food rations. Those moments still happen, but they've become almost mechanical without her.

I shake my head, willing the rising sorrow to the recesses of my thoughts. There's never a good time for the memories to reappear. All they do is remind me of what will never be again. Hopefully someday I'll be ready to reflect on happy times, instead of focusing on what we've lost.

That's one good thing about the Societal Order. Because of the structure in place, by the time we graduate, we'll all know our career paths. I'll live right here unless I choose to marry someday. And even then, my husband and I would be assigned a home somewhere within the upper division, depending on what was available. For the most part, our lives are predictable. At least I thought so, until this whole delegate thing happened.

Darting down the hallway, I escape to the isolation of my bedroom. Squeezing my eyes shut, I inhale a few deep breaths until I'm relaxed enough to face my family. Easton will be home soon. If he senses that I'm worried about this trip, he'll be upset too. Never mind that it was never a question as to if I'd go. It was an announcement, a decree, straight from the Societal Order leaders. To think that I might meet even one of them would be a once-in-a-lifetime honor.

I just hope my absence won't disrupt the household too much. The three of us have settled into comfortable patterns and habits. Now Dad and Easton will have to adjust to a temporary routine until I'm back home.

I step into the hallway just as the front door swings open. But the voice reaching out to me is not my little brother's.

"Evvvvveeerllly! Where are you? I spoke with Principal DeBrusk today," my father calls, footsteps thumping into the living room. *He's never home from work this early.* Half a step behind him, Easton slips over the threshold before the door clicks closed behind him.

"Is Everly in trouble?" My little brother perks with interest, tossing his schoolbooks aside and rushing toward us, ears tuned for a response.

"Quite the opposite, son, but I'm glad to see you've got the utmost confidence in your sister." Dad ruffles my younger brother's hair playfully.

"What's going on?" Easton's eyes dart back and forth between us. I crouch down to meet him at eye level, processing how to explain this to an eight-year-old.

"Well, bud, I got picked for a special assignment. I get to go to Centrestates to help them make sure all the Territories can work together to do what's best for everyone." His forehead crinkles with confusion.

"You're leaving?" A glassy sheen washes over his brown eyes. I grasp his shoulders and offer a brave smile.

"Yes, but not for long. I'll be back before you even know it, Easton. And I tell you what, I'll find a way to bring something back from Centrestates for you."

"Something for me? Like a gift?" My redirect works. His eyes shine with excitement now, the sadness temporarily forgotten.

"Many years ago people would buy souvenirs when they went on a trip," Dad explains. "Little tokens to help them remember places they visited. Or as gifts for those waiting back at home."

"Souvenirs?" Easton gasps, his eyes wide with wonder and anticipation. "I want a souvenir!" This time I ruffle his hair. This is the most normal I've felt all day and it's because of him.

"You got it, bud! I'm going to get you something really cool. You just wait!"

Easton wraps his arms around me and squeezes. Dad smiles and nods, a silent "thank you." Now I just have to fulfill the promise I've made.

***

After dinner, the wall receiver hums, our signal that it's almost time for tonight's information broadcast. I roll my eyes and yawn, completely uninterested in hearing reminders about ration pickups, updates on sections of the neighborhood that will be closed this week, and a list of neighbors who received infractions.

Easton and I used to make a game out of listening – trying to guess what the person speaking looked like. It's not like we'd ever find out, so we could stretch our imaginations and pretend they had purple hair or green skin. But right now, the last thing I care about is tonight's announcements and who's giving them. The humming reverberates, louder and longer.

"Hear that?" Dad asks, his eyebrows jumping. "Principal DeBrusk said they'd announce the delegation tonight! Everyone will know that you were chosen, Everly!"

"I think I'll skip listening tonight if that's okay?" His smile fades to a frown but he nods. I retreat to my room and collapse on the creaky mattress. Burying my face in the pillow, I welcome the encompassing nothingness. That is until my breathing grows ragged and my lungs demand full access to air. Flipping to my backside, I drape an arm over my eyes. It effectively blocks any remaining rays of the sinking sun that dare peek through my sagging window.

I have no outstanding assignments, so that means I don't report to school tomorrow at all. I'm sure Hayes won't be there either. He's probably worked so far ahead that he could graduate right now if he wanted to. It makes me wonder what career path he plans to follow after graduation. I guess I'll have plenty of time to ask him.

I ought to start packing, but rather than sifting through my dresser for shirts and pants, burdensome thoughts weigh on my mind, demanding attention. All my usual responsibilities will fall to my father while I'm away. Meal preparation. Weekly textile and food ration pickup. Helping Easton with his homework. *It's only two weeks.* I repeat the words in my mind, but they bring little comfort. I try another approach.

In just fourteen days, life will return to a comfortable normal. Now if only I could believe that.

CHAPTER 5 ~ KIERA

UPPER DIVISION, CENTRESTATES

*O*ne *month earlier*

"Leader Imperant, I really need to speak with you." I pause just outside his door, which hovers partially open. Swinging the door slightly wider, I peek my head through the narrow opening. "I have an update about the compliance study."

This is the third time in two days that I've tried to pin him down to discuss this. Kirill Imperant is my superior, but my patience is wearing. This conversation needs to happen now.

"Yes, of course, Kiera," he mutters, waving me in. "Close the door and have a seat."

A hint of satisfaction flickers through me. *It shouldn't have taken this much effort to gain his attention, but at least I've got it now.* I slide into the chair directly across from him. Its rigid high back and raised armrests make it feel like a throne. Although it's uncomfortable, it guides my spine so that I sit up straighter. That may help him stay focused on me and the information I have to share.

"Leader Imperant, I received a report today from our head analyst regarding the team that has been monitoring non-compliant activity in all three Territories. Their latest findings point to the compliance chips. The chips, or implants as our medical personnel prefer to call them, are injected into the forebrain to stimulate two key sections. The cerebral nuclei reward useful behaviors and the hypothalamus controls appetites, defensive behaviors and sleep-wakefulness. Obviously these are all inte—"

"Enough with the long useless explanation!" He slams a fist on the table. "What do I need to know?"

I bite back the snarky retort begging to educate him on just how lucky he is to have me on his side. I smooth back the wispy golden strands of hair tickling my forehead and channel a sense of control, letting it wash over me. If my emotions take over, he won't hear a word I say. *Stay polished.*

"Sir, the point is that our security forces have been tracking an increase in rebellious behaviors. Especially in Eastates."

"And how is this any different from what you've told me at least a dozen times already?" He stands, turning his back to me, and takes a few steps toward the window, gazing out, clearly bored. It's his verbal wave-off. But I'm not accepting it this time. He *will* listen and he *will* act. Now.

"One of our top analysts reviewed the data and noticed an intriguing pattern that points us toward the source." His gaze slides to my reflection in the window he faces. Finally, he's interested.

"It's taken years, but we can finally correlate the ages of those who have caused a spike in transgressions with the time that the elder Societal Leader Ault passed away." I pause and stand, slinking toward him. How the tables have turned. Now he listens raptly. I run my finger along the window.

"The old man was a firm believer in the brain implants, but his son, Tage, always took issue with it. We believe that when leadership passed to him, Tage quietly discontinued the program."

He rubs his chin, staring outside. Thoughts are churning in his mind. He knows I'm right, and not just because I'm rarely wrong. While he's still silent, I bolster my case.

"All he'd have to do was send an order to the head of each birthing facility in the upper and lower divisions. Stop producing the implant and destroy any remaining supply. From that moment on, no babies would receive the injection." I press my palms together and patiently wait for it all to sink in.

"He voted against it years ago," he says slowly, all of his earlier impatience drained from his tone. His gaze grows distant for just a moment before he waves a hand in the air, banishing the memory. "But Huntsman and I were in the majority so it stayed. Or so we thought."

"And perhaps it did." I pause, enjoying the intensity behind his eyes as he watches me, waiting for my next words. "But either way, we need to know for certain. Because something is changing, and if it's not the implants, then we need to shift our focus and determine the true cause."

"What makes you believe Ault could have stopped the implants?"

"The proof is in the data, as always. It's based on what we've been able to observe since Ault obviously isn't giving up any information."

"Let me guess, the solution is your delegation idea." He scoffs, moving back to his seat behind the desk.

"This is the perfect time." I spin toward him and press my lips together. *Slow down. Not too fast, not too eager.*

"The information we have makes the delegation all the more critical. I admit, it's a small sample – miniscule, in fact. But if we can verify the presence or absence of an implant, we'll have our answer. We select four delegates from each Territory, and every single one of them should have it."

He nods. Not quite the reaction I deserve. Where's the "Kiera, I am nothing without you" or "Kiera, I will never doubt or question you again"? But it will have to do. It's all he's capable of right now. But that's okay. I'm molding him into the man he can be. The process is slower than I anticipated, but I'm not one to shrink in the face of challenge.

"How do you plan to confirm whether they have it?" He feigns mild interest, but his intrigue is palpable.

"That's the beauty of it." I take a step toward him, flashing a wide smile. "There is a noninvasive way we can check. They'll never even know we looked."

"And what does that entail?" He steeples his hands, resting his elbows on the desk. What he really wants to know is, will anyone know what we're doing, or suspect anything?

"Just a simple trip to the power grid – we'll call it a tour." I turn my hand in the air in time with my words. The plan needs some detailing, but overall it's genius. "For fun, we'll pass through the X-ray machine and they can have a look at their insides while we capture images to study."

"What's your suggested timeline?" He taps a finger on the table casually, as if he isn't hanging on my every word.

"The sooner the better. I'd say by month's end we get them here. If this theory proves wrong, we'll need to pivot quickly to investigate alternate probable causes for the increase in documented defiant behavior. Whatever is happening, we must contain it to Eastates before it has a chance to spread here or to Westates."

"Put together your plan and arrange for a call with Huntsman and Ault. We'll present it as an opportunity to strengthen the Territories. Who could say no to that, after all?" The corners of his eyes crinkle as he flashes me a grin. That flicker of approval and hint of playfulness are rare but incredibly rewarding. It's why I do everything I do.

"Yes, sir. If you'll excuse me, I have a few calls to make." I turn and march out the door without looking back.

CHAPTER 6

UPPER DIVISION, EASTATES

After tossing and turning most of the night, my overactive mind finally tires. At some point, it releases me to a dreamless sleep. By the time I wake, light spills in through my windows. Half the morning is gone.

My heart flutters with panic before memories of yesterday return. I'm supposed to miss school today. It's my last full day at home before the trip to Centrestates. Rubbing my temples, I chastise myself for missing one of my last chances to spend time with Dad and Easton.

I didn't even hear them getting ready for the day. Disappointment curdles in the pit of my stomach. *How did I sleep through the usual morning routine?*

Releasing a deep sigh, I force my body out of bed. The longer I stay put, the sharper the regret will sting. As I wash and dress, I make a mental list of everything I can do to relieve some stress for my dad in the coming weeks.

After gulping down a bowl of oatmeal, I check the yard for any property violations. We're all required to maintain the inside and outside of our homes. No Enforcer has ever paid us a visit, asking to look around inside, but the outside is obviously more visible. We're really not sure how closely potential violations are monitored, if at all. But we don't want to find out either. We would never intentionally break the rules.

I push out the door and circle the house. Barehanded, I yank a few straggly weeds creeping around the perimeter. Other than four or five small patches of yellowed grass, the yard is a narrow stretch of dusty dirt. Next I check the sectioned-off garden that runs behind our house. It stretches the length of the street and each neighbor whose yard it adjoins is responsible for helping to maintain it. In the years since the local Enforcers delivered special fencing and set it up, it's barely yielded anything more than crisp twigs of failed corn stalks and mushy pink sacks of what should have been tomatoes.

Still, we're required to try. I think the plan was to reduce food rations if we could supplement our diets with fresh fruits and vegetables grown within each neighborhood. So far it's failed. My thoughts drift to early school, when we learned about the Global Infection Spread and events leading up to it nearly a century ago.

At a time when human destruction had all but completely ravaged the environment, a series of natural disasters claimed millions of lives across the country. Just as those survivors began to rebuild, a viral pandemic swept through the remaining population, decimating it further.

It was as if the Earth chose to cleanse itself.

Maybe one event caused the other, or maybe the combination of destruction and disaster proved too much for civilization to remain intact, as it once was. These were all factors that led to our Divided States. Even today, our textbooks remind us that if we want a sustainable future, we must follow the Societal Order's laws. It's the only way to ensure that resources are divided among all who need them.

A rumble of thunder startles me from my wandering thoughts. *The garden.* I've got more things to do, and I'm wasting time just standing here waiting for a storm to drench me. Darkening clouds roil in the distance, likely headed this way. It's enough motivation to quicken my pace.

After making sure the rain barrel is draining properly, watering the section we're responsible for, I retreat to the house to wash my hands and brush off any dirt that may have collected on my clothes.

My next task is to pick up our weekly rations at the Food Distribution Center. I've never been there this early in the day. By the time Dad or I usually get here, the line winds halfway around the building. But today I step right through the doors, choosing the closest counter. The small luxury makes me feel important. Mrs. Rantanen waves as she flashes me a toothy smile. She shakes a wrinkly finger in the air when she notices me.

"I know why you's here early, Miss Everly!" I can't help but smile back as she wiggles her eyebrows. "Heard it on the infurmation broadcast las' night. Ya gone and won youself a big fancy trip! And I bet ya wanna help ya pop before ya go!"

Her voice is too loud and her words run together, but I'll miss seeing her even if it's only for two weeks. She may not say the right things all the time, but her kindness is genuine.

"As usual, you're right, Mrs. R.!"

"Course I am. They say ya family get one less ration for two weeks so I ask why. I was 'fraid somethin' bad happen, then I remembured you's got the trip. I was sure happy that it was fur somethin' good." The smile disappears for a moment as her tone turns serious. "Now don't ya get no ideas 'bout staying in the Centrestates! Ya gotta come home ta us when ya done."

"Of course I'll be back! I could never leave my dad and brother and everyone else." *And if I had any say in it, I wouldn't even be going.*

She leans forward, reaching for me with her frail, bony hands. I automatically return the gesture, grasping her palms in my own. With a gentle squeeze, she dips her chin.

"I'm real proud o' ya, Everly, and ya mama would be too! I hope ya knows that!" Her gray eyes haze with sadness for a moment. Although she speaks with motherly pride, the reality stings. I don't need any reminders that my mother isn't here, or that her absence leaves a gaping sense of emptiness in every experience or achievement she'll never be a part of.

I force a smile and thank her, eager to end the conversation. Just as I'm about to ask for our packages, lightning cracks. We both startle and I take a step back.

"Oh my, that's caught me by supprise," she chuckles. It's the perfect excuse, so I take it.

"Me too. I should probably pick up our packs and be on my way, try to get home before the storm."

"Ya right," she agrees. "Just a minute and I be right back with ya food."

She winks and turns from the counter, retreating to a back room. I glance around the large open space while I wait. The other counters are empty but I can see workers bustling around in the back area where Mrs. R. just headed. They're probably sorting each family's food and bagging it. When the weather is mild, we collect our rations on portable carts that have to be returned by tomorrow morning so that they can be used for that day's pickups.

Dad usually returns ours on his way to work but this time I'm going to do it. As soon as I drop the food off at home, I'll turn around and come back here. Hopefully the storm will pass by then.

"Here ya go," Mrs. R. announces, maneuvering the wobbly metal box on wheels around her counter. "Best be on ya way, but don't fo'get 'bout us!"

I thank her and grasp the handles, pivoting toward the door. "I'll be back before you know it," I call, plastering a confident smile on my face.

She nods slowly as her eyes rake over me. It's as if she's trying to memorize every last detail from the straggling strands of hair atop my head down to my scuffed shoes. *Does she* really *think I'm not coming back?* Even if Centrestates is amazing, the only place for me is right here, with my family. Besides, it's not like they've invited me to move there. In two short weeks, everything will be right back to normal.

***

The rain holds out until I'm just a block from the house. Since the streets are still empty, I run, stumbling when the cart's teetering wheels catch on random cracks in the sidewalk. Scrambling through the front door, I unload the food as quickly as possible. Luckily it doesn't take as long as usual since it's missing my portions. After gulping down a quick lunch, I rush back out the door, ignoring the annoying spritz of rain.

I dash along the sidewalks, dragging the cart behind me. It's much lighter without its former load. This time as I approach the Food Distribution Center, I weave around the few neighbors scurrying through the doors and out of the storm. I glance toward the counters but don't see Mrs. R. She must be in the back gathering someone's pickup. My shoulders relax in relief. I'm eager to get back home.

By the time I reach our front door, my shirt and pants are drenched, courtesy of the light-but-steady sprinkling rain. Great. I barely have enough clean sets of clothes to pack and now this one is soaked. I'll have to pack it and wear it again. They must have a way for the delegates to launder our clothes while we're in Centrestates.

Here, we're issued a fresh set of clothing every seven days. That means I can only pack as many clean sets as I have. *What if I run out?* I push the thought out of my mind. It'll be the same for everyone there, so there's no sense in worrying about it. Someone somewhere decided to make this happen, so it's their responsibility to figure out how to keep us in clean clothes.

By the time I wring out my hair and tug on a dry shirt and pants, today's complete change in routine catches up with me, mentally and physically. All I crave at this moment is the warmth and comfort of my bed. Slipping under the blanket, I settle into the mattress' dipping curve that perfectly cradles my body. Within minutes, my heavy eyelids drift closed and sleep claims me.

***

The faint jiggling of the door handle tugs at the edges of my senses just before heavy footsteps barrel into the living room. That's all it takes to fully yank me from any sort of restful state. I must outweigh Easton by at least thirty pounds yet somehow that kid manages to clomp around like a fisherman on a dock, hauling his latest catch. Dad and I used to joke that we must have picked up the wrong shoes at the Textile Distribution Center because Easton's always seem to be filled with lead.

Dad follows closely behind Easton and swings the door closed. Thankfully his work schedule nearly mirrors our school schedule, so he's home for the day too. He smiles when he sees me.

"Did you have a good day, Everly? Are you all packed?" His smile fades when I shift my eyes to the wall and chew my bottom lip. He glances around, spotting a few food packages I haven't put in the cupboard yet, and frowns.

"Um, well, not yet, but I've been busy—"

"I told you not to worry about anything while you're gone. You should have spent the day packing instead of doing chores." His shoulders drop as he releases a sigh. "No more errands or chores, understand? Easton and I can take care of ourselves while you're gone."

"I know, I know, I just wanted to help."

"And you have, but now it's time to focus on getting yourself ready for this exciting adventure!" Pride reflects in his blue eyes, with no traces of worry or hints of sadness. I trust my dad more than anyone else. If he isn't sad or worried, I shouldn't be either. I nod as an appreciative smile tugs my cheeks.

I *will* push past the trepidation and accept this chance for what it is – a completely unheard of, unexpected opportunity. I would have never imagined leaving the Eastates. For any reason. And even if I never really wanted to, this is a free trip across the Xone wall and a chance to see how our government truly works. I never had that chance here. We learn from textbooks and teachings, not by visiting physical environments and observing first-hand. *How bad can something so extraordinary be?*

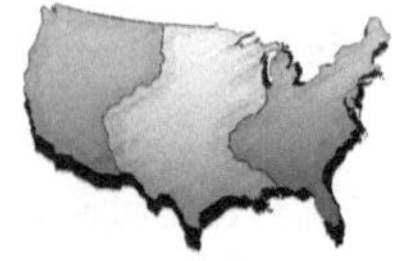

CHAPTER 7

UPPER DIVISION, EASTATES

Just as I turn toward the hallway, and my room, a sharp knock at the front door startles us all. Dad raises a hand in the air, halting me.

"Stick around for just a moment, in case this is about the delegation." I pause in place as he walks to the door and swings it open. Although it's not an official, our visitor is most definitely here to talk about my trip. My dad sidesteps out of the way as a dripping wet Josli barges past him inside.

"Hi, Mr. Scott," she calls as she beelines to my side. Easton emerges from his room to see what's going on. His curiosity dulls when he sees our guest.

"Oh, hi Josli." I'm not sure who he was expecting, but he's clearly disappointed that my best friend has paid us a visit.

"As always, thrilled to see you too, Easton!" She brushes off his slight and grabs my hand, pulling me toward my room. I practically float along behind her. I didn't expect to see her before I have to leave. The daylight hours are quickly slipping away and she needs to be home before curfew, but I'm grateful for whatever time we do have.

As I close the door, she drops onto my bed, letting her books and papers spill into a messy pile at her feet. I cringe inwardly as pages crumple and books rest against each other at unstable angles. At the end of the school year, we are responsible for returning all educational materials issued to us in the same condition that we received them. No one will believe her books were issued with bent pages and torn corners. But I'm sure she's not worried about it.

"Oh Ev, I missed you SOOO much and it's only been one day! How am I gonna do this?" She throws her hands in the air in over-embellished agony. She asks about my day but waves me off when she realizes it consisted of chores and errands. Before I can even ask, she fills me in on every detail of school, including the latest gossip.

"So, guess who's all worked up about this delegation?" She twirls a lock of hair around her finger. Unable to contain the information she came to share, she blurts it out. "Dolby Adler!"

I shrink back a little, as if the mere words sting. He's ranked second in the class, just above me and below Hayes. I'm sure he believes he should be going to Centrestates, not me. Josli leans toward me, grabbing my hands.

"But don't worry! I took care of it. I started a rumor that he has a crush on Educator Edmunds." She squeals, delighted by her genius. Educator Edmunds must be about a hundred years old. Jokes fly around the school, discreetly of course, about how long the hair on her mole grows before she gets it trimmed.

"And tomorrow I plan to release another grossly misleading, unflattering tidbit about him. I just haven't decided which one yet," Josli announces. We erupt in giggles.

"Josli, you are the best best friend ever!" While Dolby probably doesn't deserve it, I can't help but appreciate her unyielding willingness to defend me. Too soon, the laughter dissolves into tears.

"I can't believe you're leaving me alone for wildlife watching." Josli feigns a pout, already mourning the loss of our typical Saturday afternoon time together. It's one of the only approved leisure activities we can agree on, so that's what we usually do. Josli's interested to see other neighborhoods and guess how many people live in the bigger houses. But our purpose is to record any animals we see and where. It's easy enough, and it affords us a valid excuse to explore just beyond the edges of where the homes end and the woods begin. Of course, Josli always pushes for us to go farther and farther past the boundaries.

"You can borrow Easton!" I tease, knowing he'd complain of boredom within the first hour of searching for any signs of furry life. We've seen squirrels and rabbits, but not much else. And even those have been few and far between.

"It won't be the same without you here, Ev."

"I'll miss you too," I add. "And I promise to memorize every detail while I'm there. I swear, you'll feel like you were right there with me! Just wait."

"That's perfect!" Her eyes widen with excitement. "But there's one more thing I want."

"Anything," I promise, even though I don't have much else to offer.

"Once you're back, if you ever get invited to go there again, you take me with you!" She presses her palms together, like a silent plea or prayer.

"Of course! I'll just tell them I'm not going back without you!" With one last round of giggles and hugs, she dashes out the door, determined to be home by six p.m.

A wisp of sadness flickers through me. Before I have a chance to dwell on how much I'll miss my best friend, Easton offers a distraction.

"Now that she's gone, can we eat?" he calls from his bedroom.

"Yes!" I answer sharply. "Sorry to make you wait, your highness! We didn't mean to inconvenience you."

Dad rushes down the hallway, prepared to extinguish our exchange before it ignites into an argument. Easton follows eagerly at his heels.

"We're ready if you are, Everly." He glances at Easton pointedly. "We didn't want to interrupt you two. Your brother and I will prepare the rations. You sit and relax."

Easton stomps into the kitchen. This time Dad follows on his heels. I plop on the couch and remind myself that kids are impatient. I probably was too at his age and just can't remember it. It doesn't help that my emotions are a jumbled blend of sadness and anxiety. Just when the smallest bubble of hope starts to flicker within me, reality promptly pops it. As I inhale a few deep breaths, hushed conversations drift from the other room. A moment later, my brother trudges out to the living room.

"Sorry," he mutters, clearly not.

"Thanks, bud. I'm sorry too." This isn't the time to let annoyance overpower my true feelings. The moment may have gotten to me, but I want to enjoy every last minute with my family. As we settle at the table to eat, Easton spears a nugget on his tray. It must spark a question in his mind.

"What will you eat in Centrestates?" His brown eyes widen as he nibbles on the coated piece of fish. *At least he's done being mad at me.*

"I don't really know . . . I guess . . . probably the kind of stuff we eat here." I hitch a shoulder up. Eating is the last thing I'm thinking about. Dissatisfied with my non-answer, he tries another route.

"Will you go to classes there? Will it be like school?" I open my mouth to tell him I don't know that either when Dad cuts into the conversation.

"I'm sure Everly will tell us all about her trip when she gets back home. But for now, there's a lot she doesn't know yet."

When Easton's eyes drop to his tray in disappointment, Dad and I share a dejected glance. *This isn't supposed to be how my last dinner with them goes.* I decide to turn the tables on my little brother.

"Hey, why don't you tell me everything you're going to do in the next two weeks, so I don't feel like I'm missing anything?" After a moment, his posture straightens and a smile dances across his cheeks. We spend the rest of dinner laughing at the outlandish stories he invents.

***

When the last bite of food is swallowed and the conversation dwindles, I try to help clear the table. My father waves me off.

"We'll take care of that, Ev. You go pack, get yourself ready for tomorrow." At Dad's dismissal, Easton jumps out of his chair and starts gathering our food trays. He must figure that the faster he gets it done, the better. *Smart kid.*

I stroll down the short hallway to my bedroom and cross the threshold. I hesitantly sweep my gaze across the meager space. The mirror catches my eye. I smooth my hair back, revealing my worst feature – a raised, reddish-brown birthmark just below my left ear. It's shaped like a heart, which makes it even more noticeable.

My mother always brushed my hair back to show it off, claiming it made me special, different. I still hate the stupid thing, but I guess it's something I'll always have with me. Which reminds me of what I'm supposed to be doing – packing the things I'll need for a trip I don't want to take.

My heart hitches as random treasures around the room release a steady stream of memories in my mind. Some are distant while I can remember every detail of others. They all yield the same impact – an ache for moments of pure joy that can never be replicated.

A pair of orange barrettes Josli gave me for my eighth birthday. The stiff plastic molded into old-fashioned bows awed me as a child. Standing before a mirror, I'd cram as much hair as possible within the clasps. The simple accessories could never tame my unruly mane. They mostly hovered somewhere between my temples and ears, clinging to my long brown strands. Although I'd never wear them now, I'd also never part with the reminder of my best friend.

A crumpled sheet of blue-lined paper. The writing has faded, but I can clearly distinguish the word - E v e r l y - the vowels are backwards and the letters progressively grow in size. But I'll always remember that first time Easton wrote my name in his imperfect penmanship. Even then I knew that the paper was a gift, a moment I would want to remember long after the pulp crumbled to flecks of dust.

The red hourglass-shaped bottle of perfume that my mother's gentle hands once held. A remnant from her own mother, it could never be replaced. Perfume was a luxury of the past. I gently twist the cracked cap and raise the spritzer to my nose. Inhaling the stale, sweet aroma, tears pool in my eyes. I carefully replace the cap, certain that no occasion will ever warrant releasing any of the remaining precious drops. After the last splash of the scented liquid evaporates, I'll treasure the empty bottle, savoring any remaining wisps of fading lilac.

A simple square piece of frayed fabric. The pink has faded to a soft beige, nearly as pale as my arm. It was my baby blanket. Besides being the sole keepsake of that time in my life, it also bears a note from my mother. She sewed four little letters on one corner – Lyly. She's the only one who ever called me that. Even my dad and Easton have always called me Ev, never Lyly. I gulp down the sorrow catching in my throat and shift focus to one last treasure.

Warmth swells in my chest as I trace the outline of the rusty fisherman's hook with a single plume of what was once a burst of crimson feathers. In his younger days, my father carved out moments of free time to catch fish. It was considered an acceptable hobby since it provided a food source. He spotted the tattered lure tangled in a fishing line. Although it pushed the limits of curfew, he plucked the line, lashed across jagged rocks near the water's edge, until he could free the elaborate lure. He always claimed it brought him luck. He credits that luck to meeting my mother. But once they married, our family and his work in the Provisions Factory consumed his time. He gave me the lure for luck.

I carefully tuck each item into the wooden box stowed beneath my bed. None of them will go with me, but they'll all be gathered and preserved for when I return. This trip is a temporary stop along the path to my goals and the future I've earned. My father would remind me that it's a reward for the many hours I've spent studying and testing my way through classes. Just as I slide the box into its shadowy hiding place, voices carry from the kitchen, drawing my attention.

CHAPTER 8

UPPER DIVISION, EASTATES

"But Everly always helps me with my homework!" Easton protests, his pitch reaching tantrum-level decibels. Instinct tempts me to dash out there and appease my younger brother, but Dad's patient response stops me in my tracks.

"She has a lot to do, son. Besides, what makes you think I can't help? Everly's not the only smart one around here!"

Silence. I envision my little brother crossing his arms and chuffing, maybe even throwing Dad a side-eye. A chair drags along the tiled floor, followed by a faint thud. Dad's probably sitting at the kitchen table, waiting. I hover in my doorway, prepared to offer assistance if Dad will accept it. Or if Easton decides to throw a fit.

"Ooooooookay," Easton concedes. Within a few minutes, they're working through math problems. Echoes of a stray laugh or two drift down the hallway when Dad makes a joke, "Why is eight afraid of seven? Because seven ate nine." *Maybe they can handle this without me. It's not like the world will stop just because I'm leaving.*

For the first time since school ended yesterday, I think of Hayes Crimshaw. Starting tomorrow, he'll be the only person I know for the next two weeks. And I barely even know him. We've gone to school together for the past twelve years, but I can count on one hand the number of conversations we've ever had. He's always been the first one to raise his hand in class, practically bursting with the answer when an educator asks a question. And the first one to turn in an exam, as if it's a time trial.

As I carefully fold five sets of clothing, I envision him gleefully dashing around his home, investigating every shelf and drawer to ensure he hasn't left anything behind that should tag along on this trip. He wouldn't be moping around his house, wishing someone else was picked instead of him. But dread coils my stomach into knots when I slide the clothing into a sack.

I wonder what Dolby Adler is doing right now. Probably daydreaming about me missing the train and the leaders being forced to disqualify someone so careless and irresponsible. He'd be the first one to demand that they revoke my invitation to join the delegation. Then there would be no other choice but to send him in my place.

He can daydream about sabotaging me all he wants. If anyone can knock him down a few notches, it's my best friend. Josli will remind him that he wasn't selected and she'll have way too much fun doing it. I'm still nervous about the unknown and being away from my family for a few weeks. But knowing that someone else clearly wants the chance I've been given ignites my possessive side. I was offered this opportunity for a reason. If they wanted Dolby, he would be going.

By the time I exhaust the mental list of what I'll need to pack in the morning, it's practically time to brush my teeth, wash my face and change into sleep clothes. After taking my turn in the bathroom, I share a lingering goodnight with Dad and Easton before settling into bed for what I hope isn't going to be a restless night, blanketed in worry.

***

The hours trudge along at a painfully slow pace. I alternate between staring at the ceiling and flopping from one side to the other. My body rejects every attempt to settle into a comfortable position. Rest is like a wispy cloud, allowing me to merely drift in and out of random pockets of unconsciousness.

When dawn finally declares a new day and my eyes flutter open, I briefly wonder if it was all a dream – the announcement, the delegation, the trip. The sinking feeling in my stomach confirms that yesterday happened as I remember it. I'm really going to leave my family. Although I know it's not that long, right now two weeks sounds like a lifetime. Forcing myself to climb out of bed, I head for the shower. No sense in putting it off any longer.

After I dry off, I run my fingers over the scratchy blue fabric of the shirt and pants I laid out last night. Like my entire clothing selection, they're a deep cerulean hue, to represent the Territory. The color was selected to represent our skills in harvesting the ocean along our borders. Although nutrition production facilities provide more than half of our food, seafood supplements the rations. Even if it's processed and plied with additives to stretch the bounty, there's at least a hint of fresh food within our meals sometimes.

We learned in history class that the catch is only about ten percent of what it was a century ago. Overfishing and warmer waters, courtesy of climate change, severely depleted fish populations. After the Global Infection Spread, when the population reached its lowest point, the oceans were granted a temporary respite.

Over the years, nature slowly started to heal itself, although by that time the waters were overrun with chemical and plastic pollution, spawning unhealthy specimens that tainted the food chain. While life below the surface never healed completely, it's made mild progress, just enough to augment our manufactured provisions. A portion of the catch is traded to the other Territories in exchange for commodities they produce. *The other Territories! I don't have time to lose myself in history lessons right now.*

Shaking the distracting thoughts from my mind, I tug the shirt on and slip into the pants. Everything else I need to do can wait. Time beckons me to join my family. Although today will be anything but normal for me, Dad and Easton have to report for work and school as usual. Swallowing the lump in my throat, I swing the bedroom door open and cross the threshold. It's time to say goodbye. For now.

I wander to the kitchen on leaden legs. The two people I'll miss the most sit across from each other at the small round table. While Easton's slogging a spoon into his uneaten oatmeal, Dad notices my approach. His eyes hone in on my slinking shadow as I reach the fringes of daylight spilling into the room.

"There's our delegate!" A broad grin spreads across his cheeks. Genuine pride fuels his greeting. I allow a weak smile to trace my lips. He's not sad, and I shouldn't be either. Yet each footfall requires effort. When I don't respond, he continues.

"Good morning, Everly! Big day!" His greeting is excessive, but I know he's trying to be positive for my sake. I nod and slip into my seat. I can eat after they leave, for now I'll just savor these last moments.

"Everly! Don't forget to bring me a souvenir! And make it a good one!" Easton pushes the words past a spoonful of oatmeal. A white blob clings to his chin, an obvious casualty of his poor table manners. *At least he's eating.* A giggle bubbles in my chest. Maybe I should just be glad I have loved ones to miss. Tucking away my all-consuming self-pity, I scoop a blob of the tasteless breakfast into the chipped bowl already set out for me.

The day feels just like any other, until the weight of time douses our conversation. Flattening his palms on the table, my father pushes back in his seat and stands to his full six-foot height. He collects the utensils and stacks our dirty dishes in the sink. Easton pops out of his seat and dashes to his room. The stomping returns just as quickly as it faded. Slinging his school bag over his shoulder, he plows into me.

Reclaiming the air Easton knocked out of me, I wrap my brother in an embrace. Nuzzling the hair on the top of his head with my nose, I whisper words of comfort, weaving in a few usual reminders. *I'll be back soon. Be good. Help Dad, he'll have extra chores without me here. Love you, buddy.*

He clings to me, nodding and backing away when I finish speaking. Dad calls to him before turning his attention to me. "Come right home after school, son. I'll see you then."

Easton nods and backs out the door, clumsily waving a hand in the air as his other negotiates the knob, yanking it closed. Dad steps toward me, resting a rough palm on my arm.

"I'm so proud of you, Everly. And your mother would be too."

I gulp around the lump emerging in my throat. *Why did he have to say that?* I'm already treading in a sea of emotions. I don't need any added hint of sadness to trigger a wave of tears. Clamping my mouth shut, I force a weak smile to acknowledge his words.

"You go, enjoy yourself, show off your brains! Your brother and I will be right here when you're all done." He drapes his arm around me and leads me to the door. Not to escort me out, but because he can't be late for work and we both know time is a commodity we've nearly overspent this morning.

"I'll miss you, Dad." My lower lip trembles as tears swell, blurring my vision. He swipes a calloused thumb across my cheek. My eyes drop to the floor.

"Everly, this is a happy occasion. There's no room for sad tears. Nothing like this has ever happened before. And I know a lot of adults who would give anything to visit another Territory before they die." He cradles my chin with his palm, gently raising it so my eyes meet his. "If you feel sad when you're there, just remember that you'll be in the history lessons. Years from now, students will study the delegation and whatever amazing things you all do together. Years and years into the future, generations of students will read and memorize your name."

Warmth radiates from my core, settling into a peaceful calm. *He's right. I've been riding a roller coaster of emotions that I'll probably forget all about once I'm there. And this delegation will make lasting impacts.* We may be proactively preventing trade restrictions. And maybe we'll even find a way to open the borders for travel between Territories. Maybe someday I can take my dad and brother to Centrestates, and show them where I served as a delegate, where I helped make history.

***

After he leaves, Dad's parting words replay in my mind. I memorize them as I would dates and events of historical significance. They fuel a sense of purpose, which I use to clean the kitchen. I wash the dishes and wipe down the counters before checking the rest of the house for anything that needs to be picked up or put away. Satisfied everything is in place for when Easton and Dad return home, I review the instructions Principal DeBrusk gave us.

As soon as I gather everything that's coming with me, it will be time to leave for the train station. I sweep the house for any last-minute additions to pack. Just as I slip the last item into a bag, my toothbrush, a knock rattles the front door. I hover in momentary confusion as I mentally inventory everyone it couldn't be. Josli would be at school by now, just like Easton. And my dad, along with everyone else in the neighborhood, is at or on the way to work. Besides, none of them would knock with such purpose.

A swift succession of sharp raps reminds me that someone is waiting, rather impatiently. I shuffle down the hallway, toward the door. Trepidation flares in my chest, yet logic reminds me that there's nothing to be scared of. A century ago, before we were divided, people felt vulnerable nearly all the time. Crime was rampant. People carried their own weapons. Now it's not necessary.

Enforcers may remind citizens of the rules, but their jobs aren't dangerous by any means. The punishment is enough of a deterrent – no one wants to lose part of their food or supply rations. Laws are in place to keep us all fed, clothed and sheltered. In exchange for everything the Societal Order provides for us, we are expected to contribute to the community when we can and follow every law without question.

Throwing my shoulders back in a show of confidence, I twist the handle and yank the door open.

CHAPTER 9 ~ KIERA

UPPER DIVISION, CENTRESTATES

Three weeks earlier

"Leader Imperant, if I may interrupt, I wanted to discuss something with you." I pause just outside his office, unwilling to enter before he properly acknowledges me. Looking up from the stack of papers before him, he releases a breath and nods. *It's good enough. For now.* Striding through the doorway, I slip into one of the plush, high-back chairs.

"What's on your mind, Kiera?" His demeanor toward me has softened ever so slightly since I proposed creating a delegation to check for the compliance chip. Obviously we can't call it that outwardly. I've been considering calling it an inter-Territory delegation. It sounds important, with no indication of what this group truly is.

"Well, sir, I've been thinking that we could make this delegation so much more than we originally planned. This could serve as a front for several other considerations we've discussed over the past few months."

"And which ones might those be?" Resting his elbows on the desk, he folds his hands. Those dark eyes drill into me, appraising if what I have to say is worth his time.

"Our new energy alternative. We can use the existing grid for one last purpose – the X-ray machine – and then eliminate it entirely. It's the perfect time. We could do it at the end of the two weeks, just before the delegation is about to wrap up."

"I don't think we're ready for that." He waves a hand in the air dismissively. "You're proposing too much. The more variables we throw into the mix, the more likely one is to fail or negatively impact our original intent."

"Sir, I don't fail." I prop my chin on my fist and lean toward him. "You know that. It will be a lot to juggle, but I can handle it, and the payoff will be worth it. We'll get the answers we need, and we'll be in a position to act if our theory turns out to be right."

His eyes drift to the wall behind me. Pursing my lips, I consider if I should add to my argument or let it rest. Sometimes he needs a push and sometimes he needs to be alone with his thoughts before he realizes I'm right. *The trick is figuring out which he needs at that moment.* His gaze slides back to me.

"Get yourself another assistant. Fast. If we find out that the chip program stopped, we will take immediate action. That would be a blatant violation of the Alliance Agreement." A hint of defiance chases his words. *He's on board. He understands how critical this is.*

My heart rate spikes, but I have to project a calm, controlled image. He would consider any other reaction to be a sign of weakness, as if I'm ruled by emotion.

"If that is the case, sir, then we would obviously be justified in removing Societal Order Leader Ault from leadership of Eastates, but what we would do about Westates?" It's time to plant the seed and hope it grows into my own vision for the Divided States. Sitting back in the chair, I let my words sink in.

A new emotion flashes in his eyes for just a moment. Westates has always been a closer ally than Eastates, but Leader Imperant's drive for power is stronger than any alliance with another Territory.

"Westates could be doing the same thing for all we know," he says as a sly smirk crosses his lips. "We have to assume the same of them."

This is our chance to grow from one Territory to three in one strike. And when it happens, Leader Imperant will need as much of my help as he can get.

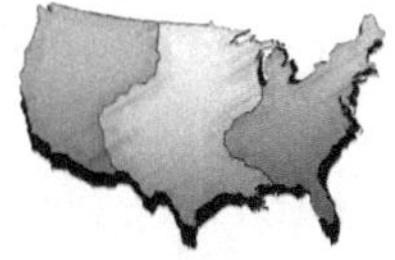

CHAPTER 10

UPPER DIVISION, EASTATES

"Are you ready?" Hayes Crimshaw stands before me, his lanky frame nearly buzzing with anticipation. His palms shoot up, accentuating his question. Actively taming the surprise of this unexpected visitor, I concentrate on painting a neutral look across my face.

"Um, almost." *What's he even doing here?* We barely know each other. I would never just show up at his house, even in this particular situation. I guess this shared adventure has officially made us friends. I don't have any strong opinions of Hayes, either positive or negative. I don't really know much about him. Other than that he's smart. Really smart.

"Then let's get your stuff!" He pushes past me, effortlessly invading my home. His presence injects an urgency to my previous leisurely pace. I tug the door closed and follow him. His aggressiveness slows as he enters the kitchen. My father says that all the homes on this block are copies of each other. Each is a one-story box with the same basic floor plan.

As long as your family is contributing to the Societal Order, by going to school and work, you don't have to worry about housing or food. When citizens grow too old to work, they're moved to a larger building with multiple smaller homes within it.

So while Hayes' intrusion is odd, it's no surprise the layout is familiar to him, as well as the invisible barriers of what is socially acceptable. Unspoken understanding halts him before he reaches our bedrooms. The family room and kitchen are common areas that host shared necessities – food storage and preparation devices, as well as seating areas for meals and schoolwork. But privacy reigns with one's bedroom. Even though the space is cramped with a narrow bed, a weathered dresser and a sagging desk, it's all mine.

The uniformity of our homes and possessions is by design. Our neighbors are our equals. There's little incentive to compare yourself to anyone else when we all have the same lifestyle – house, clothes, food. This makes special mementos, tiny trinkets hidden beneath layers of the mundane, special and private.

Our homes were modified for efficient heating and cooling as a way to balance times of the year when power can be conserved and when an upsurge becomes necessary. Extreme weather can be challenging, but the Societal Order prioritizes blanket and coat distribution in the colder months. So even if our homes aren't comfortably warm, we have plenty of layers to wrap ourselves in.

It maximizes our own body heat and minimizes our reliance on the grid. For three months each year, during the summer, we are allotted the least amount of power access. It's a conservation time, which makes up for the increase in energy needed to maintain minimal warmth during the colder months. Each home's underground shelter offers relief when nature delivers sweltering heat, especially those who have aged or feel choked by the inescapable humid air.

A hand flashes just inches from my face, slender fingers waggling. "Everly! Did you hear me? I hope you're not planning to act like this in Centrestates. You'll single-handedly embarrass our whole Territory." Hayes crosses his arms and taps his foot impatiently. *Who invited him anyway? I never offered to play host – he just barged right in.* When annoyance seeps from my narrowed gaze trained on him, he raises his eyebrows. He gulps and slides his glasses farther up the bridge of his nose.

"Hey, where are your bags? I'll help you carry them to the train." I sense it's a peace offering, but I'm not accepting it just yet. I shake my head.

"You have your own stuff to carry. You don't have to help with mine."

Hayes blows out a frustrated breath and rolls his eyes as if that's the dumbest response I could have provided.

"I told you, I already took my bags to the train. They're on board, just waiting for me. And I'm waiting for you, so let's go!"

I nod, chewing my lower lip. He must have mentioned that while my mind was consumed with architecture and electricity.

***

Our walk to the train station is surprisingly comfortable. Hayes is fluent in honesty and speaks whenever a thought pops into his head.

"Everly, we have to watch each other's backs when we get there," he says. "I have a theory, wanna hear it?"

"Sure."

"When you bring together a group of strangers – and teenagers, at that – they are likely to feel insecure or competitive." He glances my way, probably checking to see if I'm paying attention.

"Yeah, that makes sense," I agree.

"But we can't be like that. We've had the same educators, walked the same hallways, sat in the same classrooms, and eaten the same rations. And we have something else in common too."

"Oh really? And what's that?" He's definitely piqued my interest.

"I happen to know that my sister has a crush on your brother." His eyes widen as he awaits my reaction. An uncontrollable giggle escapes me.

"That's so cute! I bet Easton has no idea!" I can't help but gush. "Maybe he likes her too. I can ask him when we get back."

"No, Everly, you can't. My sister is younger but she's vicious. I'm not supposed to know, I sort of overheard her talking. We have to keep this a secret until she tells him herself."

"Oooookay," I hesitantly agree. *He's afraid of his little sister.* I hold back the chuckle building in my throat. Thank goodness Josli didn't hear him admit that. She'd have burst out laughing. I swallow any humor I find in it and paint a serious look across my face. Hayes told me that in confidence. I can keep the secret. And maybe Easton will find out on his own somehow before I get back.

The rest of the way, we chatter about our classmates and what they're probably doing – and thinking – right now. Although I mostly listen, I settle into a comfortable companionship with

Hayes much faster than I expected. Sharing this experience of leaving everything we've ever known and jumping directly into the all-encompassing unknown is definitely speeding up what could be a friendship.

When we arrive at the train station, Hayes takes command of my baggage. It's a relief – one less thing I have to figure out. Having done this very recently, he knows exactly where to deliver the bags and where to board. We find our seats and settle in for the ride. My eyes sweep over the other passengers. There aren't many, but they all wear the customary cerulean blue that represents Eastates.

Dad's always wondered why our clothes aren't more of a murky green. He says that shade would better portray the bordering coastal waters struggling to revive from decades of festering contamination. Although I haven't seen the ocean myself, a portion of our citizens still command fishing boats, sweeping the seas for sustenance to support the region without completely depleting the source. I shake away the thoughts when a tall woman with deep red hair that sweeps just below her chin approaches us.

"Ah, Hayes, good to see you again. I presume this is Everly with you. The other delegate selected for the inter-Territory delegation?"

"Yes, and we already loaded her bags," he answers. She reaches toward me with a hand extended.

"Excellent." She meets his gaze before shifting her attention to me. "Well, it's nice to meet you, Everly. I'm Galia and I'll make sure you get where you need to be today. Just sit back and enjoy the ride. If you have any questions, I'll be seated right back there." She points a few rows behind us, where about eight seats span the area from window to window. "Just come get me if anything comes up."

"Thank you," Hayes says. "We will." With that confirmation, she turns and heads to the seating area she just pointed out.

It never occurred to me that *we* might be considered cargo for an overseer to manage, just like a bushel of apples or a carton of socks. Was anyone else secretly watching over us before she introduced herself? I glance back to where Galia sits. The few others around her looked bored and completely uninterested in us. Hayes notices me watching them.

"Hey, at least we'll be able to tell which delegates are from each Territory." He nudges my elbow. He's right. Citizens from Centrestates wear tan while those from Westates wear green. Although our clothes blend in with the others' on this train, as soon as we reach our destination, it will be simple to distinguish the other arriving delegates.

I wonder if we'll feel any sort of kinship toward the other two students selected from the Eastates, from the lower division. Although this inter-Territory delegation is new, the representation almost mirrors the Societal Order leaders' balance of power. Four delegates will represent each of the three Territories. There must be a plan in place to prevent any possibility of a deadlocked disagreement. An odd number of voices would tip the balance of decisions one way or the other. I guess I'll find out how it will all work soon enough.

This delegation has exactly two weeks to fulfill whatever the leaders expect of us. *Hopefully the road ahead is a smooth one.*

A deep rumble signals that the beast whose belly we reside inside has awakened. Hayes and I share a wide-eyed look as excitement passes between us. He offered me the window seat when we first climbed aboard, and I had no intention of rejecting that offer. The only condition was that he gets the window seat on the way home. It's worth the trade-off. By that time, I plan to sit back and enjoy every minute that brings me closer to my family. I'll spend that time replaying the moment when the Societal Order congratulates us on our epically genius contributions.

My mind begs to wander but before a daydream can claim my thoughts, I press my palms to the window. Dusty, dry land stretches for miles, but we've barely breached the division's boundaries. How soon will the overwhelming brown yield to patches, and eventually fields, of green? Around here spindly trees clump together in wayward groupings. But the land can't all be exactly like this between here and Centrestates. There must be some variations.

Hayes and I are the only ones even remotely aware of the rush of landscape just beyond the other side of the glass. The few other passengers chat with the person beside them or slouch in the seat, attempting to pass the time while drifting off to a state of unawareness. The last thing I'd do right now is close my eyes. I'm not willing to miss any stretch of land, fields or buildings that I may never see again.

The others on board must be transport overseers, those who spend their work hours traveling back and forth to exchange goods between Territories. While they wear the Eastates standard-issue pants and shirts, they do appear to be somewhat official and they're all adults. I guess if you made this trip every time you went to work, it wouldn't be so interesting anymore.

I turn my attention from them and return it to the world just beyond the windows. Hayes adjusts his glasses, hovering just behind me, mirroring my fascination. The landscape blurs as the train rockets westward. In the distance, the sound barriers slice through the atmosphere. They're like smaller versions of the Xone walls, but they aren't so small as we race toward them. The towering giants divide the upper and lower divisions, eliminating, or at the very least reducing, noise pollution from either side. I wonder if the southern delegates ride on a similar train at this very moment, clinging to the sights rushing by. *Are they struggling to keep their eyes open?* Or maybe they'll be transported at night, when they're accustomed to being awake.

If only time could freeze, we could properly investigate every speck of the unknown.

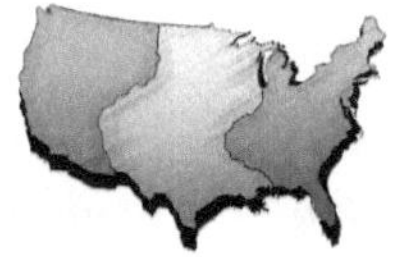

CHAPTER 11

UPPER DIVISION, EASTATES

We surge by more scraggly bushes and trees, our division's typical vegetation. I can practically feel the yellowed grass crunch beneath our shoes if we were out there right now. While the scenery is familiar, whizzing past it at this pace is exhilarating. *I wish my dad and Easton could be here. And Josli. She'd probably be giggling the whole time, which would quickly overtake me too.* Giddiness bubbles in my chest, washing away the anxiety and homesickness. At least for now.

Each neighborhood beyond the glass appears nearly identical to our own. Boxy houses line nondescript streets, which are mostly empty. It's no surprise to see the sidewalks and roads dormant. I imagine most of the residents are either at work or school. *Like we would normally be.*

Larger buildings loom in close proximity to the homes. Those must be schools, food production facilities and textile factories. Plots of open space stretch between communities, like invisible barriers, clearly marking where one ends and the next begins. Each community is meant to be self-sustaining, with no need to mix people or products.

I guess my life would be exactly the same no matter where we lived.

Sooner than I expect, the populated areas fade into what looks like uninhabited terrain. Abandoned buildings lurk in the distance, draped with random openings that stretch into complete darkness. I imagine what they looked like a hundred years ago, when they could withstand wind, rain and snow. Now I wonder if a single tattered leaf drifting through the air could crumble them. Gnarled vines streak the sides, clawing their way to the melancholy sky.

And just like that, the pitiful shacks disappear into the blur of everything else we've passed. Forgotten once again. I'm surprised the Societal Order would allow decrepit buildings like that to stand. Surely they could be reinforced and converted into something useful. Maybe that's something I could bring up with the delegation – proposing a use for abandoned structures. There must be some in the other Territories too. I tuck the thought into the corner of my mind in case I need an idea to contribute at some point.

A lanky arm rockets past me as a rush of warm breath flutters over my cheek.

"Everly, look! The trees and bushes look a little healthier here." Hayes taps a finger against the window, completely oblivious to the personal space he invades. Namely, mine. "That means we're getting closer to a water source." He pushes his glasses higher on the bridge of his nose. I shrink as far as I can into my seat and turn back toward the surrounding landscape. Although it still drowns in varying shades of brown, a few green patches sprout – bushes and trees that breach the otherwise monochromatic terrain.

"You're right." Sweat beads along my forehead as I scramble for a nice way to tell him to back off. "Do you want to switch seats for a little while? So you can get a closer look without me being in the way?" His features drop as he suddenly notices my awkward posture. Understanding sweeps through him. His back straightens as he detaches himself from the window and sinks into his seat.

"Nah, we made a deal. You get the window now and I'll get it the whole way home." He faces forward, as if he's not even allowed to glance my way or peer outside. Guilt slithers through me. Just like when Easton is upset. Maybe a little distraction technique could banish the awkwardness. It typically works with my eight-year-old brother. I decide to pose one of Easton's questions from last night on Hayes.

"Hey, I wonder what kind of food we'll eat in Centrestates. What do you think?" He turns toward me, his expression a clear acceptance of the challenge. *He actually wants to process this.* He tilts his head back in thought for just a moment.

"I have a theory. Wanna hear it?" His whole stance relaxes as he prepares for what, I fear, could become a dissertation.

"Sure." *I asked the question, didn't I?* Even if it was just to move us past the indirect but still uncomfortable invading-my-personal-space incident.

"I think they'll put on a big show for us." He raises his hands in the air to emphasize his words. "They'll bring out the best food, give us the best accommodations and treat us like royalty. All so they can show us all just how superior they are."

I raise an eyebrow. "You think they're superior to us?"

He grunts. "Of course not, but don't we all think our own Territory is the best? And this is their chance to show us how they've mastered food production – they've probably got a whole quadrant of greenhouses that function year-round."

Just the thought awakens my taste buds. A sweet, fruity aroma tickles my nose as my overactive imagination anticipates what might be grown, harvested and offered to us. Hayes is probably right. They'll want to impress us. Freshly grown food is definitely one way to do it. That is, if they have any idea of the mush we typically eat.

I remind myself to commit every detail of the next two weeks to memory. Everyone back home will have a zillion questions, and hopefully I'll have some impressive stories about this delegation to share with them.

Returning my attention to the window, Hayes and I settle into a comfortable silence. He's right, the closer we get to Centrestates, the healthier the landscape appears. Before my eyes, the browns blend into rich shades of green. I can't help but smile as my eyes seek out every bit of nature that we only see in books back home. *How can everything be so healthy out here when we can't even grow a tomato?*

Movement within the foliage snags my attention. I press closer to the glass, squinting and craning my neck to get a better view. For just a moment, I catch a glimpse. The four-legged creature freezes in place as the train blasts by. White spots dot its brown coat. A larger, darker brown version of the frightened animal emerges and nudges the younger one. Together, they turn tail and run.

On all those afternoons Josli and I spent wildlife watching, we never once saw anything bigger than a rabbit. I blink in disbelief. It happened so fast but I'm certain I saw a deer. Two of them. I'd tell Hayes but he probably wouldn't believe me.

***

The closer we get, the higher the mighty Xone wall rises. Somehow it seems to beckon us onward. I've never thought of them as welcoming, but excitement races through me as the reality of crossing the barrier grows. *This is really happening.*

When I stretch in my seat, Hayes turns toward me.

"I have a theory about the night dwellers' appearance. Wanna hear it?" He bobs a shoulder up in question.

"Sure." Of course I agree, although I'd rather get back to plastering my face to the window.

"So if night dwellers mostly see the sun when it's setting or rising, they'd have a very low risk of a sunburn. In fact, they would be more likely to have pale skin and dark hair. But day dwellers, on the other hand, would likely have lighter hair and darker skin."

"How does that explain your red hair?" I don't mention it, but my mousy brown locks don't exactly scream *sun bleached.*

"I guess I'm an anomaly. I must have unique genes." He waves the explanation off and jumps back to his real topic of interest. "As generations adjusted to the sun and moon cycles and environmental conditions within the timeframes they experienced, it must have created genetic predispositions to certain traits." He slides his glasses back along the bridge of his nose and smirks. "I plan to ask about it when we get to Centrestates."

"Well, how about you wait until they tell us what's going on?" This guy's building theories in his head while all I want to know is where I'll be sleeping, eating and spending my days.

"Of course. I just plan to get as much out of this experience as possible. We're almost done with school now, Everly. And if they're considering expanding inter-Territory trade and commerce, maybe that means we'll have the option to take a job in Centrestates."

Before I realize it, my face scrunches into a cringe. "You'd want to move there? You haven't even seen it yet."

"All of our lives we had the same options – go to one school, live in one house, prepare for one career. What if we had a choice? What if we could live wherever we wanted to?"

I shake my head. We aren't supposed to talk like this. Maybe the delegation will change things, but right now the stuff he's saying is not possible. I shrug nonchalantly, tempering my uneasiness. Before I can formulate a response that acknowledges his question yet doesn't speak poorly of the Societal Order, he continues.

"Who knows what this delegation might accomplish? If the leaders know we'd like to visit and maybe even live in other Territories, maybe we can be the voice for those who would never have a chance to say it."

I shake my head slowly, giving his words thoughtful consideration. "Maybe you're right." He drops his chin with a single nod of satisfied agreement. "I mean, you can't be the only one who's ever thought of living in another Territory. Or even just visiting."

I lean closer, whispering my next words. "But I don't think we're really supposed to talk about it. People might be fearful to even question something like that." We've been taught, from our first days of school, that the Societal Order was put into place to protect us from mistakes that previous leaders made. To criticize the rules puts us all at risk to repeat history – one that includes wars, food and supply shortages, environmental collapse and rampant disease.

Besides the principles that have been ingrained in us, we've all heard the rumors of what happens to those who question the Societal Order. Some lose electricity rations, get extra working hours or worse. Supposedly a few people have disappeared over the years, never heard from again. Just the thought makes me shudder.

"Well, Everly, maybe it's time we started talking about it." With finality, Hayes settles into his seat and yawns. "I guess I've been awake longer than I realized." He stretches and shakes his head. Shadows droop beneath his eyes. "If I take a quick nap, will you wake me when we get to the Xone wall? I want to see how we pass through it."

"Sure." With that one-word promise, he tilts his head back and lets his eyes fall closed. He was probably awake most of last night, just like me. Only his insomnia would have been fueled by excitement and anticipation. Mine was rooted in worry and fear.

My energy fizzles slightly as I realize how easily I've adjusted to the train's rhythmic chugging. I understand Hayes' submission to exhaustion. He must have been riding an adrenaline high for who knows how long. How else could he, the same person who practically pushed me out the door of my own home, be willing to take a nap when there's still so much to see?

A hush descends, giving way to the transport overseers' conversation. Tuning out the train's steady hum, I focus on a female voice. It must be Galia. Her statement sounds more like a question to the others.

"Those kids up there." When she pauses. I imagine her beckoning toward us. "So they're on the list for transport in today, but they're nowhere to be found on the transport out list."

I keep my head still and my eyes forward. No need for them to know that my senses reach out like antennae toward them, desperate to hear more of this discussion. I nearly flinch when I hear a shuffling. A male responds. From the sounds of it, he's snatched the papers from the person who first spoke.

"Two weeks is the maximum amount of time they've been granted to cross the wall. It says so right here under their names and purpose." He pauses. In those moments, the only sound is my thumping heart, ready to catapult through my chest. His next words do nothing to steady my rocketing pulse.

"But you're right. The schedule for the next three weeks is right here. And they aren't on it."

CHAPTER 12

UPPER DIVISION, EASTATES

Their conversation drops to whispers. I can no longer hear even snippets of their words. I don't know which is worse – that they're talking about us and our fate, or wondering why they don't know what's going to happen to us.

Shifting in my seat, I turn back toward the window and attempt to focus on what exists mere yards away from me. When a soft snoring reaches my ears, I glance at Hayes. Sure enough, his head lolls toward his shoulder and his mouth gapes open. *Should I wake him and tell him what I overheard?*

After a few indecisive minutes, I leave him be. It must be a mistake. Someone just forgot to add our return trip to the list. Everything else on that list is probably the same stuff, week in and week out. And this one time, since it's so unusual, no one thought to add us. *But we're on the list right now to leave.*

Farther-reaching justifications swirl in my mind. Someone somewhere made a mistake. That's all it is, and they have two weeks to figure it out. *That's plenty of time.* At least that's what I've got to tell myself. We'll get this fixed. We have to, but there's nothing I can do about it right now.

I force my eyes to once again focus on the landscape we barrel past. It grows slightly greener with each mile, making me wonder how much more it will change by the time we reach Centrestates. The slight hum of hushed conversations drifts through the compartment, but I refuse to allow it to distract me from the world I never imagined I'd see. If more trees and plants grow as we move farther from the heart of our division, maybe this whole area is healthier – cleaner air, richer soil, purer water?

Maybe Centrestates is bathed in lush foliage and crystal lakes. A twinge of jealousy tugs at my gut. No, we've always been told that the Territories are equal. Each one has its strengths, but all are needed to meet the needs of citizens throughout the Divided States. And that happens through trade, heavily regulated trade.

The main reason this train even exists is for transporting items, not people. I search the compartment with a renewed purpose, seeking hints of past travelers, but nothing stands out among the monochromatic tan interior.

The seating area is small, which makes sense since the only ones who would use it are those responsible for accompanying deliveries to Centrestates. Worn fabric seats dimple in the center, their cushions permanently flattened by years of wear. The edges of the tattered carpet curl, reaching toward the ceiling. Dents and marks pepper the walls. It's by no means luxurious, but it serves its purpose.

The transport overseers don't seem to mind. Or maybe they're just so used to the same surroundings day in and day out that they don't even notice the imperfections. As long as supplies are sent out of Eastates and inventory is received, they probably don't care about much else. Their job is to travel between the Territory's upper and lower divisions, as well as to Centrestates, to ensure that promised trade transactions are completed.

Of course this train isn't just carrying me, Hayes and a few overseers. Stacks of cartons probably line the other cars, stowed until they're unloaded in Centrestates and swapped for whatever offerings they have for us. While Eastates supplies the other Territories with a minimal amount of seafood, our factories weave textiles that reach citizens beyond the Xone walls. They rely on us mostly for clothing, shoes, towels, sheets and blankets.

Some of our day dweller neighbors farther east in the upper division have achieved some success in coaxing apples to grow in scrappy orchards. The bounty is less than plentiful, but both the upper and lower Eastates' divisions are allotted a share of the harvest. The rest is sent westward to Centrestates.

I briefly wonder if any of our apples travel all the way to Westates. *Probably not.* Because of the distance between us and Westates, it wouldn't be practical to ship fresh food one way or the other. Centrestates serves as the "middle man," enabling trade from one end of the country to the other.

Like us, Westates is known for fishing along the coast, but supposedly they've been able to grow oranges, resuscitating the groves that prevailed many years ago. But like us, their primary contribution to the Divided States isn't food. They are responsible for manufacturing hard goods like tools, housing structures and machine parts. Most of their output is repurposed from the past.

In exchange for textiles and remanufactured parts, Centrestates provides the other Territories with grains, along with their main commodity – maintaining the power grid. It's a balance of supplying for each other's needs. Maybe we'll review all of this when the delegation convenes. And maybe we'll talk about other possibilities for trade.

Easing my neck back against the headrest, I let my gaze track the scenery racing by as I consider what these parts may have looked like a hundred years ago.

In an instant, worrisome thoughts creep back in – our names aren't on the list to return home in two weeks. I inhale a deep breath and squeeze my eyes shut. Learning has always been an escape for me. I will my thoughts to recall history lessons and lose myself in what once was and how it brought us to today.

At the time, the United States had one leader, called a president. The system was in place for centuries, but that fell apart when the Global Infection Spread jumped across continents, claiming lives until more were lost than saved. Borders closed and barriers rose. Nations isolated themselves, creating independent silos for their citizens. Canada and Mexico sealed their borders, eliminating immigration permanently.

The president relied on other governing bodies for support, but the virus was always one step ahead. Medical experts raced to study and eradicate the original virus and its mutations. They might have been able to wipe it out completely if not for a wave of natural disasters that struck a population already struggling to overcome a contagion with no boundaries.

Although at the time, citizens were unprepared for the series of events that claimed millions of lives, our history classes clearly outlined actions that led to the devastation. Weakened regulations practically invited environmental deterioration. Uncontrolled deforestation and pollution set the course for heat waves, droughts, fires, floods and storms that battered the land, sea and air. Even as those left adapted to new strains of the virus, public health was sabotaged by climate change.

When the Divided States formed, the Societal Order Leaders adopted an Alliance Agreement so that relations between the Territories were clearly defined. It's worked just fine for nearly a century. But somehow Hayes and I, and a bunch of our peers, are supposed to know how to make it better.

A wave of exhaustion washes over me. So much has happened in such a short amount of time, and this trip has barely begun. As I sink into my seat, I imagine the train's wheels pulling us along the track. It's a steady tugging motion, and even though it's not exactly a gentle glide, my muscles relax, submitting to the rhythmic movement.

I glance at Hayes. His neck cranes toward the aisle at an awkward angle. *That's gonna be sore when he wakes up.* Curly red bangs hang in suspension just over his glasses. For a moment I wonder if this is the only time he isn't thinking or processing information. *Nah, he's probably dreaming about solving math equations.* I stifle a giggle.

Even though I'd trade him for Josli in a second, my counterpart could be much worse. Some others, like Dolby Adler, would probably try to undermine me before we even stepped foot in Centrestates, just to make themselves look better. I don't get the sense that Hayes would do that. Granted, I barely know him, but I've talked to him more today than I have in the past seventeen years combined. He's not so bad. I just have to get used to someone who'd rather process theories instead of sharing gossip.

I try to envision the other delegates we'll meet, but all my mind can conjure is familiar faces from school. I'm not sure which ones I'm most curious about meeting. While it feels like the Westates delegates live two worlds away, and I'd love to know what their daily life is like, the night dwellers captivate my interest. Even the ones from Eastates. I've never met one, and now there's Hayes' theory about their appearance to consider.

Yawning and extending my arms, I stretch out a kink in my lower back. My overtaxed mind drifts back to the night dwellers, or nocts, as Josli would say. We've never had a reason to meet anyone from the lower division. *It was never a possibility. Until now.*

Some resources are shared between the nocts and the dayds, their slang term for us. Efforts to grow fruits and vegetables are focused in the upper division since they are best tended to during daylight hours. Even if the sun's rays are forced to slice through a hazy atmosphere, our produce workers can monitor them without the need for electricity. By the time the Divided States was formed, the land was virtually barren. With time and care, it slowly started to heal. The few orchards that have actually grown and harvested apples are proof that renewal is possible. Even if the process is slow.

The lower division is worse off than us. Decades ago, the region suffered an exceptional drought period that caused water shortages and widespread pasture and crop losses. Farming was deemed a lost cause, with such a low probability of success that it wasn't worth expending labor and land on it. Instead, the division was earmarked for textile factories. This way, the night dwellers work inside, relying on the electricity that we forgo during the overnight hours.

Another yawn tugs my lips apart. I glance out the window with leaden eyelids, too tired to focus on anything within view. Before I even realize it, my senses start to fade. Sound blurs into the perpetual mechanical hum. My breathing slows until the clearest sound I hear is my own deep breaths. Finally, my body slackens, melding to the seat for support.

***

"What the?! Are you kidding me?" Angry grumbling drifts to my ears as an abrupt nudge jostles my shoulder. My eyes flutter open, coaxing my body to follow suit. I blink away the confusion as my memory returns. I'm sitting next to Hayes Crimshaw.

"Everly! You were supposed to wake me up! We're already in Centrestates. We crossed the Xone wall!"

My eyes open wider and search the window. We've stopped at what appears to be a train station much like the one we boarded this morning. *How much of the ride did I miss?*

"I fell asleep," I admit. The one thing I had planned *not* to do. Annoyance flares, replacing my disappointment.

Hayes crosses his arms and pouts. Josli would probably burst out laughing at how childish he's acting. I cross my arms and deflect his attitude with my own.

"Look, I didn't mean to fall asleep, but how is it any different from what you did?"

With no valid retort, his eyes narrow and his mouth opens and closes a few times. Satisfied my point's been made, I face the window and watch the buzz of activity just outside our compartment.

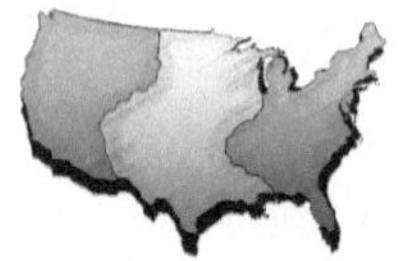

CHAPTER 13 ~ KIERA

UPPER DIVISION, CENTRESTATES

Two weeks earlier

"Wynter, please join us," I call to my assistant when she pads down the hallway past my office door. When she peeks her head in, I wave a hand in the air, encouraging her to join us. It's time for her to meet the newest member of our little team. It's like I'm introducing my left hand to my right hand. "This is Lisum. She's come to us all the way from Westates."

Lisum rises from the chair across from me. The two shake hands, sharing nervous but polite smiles. *I hope they get along. It will make everything so much easier.*

"The Westates! This is so exciting, Kiera!" Wynter claps her hands together. "I've never met a citizen from there! Lisum is the first."

"She actually came highly recommended from Societal Order Leader Huntsman's office," I brag. "Just hours after he agreed to the delegation, one of his staff members reached out and offered to send one of his highly recommended assistants."

"Yes, as soon as I learned about the initiative, I requested to be a part of it," Lisum explains. "This sort of collaboration is long overdue, in my opinion. It was a wonderful idea, for whoever came up with it."

I nod in agreement but say nothing. *She'll find out soon enough that this whole thing was my idea.* I'm already pleased with her enthusiasm. We can leverage it to gain buy-in from the other departments in the building.

"Well, you couldn't have come at a better time," Wynter says, jutting her chin in my direction. "Kiera here has been working me night and day."

"We have much to do in very little time," I say. "But it sounds like we're all in agreement. Lisum will be an integral part of this process, which will cut Wynter's workload by half."

"That sounds great to me!" Wynter chirps.

"Me too," Lisum smiles and nods, her gaze jumping between us.

"Wynter, if you could get Lisum all set up with a workspace near yours, you can start showing her all the arrangements you've been making for transportation, accommodations, conference room reservations, meal blocks and all the other logistics. I could go on and on, but you are obviously more than familiar with all the tasks at hand. We don't have much time left before the delegates arrive, so you both might as well dig right into your work."

With that, they're dismissed. Now it's time to finalize the list of delegates. All that's left is to review it with Leader Imperant, but he won't challenge any names I suggest. If anything, he'll congratulate me on why I selected each individual. What started as an initial task of confirming the absence or presence of a compliance chip has grown into so much more.

In two weeks, I've doubled our testable hypotheses. And I'm just getting started.

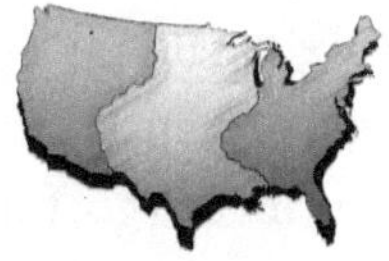

CHAPTER 14

TRAVEL TO THE UPPER DIVISION, CENTRESTATES

Voices and rustling draw my attention behind us. The other passengers in our car rise, clipboards in hand. Yep, they all must be transport overseers, ready to check their inventory and exchange it for something else. They march past us and file out the door. All but one. Galia. She pauses next to our seats and glances at her clipboard.

"Well, you two. It's time to switch trains. I'll escort you there and get you some food to eat on that leg of the trip. And I'll make sure your belongings are transferred as well." She nods once and politely waits for an appropriate response.

"Okay," Hayes hesitantly agrees. "I didn't know we had to switch trains. Is it just one more we're taking?"

Galia smiles and her serious demeanor softens. "Just one more. This is as far as an Eastates train can go, for security measures. This train will unload cargo and replace it with goods from Centrestates and then we're headed back home. You two, on the other hand, will board a railcar that runs directly to the heart of the Territory."

Hayes and I share a wide-eyed glance, curiosity passing between us. It's only a matter of seconds before his overflows and a question spills out of him.

"So if this railcar goes from here to the capital of Centrestates, does that mean we'll be the first ones from Eastates to ride in it?" His eyebrows jump in anticipation of Galia's answer.

"Close, but not exactly. Our own Societal Order Leader Ault has traveled to Centrestates for meetings. And of course his security detail accompanies him on those trips. But, really, other than them..." She smirks and cocks her head to one side. "Actually, we could say that you two are the first citizens, not in a governmental position, to visit Centrestates."

Brimming with pride, Hayes straightens his back and raises his chin. He's nearly glowing. Galia flattens the clipboard against her chest and leans toward us.

"This really is something." Then, in a near-whisper, she adds, "I think some of the other overseers are jealous of you two. Take every second of this for what it's worth – the chance of a lifetime."

She pulls back suddenly, as if she's crossed an invisible line. I can't speak for Hayes, but her honesty doesn't offend me in any way. Her green eyes dart around the cabin before she glances at the clipboard once more. She clears her throat as her posture visibly stiffens.

"If you'll meet me outside, we'll get you situated for the remainder of your trip." Without awaiting a response, she turns on her heel and strides to the door.

I stand shakily, my legs cramped from hours of disuse. After taking a moment to stretch and smooth out some wrinkles in my pants, I'm ready. Hayes watches me impatiently. I throw a hand in the air, motioning for him to go. He obliges without hesitation.

The first part of our trip is over.

***

The instant I step foot off the train, I freeze. Pairs of overseers litter the platform. The ones from Centrestates wear tan while their Eastates counterparts wear blue, like us. Some compare lists while others point and motion from one car to another. A few workers command loud, rumbling machines that unload cartons and stack them in a sectioned-off space. It's like a stall, the front completely open with back and side walls – maybe some sort of holding area.

Gray and white tiles pattern the floor in a subtle checkerboard. It's surprisingly clean considering all the shoes and machinery that must pass over it during a typical day. A few bear scuff marks, but they're barely noticeable on the darker-shaded tiles.

Fading white signs litter the walls. Their once-stark black letters announce that we've reached the Exchange Zone. The smaller ones give cautions and warnings to be watchful for moving equipment and heavy loads. I'm too busy absorbing all the sights and sounds that I don't even notice our guide is already on the move until Hayes scolds me.

"Come on, Everly!" he snaps. "We don't have time to stand around and gawk at everyone!"

A small part of me wants to stick my tongue out at him and roll my eyes, but I temper the annoyance and follow as he chases after Galia. Every few steps, she throws a glance over her shoulder, ensuring that she hasn't misplaced her charges.

Each step we take draws us farther from the hive of activity. It's not long before Galia leads us down an isolated hallway. The dominant sound in this section of the station is the echo of our shoes chasing each step we take. *Why is it so quiet all of a sudden?*

The overhead light grows brighter as we reach the end of the hallway. The opening spills into a completely different space than what we just left. There are no brick walls, loud machines, cartons of supplies or workers bustling around. The pristine white walls radiate a welcoming glow. A dozen small, round glass tables are spread throughout the room. The tan chairs tucked beneath them are overstuffed, as if they're filled with clouds. Doors line the walls, some labeled, some not. Connecting hallways stretch out on the right and left like a maze. *How big is this place?*

"We'll stop here for a restroom break so you two can freshen up." Galia motions toward a set of doors a few feet away from us. "I've got to pick up your lunches. If you just wait right here when you're done, I'll be back in a few minutes."

True to her word, Galia returns soon after Hayes and I finish up. She thrusts a small cardboard box toward each of us.

"There are grain bowls, fruit and drinks in these. You can eat on the next train."

We both thank her and take the packed lunches. A spicy scent tickles my nose and makes my mouth water. Even through packaging, this already smells better than the food back home.

Galia waves a hand over her shoulder, gesturing for us to follow her down a connecting corridor. With each step, the walls seem to creep closer, enclosing us in a chute. After a few dozen yards, the hallway opens up again, this time to a platform.

Two identical trains, both smaller than the one we just left, mirror each other on the tracks. A flutter of excitement swirls through me. These are clearly not meant for supply transport. Literally. Other than the framework necessary to secure the glass, windows encapsulate the roof and sides of this locomotive. It makes the first train look old and dingy, and we haven't even stepped inside this one yet.

Galia leads us to two tan-clothed workers, presumably guards, who stand on either side of the platform. I sense that no one's getting on a train without gaining their approval to pass.

"Good day," Galia calls, greeting the men. "I am here to deliver two passengers for transport to Centrel Hall. They are the upper division inter-Territory delegates."

One guard trails his beady dark eyes over us while the other one runs a hand over his short red beard and nods.

"Yes, we've been expecting you." He smiles, but it's clearly forced. "I'll escort them aboard while Kylan here locates their luggage." He nods to the beady-eyed man, who looks less than thrilled to retrieve our bags.

"All right, well, good luck to you, Hayes and Everly. Safe travels." Galia flashes a nod and smile before turning to Kylan. "I can show you where their belongings were unloaded."

He huffs out an impassive grunt but follows as she walks back toward the hallway we just left.

Red beard leads the way, not bothering to introduce himself. It's probably better that way, considering we're about to meet ten other delegates, not to mention whoever is in charge of us all. By the time I can remember all their names, our two weeks will probably be just about done. *That is, if we have a ride back home.* My stomach churns at the reminder that we weren't on the overseer's list. We'll have to ask about that when we get to Centrestates.

"You can wait in here. It'll just be a moment while we load your luggage and disconnect the other cars. You are our only passengers for this ride, so make yourselves comfortable. If you need anything, I'll be right out there." He points toward the platform. "If not, just sit back and you'll be on your way soon."

"Thank you," Hayes calls as the man retreats. I echo his sentiment, but doubt the man hears. He seems to be in a hurry to leave us.

Spinning toward me, Hayes wears a goofy grin. "Do you know what this means, Everly?"

"No one's babysitting us for a little while?" My guess makes him scowl. His question could mean anything, but my response is clearly not what he expected.

"No! We have the whole compartment to ourselves, which means we can sit anywhere, which means we both get a window seat!" His frustration is quickly replaced with excitement.

"Oh, right!" *Of course! Who would have thought we'd have this whole car to ourselves?*

Hayes wanders up and down the aisle, assessing his options. When he settles in a row right around the middle of the car, I choose the seat right behind him. I don't really care where I am as long as I have a window. Since we're not moving yet, I focus my exploration inward.

The cloth seats are tan, like the first train we boarded, but that's where the similarities end. Sliding a hand over the silky texture, I admire the golden flecks and shiny, raised swirls. I've never seen a fabric like this, but it must have come from Eastates – that's where all the textiles are woven and reconstructed into useful supplies. *Maybe there are special batches of fancier materials for purposes like this?*

Lowering my gaze, I realize the carpet is in better condition than the seating options were on our earlier ride. Sinking my shoes deeper into the cushiony surface, I wonder if this level of luxury is truly needed. The perfectly smooth walls are also tan, but the neutral shade provides a simple backdrop for ornate vines, painted in a shiny gold tone, that climb from the floor to the window's lower edge.

"So this is what it's like to be important," Hayes mutters, catching my eye. He reclines in his seat, hands folded beneath his head, elbows turned out. "This is just the start of it for me, Everly." When I narrow my eyes at him, he half-heartedly adds, "And probably you too."

Before I can roll my eyes in response to his afterthought, the engine rumbles, emitting a slightly audible churning. Even the engine's quieter on this thing. A fresh rush of adrenaline courses through me. If just traveling to this place is an adventure, what will it actually be like when we're there?

We roll forward, slowly at first, but steadily picking up speed. Within a minute, we rush past the platform and through a narrow tunnel. A glow of light awaits on the other end. As we breach the outside, a new world opens before our eyes. Hayes jumps from his seat, pointing and gawking.

"The Xone wall! We came right through it! The train station is inside the Xone wall!"

I need only recline my neck to see the mighty Xone wall rising behind us. It climbs to the sky, claiming the clouds. Just as I've seen in pictures, the honeycomb pattern is perfectly etched in the stone but fades as the length runs nearly out of sight.

So there is a hole in the wall, for the trains. But like Galia said, travel beyond the wall is extremely limited. A satisfied smile curls my lips as I consider how few others have been in this very place I sit. If only Dad, Easton and Josli could be here. *How could I ever describe what I see and feel to any degree that they would understand? And how much will I forget by the time I get home?* I already mourn the lost memories that will pass through my mind too quickly, even though they haven't happened yet.

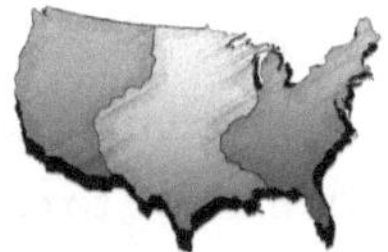

CHAPTER 15

TRAVEL TO THE UPPER DIVISION, CENTRESTATES

Hayes and I both stare at the Xone wall, under its imposing glare, until the scenery rushing past commands our attention. What starts as patches of green quickly yields to sprawling acres. Repositioning in my seat, I face forward. I'll get to see the Xone wall up close again on the way home. Hayes slides into his seat, bobbing his head back and forth to monitor the views from both sides of the train.

In that moment, an impatient growl erupts from my stomach. Hayes looks over and chuckles.

"Guess we should eat, huh?" He picks up his lunch package and sets it on his lap, carefully opening the flaps. Leaning against the seat directly in front of mine, I reach for my own box. As soon as I retrieve it, movement catches my eye. A small rectangular tray silently lowers itself before me – coming right out of the seat back.

"Hayes! Look at this!" I don't have to explain. As soon as his eyes land on it, they widen and he jumps out of his seat.

"Whoa! How'd you get that?" He knocks on it before raising it at an angle.

"I just touched the back of the seat. You try it."

Leaping back into his seat, he presses a hand against the seat in front of him. We both watch in awe when the attached tray gently lowers itself to a ninety-degree angle just above his lap.

"Trays so we can eat! On a train." He slides his glasses up the bridge of his nose.

Distracted by the wonders of the little tray tables, we devour every ounce of our delicious lunch.

***

"You know, Everly, Centrestates grows the most fresh food. It's all about their geography and history. Even before the Global Infection Spread, their land was always best suited for farming."

I roll my eyes but he doesn't notice. Of course I know all this. I've attended the same school and listened to the same lessons as him. Besides that, it's relaxing just looking out the window. I mutter a neutral "Uh-huh" in hopes he'll keep his thoughts to himself, but instead of discouraging him, he continues, completely oblivious to my disinterest.

"So even though we all had to deal with the effects of long-term pollution and harmful, wasteful practices, they were best positioned to rebuild. Before we were divided, the midwestern region of the country was known for crop growth – corn, soybeans, wheat." He pauses, actually looking at me. Maybe just to ensure someone's listening to his rambling.

I nod, unsure what to say. Is he looking for confirmation that I want to talk about this? Because I don't.

"I have a theory. Wanna hear it?" He raises his eyebrows in anticipation of the only polite answer I can give. He can be annoying, but he's harmless. And he's all I've got right now.

"Sure."

"So, we know that a majority of the Centrestates' farmland was completely ravaged, but generations of farming experience was their advantage. Those who survived disease and natural disasters developed new methods to adapt their profession and teach it to younger generations."

"Yeah, that makes sense," I agree. "But I'm sure that's not exactly news to anyone here. And I don't think it's really anything that will come up when the delegation meets."

It's not like he's made some major discovery. *Maybe he just wanted to delve into a deeper discussion?* Either my tone or facial expression are too transparent, giving away my lack of enthusiasm for this conversation. His demeanor instantly deflates.

For the first time, I wonder if he's disappointed that I was chosen as his counterpart.

Hayes shuffles to a seat on the other side of the aisle, stares out the window and sits in silence. Awkward, painful silence. Any excitement in watching the scenery pass by has been squashed. My guilt smothers the air. As much as it pains me, I've got to get Hayes talking again. Somehow in our short time together, we've developed a bubble of normalcy and it just popped.

As I scan the hills and valleys, an igloo-shaped dome rises in the distance. I'd guess it's about three train cars high as well as wide. It's surrounded by three other domes, creating a formation. I've never seen anything like it. *And it's the perfect conversation starter.*

"Hayes, check that out," I point, even though he doesn't turn to face me. "What do you think those are?"

Even if he's still mad, curiosity outweighs any grudge he holds. He rises, crossing the aisle, and slides into the seat in front of me. Pushing his glasses up the bridge of his nose, he squints and nearly presses his face to the glass.

"Those domes," I start. "What do you think they are?"

He taps a pointer finger to his lips for several beats before confidently stating, "I bet they're greenhouses. Enormous greenhouses."

Before I can agree or interject an opinion, he continues.

"After the growing fields here became contaminated, they were considered barren. The Societal Order leader at the time designated area in the Territory for greenhouses. They needed a completely controlled, protected environment to restart the processes that once occurred naturally."

"Do you think there are more than just those?" If I can just keep him talking long enough, maybe we can get back to what's become our normal. He pauses again, considering my question. Slowly, he starts nodding.

"Yes, there are probably a lot more. But you know what the real question should be, Everly?"

I gulp, certain my brain won't produce whatever answer he's looking for. Raising my shoulders, I shake my head.

"Why don't we have those?" His finger taps the window, motioning toward the structures. "Both Eastates and Westates have the advantage of coastal fishing. And even though we can incorporate fresh catch into food production, our land has yet to recover from the environmental breakdown. We can barely grow anything, so why aren't we doing that too?"

Now it's my turn to ponder his question. I chew my bottom lip.

"Maybe because we're focused on textile production? One Territory can't do it all. Each one has its strengths, it's why we all depend on each other." Even as the explanation passes over my lips, almost automatically, it doesn't feel true. Food is such a basic need for every single citizen. Shouldn't it be more of a priority than hoping neighborhoods can grow a few random vegetables in their backyard?

"I don't know, it just doesn't seem that hard. If they can do it here, we should be able to do it there." With that, Hayes slinks back into his seat. I can tell his mind is turning this over, dissecting theories and arguments for and against his theory. Maybe this is something to discuss with the delegation. Either way, I sense it's best to let him be. At least this time his silence isn't due to any unintentional offense I've caused.

***

My own thoughts wander as I watch the cluster of igloo greenhouses fade in the distance. Maybe Hayes is right. All three Territories allot acreage for farm fields, but Centrestates is responsible for about eighty percent of natural crop growth. According to our agriculture classes, citizens throughout the Divided States share the same, mostly plant-based, diet. Although our rations don't look like they come from plants. At least not healthy ones.

I can't be sure about the other Territories, but in Eastates, our rations are processed in the production facility. As a measure of efficiency, everyone gets the same meals. Additives are part of the process. This allows the Societal Order to ensure that we're all getting needed vitamins and minerals to maintain healthy bodies. I just wish the final product was more appetizing. *Unless it isn't meant to be.*

Many years ago people faced obesity and a range of diseases caused by it. There were too many unhealthy options – greasy, fatty, sugary – on every corner. Food stores sold all kinds of fresh and frozen foods, but the Global Infection Spread gradually put an end to that. It reached every state and nation, dissolving critical links to products and processes. Rebuilding required sacrifices, like giving up a slew of unnecessary choices. Survival became the ultimate goal.

Our diets afford us the ideal calorie intake for each day. Our breakfast and evening meal rations are provided for specific people in each family. In ours, we know that the lightest blue cartons are for Easton. *Maybe the lighter color signifies less calories or portions?* My cartons are a purplish cornflower shade while Dad's are a deep navy blue.

If I'm accepted for employment at the nutrition production facility, I'll learn all about what the different colors mean and how the Societal Order organizes food sorting and packaging. Although we don't have any dietary restrictions in our family, I know others do. Josli's younger sister is allergic to fish, so her rations don't contain any. Her cartons are bright yellow. Seeing the different colors tugs at my curiosity. I want to know what each one means and how production is organized to ensure everyone gets exactly what they need.

If I actually get the job I want, I'll probably start as an apprentice, learning all there is to know about how our food is produced. But my ultimate goal is to become a nutritional scientist. I want to create rations that provide the necessary nutrients while also being palatable.

A hint of Hayes' skepticism drifts through my thoughts. The Societal Order controls everything. *If they wanted our food to taste better, couldn't they do it? Are there just not enough tasty ingredients? Is this the best we can have? What if our food was more appetizing? Would people complain that they wanted more?* With the current system, there's no opportunity, or motivation, to overindulge.

I'm bordering on forbidden questions. I could never ask any of them even if I was employed at the nutrition production facility. I would be told whatever I needed to know in order to perform my duties. I imagine it's a fine balance between contributing to change without breaching unspoken boundaries.

The Societal Order's rules and processes are in place to help each Territory thrive. And we aren't supposed to question those decisions. They are greater than any individual, and necessary to ensure an equitable lifestyle for all citizens. It's the reason that all three leaders meet throughout the year, so that each Territory continues to contribute and receive what is fair.

As I run my gaze over the unnecessary extravagance surrounding me, I wonder how equitable lifestyles are when only a select few get to ride on trains like this.

Hayes must be lost in his thoughts because he keeps to himself for the rest of the trip. I memorize every growing field and count each greenhouse igloo we rush past. I reach sixteen by the time the train begins to slow down.

"There's the station," Hayes declares, pointing ahead to the right. The three-story brick building is brimming with windows. *Is someone waiting for us in there?*

We glide toward a platform. Another train rests idle on a parallel track. My insides twist at the mere sight of our final destination. *We actually made it. I'm really in the heart of Centrestates.*

A few people stride across the long, rectangular platform. They wear outfits just like ours – pants and a pullover long-sleeved shirt – but shaded tan instead of blue. I assume they're all workers until two gesture and motion toward our train excitedly. Most of the workers we've seen today weren't even remotely interested in us. *Do they know it's just two teenagers arriving or do they think a Societal Order leader is in this car?*

The train crawls to a stop as the engine's light rumble ceases. Just as I wonder how we're supposed to know what to do and where to go, the door slides open. A petite woman with short dark hair traipses into the car, focused solely on us. Not surprising, since we're the only occupants.

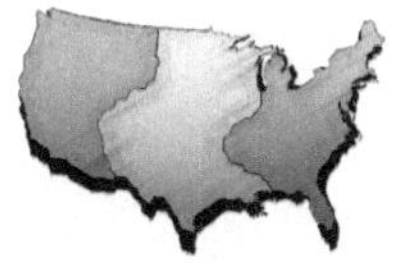

CHAPTER 16

UPPER DIVISION, CENTRESTATES

"Everly Scott and Hayes Crimshaw, welcome to Centrestates!" Smiling broadly, she throws her hands in the air as if she's presenting the whole Territory to us. Even though we're still inside the same enclosed space we entered hours ago. Hayes and I both respond at the same time, our words spilling over each other in a jumble of greetings. She continues, unfazed.

"My name is Lisum and I am thrilled to meet you." She offers an outstretched hand, which we take turns shaking. "I'd be happy to take you to the other delegates as soon as you're ready to disembark." She motions toward the train station. "I believe you're the last ones to arrive. I'm sure you can't wait to meet everyone!"

Hayes turns to me, a hint of a question reflecting in his wide eyes. He clearly cannot wait to join the others. I nod and gulp. *Why are we the last ones here? They'll all be staring at us when we walk in. Where's Josli when I need her?*

"Yes, we're ready!" Hayes answers without hesitation. I straighten and pull my shoulders back, as if holding a confident posture will somehow mask my insecurity.

"All right then, let's go join the rest of our honored guests." She turns in place and glides out the door, with Hayes following about half a step behind. My legs seem to bear the weight of my growing anxiety. Now that we're this close, my pulse skyrockets. I smooth my hair, take a deep breath and focus on the simple act of moving one foot in front of the other.

***

Sights and sounds bombard my senses as my feet brush solid ground. My first step is a graceless stumble, but I'm not the only one. It seems after sitting so idly for much of the day, Hayes' legs have forgotten how to work too. It doesn't help that we aren't exactly accustomed to railroad travel either.

Lisum seamlessly weaves around the workers on the platform, leading us to the large glass doors spilling into the train station. As we pass, I watch their methodical routine. Three men and one woman unload baggage from the immobile trains, neatly stacking each armful into an organized pile. *I wonder if our bags will be added to it soon.*

Moments later, the station's entrance looms before us. The doors part as we breach the threshold, delivering us into a large open space.

Our shoes echo on the white tile floor. Columns of pink bricks stretch to the ceiling, split by window pairs every few feet. A few workers bustle past us. They glance at us curiously as they continue on their path.

"This way," Lisum calls over her shoulder. We gravitate toward a group clustered together in the middle of the spacious room. They stand in clear contrast to the tan-clothed Centrestates citizens, forming a small but colorful sea of earth tones. I've never seen people from all three Territories together like this. Textbooks had pictures here and there, and facts about each area, but actively being a part of something like this feels surreal. Wrong somehow.

A woman stands at the center of the group speaking, hands in constant motion, punctuating her words. Two other Centrestates adults stand a few feet from the group. Circling, hovering and observing. I recognize them from the platform – the people who were watching our train when we arrived. I guess they did know who was on board. As soon as they notice Lisum's approach with us in tow, one pulls a camera out of a bag slung over her shoulder while the other raises a black rectangular device to his mouth and begins speaking into it.

"I see the last of our delegates have arrived." All eyes turn toward us as the woman in the center of the group announces our presence. Collectively, they watch us with fascination, evaluating us. Maybe wondering if we're soon-to-be friends or competitors.

The perky blonde we can thank for this awkward attention clasps her hands together and takes a few steps toward us, naturally widening the circle formed around her. She turns, waving a hand in the air to signal she's addressing us all.

"I'm Kiera Saign and I'll be your guide throughout this important assignment. Don't worry about your baggage. Transport workers are gathering it right now and it will be delivered to your rooms, probably before you even get there." As she speaks, her eyes travel across the group, pinning each of us with a moment of individual attention.

Hayes nudges my elbow and shoots me a sly grin when I glance his way. He can barely contain his enthusiasm. I should be feeling that way right now. It's an honor to just be standing here. Even if I were dismissed in the next five minutes, I've actually crossed a Xone wall and visited another Territory. I've barely just arrived and this trip has already been more amazing than I was willing to imagine it could be.

Yet, deep down, my insides twist with something more than nerves. My intuition urges caution; maybe it's just a reminder to not embarrass myself, or the Territory I represent.

I'm not sure what I was expecting, but the other delegates aren't very different from us. Some mirror Hayes' excitement while others shift their eyes back and forth uneasily, from their surroundings to each other. In contrast, a few radiate confidence, as if they belong here. And it's not just those wearing the telltale Centrestates tan clothing.

Kiera introduces some others who have joined our entourage. The two people who were outside on the platform when our train arrived are from the Centrestates' information broadcast. They will visit with us throughout our time as a delegation to capture the experience on film and collect details to share throughout all three Territories.

The word "film" catches me off guard. At home the information broadcast is only voices, not pictures. *It would be bad enough if I had to just talk to them, but now they'll also be taking pictures or videos?*

We're instructed to pretend they aren't here unless we're specifically asked for an interview. *Great, so they'll have proof if I say something stupid.*

Next Kiera presents her two assistants. I recognize one face – Lisum. She and another woman, Wynter, will help us get settled but for the most part, Kiera will oversee our day-to-day activities. As they arrange us for some photos, Hayes is whisked to the back row. They position me right in front of him, grouping the other Eastates delegates beside us.

As our three hosts smooth out any stray wrinkles and wrangle any unkempt bangs, I wonder how different the trip home will be. *Will I miss any of these people? Will I be sad to leave? I'll definitely be anxious to see Dad, Easton and Josli, but will I form any friendships here? Real friendships with people I'll never see again?* That is, if I even have a ride home. I can't forget to ask about that.

Everything I'll learn about the Territories, and their divisions, is now a living, breathing lesson. The other delegates here will inform our initial, and probably only, impressions of the other Territories. Just as we will likely influence their opinions about Eastates. Nervous energy buzzes in my veins as an invisible microscope seems to scrutinize my every move. It's not just the leaders we have to impress; it's also each other. Everyone here was chosen, selected for their academic achievements as well as the manner in which they exemplify the Societal Order's rules. Or at least that's what it said in the papers Principal DeBrusk gave us.

A few of us may someday lead future waves of citizens within the Territories. And the peace treaty we develop may lay the foundation for unsecured travel beyond the Xone walls. Maybe they could even be crumbled to dust, and citizens could move freely throughout any part of the country. *Then the delegates could visit each other again someday. If we wanted to.*

I observe my surroundings with a fresh perspective, with a newfound eagerness to begin this assignment pulsing through me. In just two weeks' time, someone may be earmarked as a future leader. Maybe it will be me. Or Hayes. Everyone here is probably thinking the same thing. Raking a casual gaze over my peers, a few stand out. One plants a hand on her hip while jutting the opposite leg forward. Doesn't look like she has any doubts about being here.

After what feels like a hundred photos, Kiera announces we can break our pose and relax for a moment.

"That's enough pictures for now. Some of you have been cooped up on a train for several hours. Our first stop will be restrooms and the cafeteria. Once you've had a chance to refuel, we'll take a tour of the building. You'll spend much of your time in Centrel Hall. It's the most prestigious landmark in Centrestates."

Her shoulders square slightly, as if pride seeps out of her just by mentioning where we're headed. She continues as we trail behind her and follow as she takes a few tentative steps toward the door. She twists slightly, speaking as she walks.

"Follow me, everyone. Centrel Hall isn't far from here, so we'll walk." As a group, we collectively quicken our pace to keep up with her long stride. We trail her for four blocks, a string of people in perpetual motion stretching across the wide sidewalks. A few delegates stumble as they struggle to maintain the pace while absorbing the sights and sounds. Casting only brief glances downward, I notice a few veiny cracks in the concrete. Stray blades of grassy weeds burst through the narrow openings. *Maybe this place isn't as perfect as I thought.*

Citizens hustle around us, some pushing through glass entrances to ornate buildings, while others rush onward to an unknown endpoint. They mostly keep to themselves, but a few smile at us as they pass. It makes me wonder what has been said about the delegation on their information broadcast already. They must know who we are, if not for the color of our clothes alone.

Other than those in our cluster, everyone else wears the standard-issue tan. But many manage to personalize the look with a belt looped around their waists or a colorful metal insignia pinned near their collarbones. *I wonder what those mean?*

Adding embellishments to our clothing is discouraged in Eastates. Every year at least one student attempts to stand out by arranging a paper-clip pattern along their collar or drawing a swirly design on their sleeve. As harmless as it seems, educators act quickly to correct the behavior – sending the guilty party to the principal's office. I'm sure their parents are contacted and the family likely loses rations or are subjected to an earlier curfew for the punishment period.

I shake my head, willing away the thoughts. It never happened to our family or Josli's, so I don't know for sure, and there's no point thinking about it. Refocusing my senses on the world around me, I search our small group for Hayes. I recognize his gangly frame a few steps ahead of me. His head pivots back and forth, showing off the goofy smile he wears.

As if an idea just popped into his head, he pinpoints his focus to our guide and brushes past the others to reach her.

"Um, Kiera, can I ask a question?" Hayes adjusts his glasses and patiently waits for permission to ask away. I chuckle to myself. Of course he's first on the list to learn more about this place. *I wish I had a pinch of his confidence.*

CHAPTER 17

UPPER DIVISION, CENTRESTATES

"What's so funny?" A deep voice startles me, washing the smirk from my face and launching my heart into overdrive. I turn toward the source of the abrupt question, gulping as I take in his wavy dark hair and startling blue eyes. They match his clothing. Perfectly. It's one of the Westates delegates. His intent gaze pins me in place as he awaits an answer.

"Um, nothing. I was just thinking about something my little brother said." It's the best lie I can come up with, so it will have to do. I'm not going to openly admit I was laughing about Hayes' incessant pursuit of knowledge.

"Oh. Then I'll let you get back to your entertaining inner thoughts." His right cheek tugs into a lopsided smile. It only makes him look cuter. A hint of pine tickles my nose. *Is it him?* Of course, we are outside, so the scent could be drifting in the air. I don't see anything more than waves of grass and an assortment of small decorative bushes around here though. The handsome stranger drops back into the group just as quickly as he seemed to appear beside me. *Oooookay.*

I shift my focus from the odd Westates guy to the other delegates. Mostly the girls from Centrestates.

Ancient history springs to my mind. Women used to color their fingernails and paint their faces to look more attractive. During the Global Infection Spread, priorities shifted to necessities. Extravagances like those were quietly discontinued. I don't think many people minded or even noticed. Those who survived had to accept a new way of life, born of fear and loss.

Yet makeup and nail color exist in Centrestates. It's not manufactured in Eastates – we're only supposed to focus on necessities. So does that mean Centrestates produces it? *If so, what else do they have that we don't?* The Territories are supposed to be equal. Well, I mostly believed that until I saw the second train we took today.

Quickening my pace, I merge into the center of the group. We move as one gawking, distracted sea of bodies, trying to keep up with Kiera while absorbing the avalanche of new sights and sounds. Even though everyone but Hayes is a complete stranger, I feel a slight connection to the others already. We're similar enough – all around sixteen or seventeen, the majority of us plucked from home and dropped into an unfamiliar place.

Even those who were poised with confidence back at the train station allow awe and wonder to cross their features. Eyes widen and mouths drop as they take in the heart of the division. We have to crane our necks to see the top of any building within viewing distance. Although they all have unique features, every one of them is made of a sleek polished metal and glass. Our reflections bounce back at us as we scamper down the sidewalk.

The churn of approaching engines draws my eyes to the street. Cars roll along as if it's just another day. A few heads in our group turn, watching the vehicles pass with interest. We have cars in Eastates, but they are only used by government officials. Fuel and replacement parts for required upkeep are rare commodities, so not many citizens drive. Considering we're in the heart of the Territory, maybe these drivers *are* all government officials.

I count six of them before we turn a corner and face a new series of buildings. I'm used to endless rows of squat homes and centrally placed warehouses for ration pickup. My eyes bounce from one building to the next, sweeping across the road to find mirror images lining the other sidewalk as well. The structures reach to the sky, floors upon floors stacked on top of each other.

We draw nearer to what is clearly the tallest structure in the entire city. Its ivory exterior climbs toward the clouds. I imagine a fairy tale king sitting atop an ornate throne inside it when Kiera stops abruptly, turning to face us in a dramatic whirl. She throws both arms out at her sides. "This," she gestures toward the tower, "is Centrel Hall." She pauses, scanning our group. *Is she trying to gauge our reaction?* I can't be sure if my jaw gapes as I slowly tilt my head back, following the sleek lines of each floor's wall of windows.

"This is where formal meetings are held between Territories, where our three leaders come together. Decisions that impact each and every one of us are made within these walls. It's really quite remarkable, and not a place that many citizens have been invited to visit." With those final words, she charges forward. Our small group rushes to follow.

"Should we curtsy or bow or something?" Warm breath tickles my neck as the deep voice from earlier whispers in my ear. The Westates guy brushes past me, smirking and raising an eyebrow. I narrow my eyes at him, brushing my hair back to scratch the itch he left. Before he can turn away, his eyes lock on the skin just below my earlobe. *My stupid birthmark. No one at home notices it anymore, which makes me forget . . . until someone sees it for the first time, and stares.*

Raking a hand through my stick-straight mane, I flick it back into place, hiding the raised, heart-shaped bump. The Westates guy peers at me curiously once more, then picks up his pace, effectively putting a row of bodies between us. *Has he never seen a birthmark before? Something's wrong with that guy and this is probably my cue to stay away from him. Far away.*

***

Kiera stops just outside the elaborate structure and pauses. When she spins to face us, the street noise seems to mute to a whisper. This woman commands attention, even from inanimate objects.

"This is it! This is the most important building in the whole Territory! I assume each and every one of you is ready to fully immerse yourself in this experience." She purses her lips, poised to continue. But before she can, an outburst yanks everyone's attention to the delegate standing closest to her.

"Yes!" Without hesitation, Hayes punches a fist into the air. A few delegates chuckle but fall silent when they notice Kiera's glare. With a blink, she recovers, instantly shifting from annoyance to amusement. A fresh smile softens her features, and she nods to Hayes.

"I appreciate that enthusiasm. I hope to see it from all of you in the coming days."

Somehow her words feel more like a command than a statement.

As if on cue, Kiera's assistants – Lisum and Wynter – plunge ahead, triggering the automatic glass doors to swoosh open. Kiera nods and they spring through the threshold, positioning themselves on either side to herd us to our next stop. A moment later, Kiera breezes through the open entryway, Hayes maintaining his role as her shadow.

Those of us at the back of the line linger, waiting for the bodies in front to shuffle inside. Just as I'm about to step forward, a frantic voice yanks my attention to the row of tall bushes flanking the entrance.

"Hey!" The single syllable whisper-shout is both a warning and a demand. A wiry old man emerges from the foliage. Loose, tattered clothing hangs from his tanned, wrinkly arms and legs.

"I know why yer all here and yeh better be careful." He jerks his head toward the open doors. "They don't care 'bout no one. Ain't what they say they er."

Desperate to look away from the man, I glance to the delegate standing behind me. It's the other boy from Eastates, the night dweller. A spark of comfort blooms inside me. Just seeing the familiar blue clothing reminds me that I'm not here alone. His eyes narrow on the stranger and he responds.

"Thanks for the warning, but we'll form our own opinions based on facts." The boy motions for me to move along, to the safety of the building.

"Yeh sure will." The man smiles as we pass, revealing two rows of crooked, rotting teeth. An empty gap marks a space that once held a tooth.

How could someone like that even exist here? Everyone in our Territory gets rations that include food, clothing and hygiene products.

Just as stealthily as he appeared, the old man slips away. I focus on the entranceway before me, eager to pass through it.

"Hey, don't let that guy get to you. He doesn't know what he's talking about," the boy says, shrugging off the encounter. "And he should probably start worrying about himself, not us."

"I can't argue with that." I search his dark eyes, sensing honesty with a hint of concern. "Thanks for stepping in though. I wasn't really sure what to say."

"No problem." He thrusts a hand toward me. "I'm Vanen."

"Everly." We shake, exchanging brief smiles. He's slightly taller than me, with a strong grip. Josli would be disappointed. Nothing about him stands out as a night dweller. He could pass for anyone at school back home.

Okay, that wasn't so bad. I've officially met one delegate. Counting him and Hayes, there's only nine more to go.

***

The breath rushes from my lungs as I take in Centrel Hall's illustrious interior. The crisp surroundings awaken my senses, breaking through the emotional fog of the morning. The entire building is encapsulated in glass. All four walls sparkle from their crystal coating. The entire space is open and airy, not at all like the stuffy classrooms I expected.

Rooms offshoot in every direction from the main entryway, and a stairway rises in the center of the first floor, leading up seven stories. The polished rails wink at us, reflected in the golden frames lining the windows. Nature invades the building, bathing the interior in warm sunlight. Jade leaves reach toward the sky, rising from golden pots placed every few feet. A spiral staircase swirls upward, branching off to each floor above. An enormous tree sprouts within the center of the staircase, stretching all the way to the top floor.

So many plants. Healthy too. My thoughts flicker to the pitiful gardens back home. We're tasked with growing food, never mind we're not very good at it, while Centrestates uses plants as decorations? I swallow my incredulity, reminding myself that we are in *the* most important building in the whole Territory. For all I know, Societal Order Leader Ault sits on a sterling silver throne while he rules over Eastates. Or maybe his capitol building mirrors this one. Those kinds of details were never taught at school.

Echoes of our footfalls chase us down the hallway as we rush to keep up with Lisum and Wynter. They herd us toward the restrooms and direct us to the dining room after we've washed up. The bright, expansive space is a grown-up version of the school cafeteria back home. Instead of parallel rows of long tables with stiff stools attached, dozens of tables alternate throughout the space. They vary in size and shape – square, circular, rectangular, and able to seat four, six or eight people.

A few tan-clad men and women sit at scattered tables throughout the large room, but I'm guessing we've arrived at an off-time as we easily outnumber the people who look like they belong here. They whisper, nodding toward us and flashing encouraging smiles. While they're obviously aware of our presence, they make no effort to approach.

The grins slip away when our observers notice Kiera flurrying around us. *Looks like she's known around here. And based on their reactions, they aren't happy to see her.*

"I've reserved space for our group." Kiera waves a hand toward the center of the room, where three rectangular tables have been pushed together with twelve seats evenly spaced around them. "Now, take some time to refuel before we tour the building." With that, she turns and strides out of the room. *I guess our first official act is eating and she's not sticking around for it.*

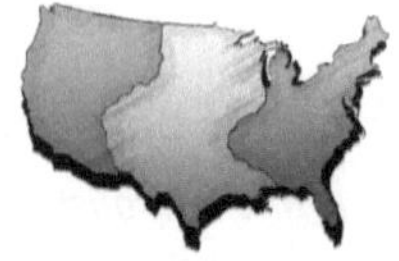

CHAPTER 18

UPPER DIVISION, CENTRESTATES

Lisum and Wynter hover like overprotective parents, shooing us into a line that mimics the school cafeteria back home. We file through the chute and select small plates of colorful offerings – orange and green clusters of vegetables, golden potato cubes and pink slices of meat.

I follow the girl in front of me, filling in the next empty seat at our designated table. Settling into the chair, I glance around. Each side of the table blends into a mosaic of faces and features – from dark complexions to square chins to pointy noses, from curly red locks to mousy brown strands like my stringy mane. Most of the delegates are quiet, seemingly still taking in their surroundings.

Before too long, laughter draws my attention to the other end of the table. Of course Hayes has already made some friends. He happily chats in between bites of food, looking completely relaxed, while I remind myself to drop my shoulders, releasing them from their perpetual hunched state.

Shifting focus to the magnificent scents wafting from each plate, I stab a forkful of vegetables. My mouth waters in anticipation. The buttery, savory flavor ignites my taste buds. *This is nothing like what we eat in Eastates.*

I steal glances at the others, anticipating wide-eyed surprise to match my own, but no one else seems to be impressed by their food. *Do they eat like this back home? Or are they so uptight that they don't dare express any wonder or excitement?*

A few share sporadic chitchat, but much of it is drowned out by the clanking of silverware on plates. After a few minutes, a voice cuts through the background noise. It's one of the Westates girls, complaining about how long and slow the train ride was. She twirls a lock of chestnut hair around her finger as she announces, "It better have been worth it!"

A few delegates chuckle, while others quickly offer their own gripes: "My family couldn't come to see me off," or "The ride made me dizzy, I felt like I'd throw up." *Were Hayes and I the only ones amazed by the scenery?* I keep quiet, unwilling to join in what feels like a disrespectful path that I'd rather not take. The train was a whole new experience, but it didn't make either of us sick, or dizzy.

As if summoned by the negative spiral the conversation has suddenly taken, Wynter dashes to the head of the table, dramatically throwing her arms into the air. "Why don't you all take turns introducing yourselves? You'll be working together very closely over the next two weeks. Might as well start getting to know each other."

She nods enthusiastically before zeroing in on my classmate, raising her eyebrows expectantly. He's more than happy to accommodate.

"I'm Hayes Crimshaw and I'm from Eastates, the Upper Division."

Like a relay, each delegate takes a turn, defining themselves in less than a minute. Each introduction spills into the next one. I watch and listen, but the names run together, passing through my mind nearly as quickly as they fall from each delegate's lips. My stomach churns as I fail to remember most of their names.

Once the last person finishes his introduction, it appears that the simple icebreaker effectively shifted the mood at the table. Inquisitive chatter grows all around me. I let out a deep breath, knowing I should ask someone a question or somehow start talking to one of the other delegates. Before I have the chance, the girl sitting beside me strikes first.

"So you're from Eastates," she says, turning to face me.

"Yes, I . . . I came with Hayes." I point to my counterpart at the head of the table. "He seems to be pretty popular right about now."

She's wearing tan, so she's from here. *What was her name? I think it started with an S.*

"I'd say he fits in just fine. He'll probably be named head delegate by mid-afternoon and be bossing Lisum and Wynter around by dinner," she giggles, instantly relaxing my nerves. As a laugh escapes me, I glance around but no one notices. They're all engaged in their own animated conversations, relaxed enough to talk and joke.

As brief as the introductions were, they somehow dissolved the tension.

***

Just as we ease into a comfortable, if slightly guarded, companionship, Kiera sweeps into the room. Whispered conversations die as they're replaced by the steady clack of her heels approaching the table.

"All right." Kiera stops behind Hayes, pressing her palms together and pursing her lips. "Looks like we're just about done here. Let's clean up and get on with the tour. We don't have much time right now, so we'll have to be quick about it."

She waves her hands in the air and gestures toward the door, coaxing us to hurry. One by one, we rise. A few barrel away from the table, eager to fall into step behind Kiera. Others, like me, stand uncertainly. *Do we just leave everything here?*

Lisum and Wynter swarm around us once again, directing everyone on where to deposit used utensils and stack dirty plates. They gather what was left behind by those trailing Kiera, who's clearly eager to show off her habitat. She charges into the hallways, headed straight for the winding staircase.

Once we've all caught up, she starts up the steps, throwing out brief phrase descriptions of each level we pass.

"This first floor is where all agricultural planning happens." Her heels clack with each step she climbs. "Each department is composed of the most knowledgeable experts in the Territory. They inform Leader Imperant on strategies to execute and all possible courses of action and outcomes."

She continues as Hayes and the rest of us eagerly follow, our eyes scanning and our ears perked for every last detail she provides. We pass floors that house experts on labor and production, trade and finance, and security and defense. That announcement makes Hayes stop in his tracks.

"Um, Kiera, why would Centrestates need security and defense?" he eagerly asks.

"Besides overseeing the distribution of Enforcers throughout the Territory, that staff ensures that we are well protected from any threats from the northern or southern borders," she coolly explains. I've never thought about that in Eastates. Maybe those who live closer to those borders would understand the need.

The remaining levels are reserved for visiting leaders, meeting space for those who work in the building and Leader Imperant's immediate staff.

When we reach the top floor, Kiera flashes us a sly smile before leading us down the hallway. She stops at the first door on the left and swings it open, waving a hand to gesture us all inside. Unlike the rest of the building, the stark tang of antiseptic burns my nose. Whoever is responsible for cleaning this room must be very good at their job.

"This is where you'll spend the duration of your time here. This room has been reserved for the exclusive use of the delegation for the next two weeks." We file past her, toward the massive table that takes up most of the room. At least twenty chairs surround it. Everything about them looks comfortable – from the cushioned seats to the wide armrests and the high backs. But best of all, each chair's star-shaped base rests on five small wheels. Easton would love to hop on one of these and roll around the whole room, probably crashing into anyone who got in his way.

I catch myself smirking as I imagine my little brother's antics if he were here. Pressing a hand to my mouth, I cover any evidence of my amusement. I'm not prepared to let my guard down. Not just yet. Thankfully no one notices.

Like mindless drones, everyone migrates toward the wall-size window, their gazes fixed on the sprawling world beyond the glass that seems to stretch on forever. Almost in a trance, I wander forward and stop next to Hayes. I've got to remember this moment so I can tell Josli, Easton and Dad all about it.

"Take it all in," Kiera says. Her words ooze with pride. I can practically hear the smirk tugging at her cheeks without even glancing her way. "Enjoy the view! I will be right back, I've just got to step out for a moment."

As soon as Kiera exits the room, a few delegates allow their thoughts to spill into words.

"I can't believe we're really here," a girl from Westates mutters as her eyes rove from one corner of the elaborate room to the next.

"Is this what our capitol building is like?" the other girl from Eastates questions.

"Doubt it," a boy from Centrestates says, arrogance dripping from each syllable.

"I have a theory that each capitol building was created based on the Societal Order leader's taste at that time," Hayes starts. "They probably started from an existing structure and just enhanced it to meet..."

I've heard enough of that guy's theories for the day. I tune out my counterpart's voice and fully take in my surroundings. This is by far the fanciest building I've ever seen, let alone stepped foot inside. Ornate gold-framed portraits line three of the stark white walls. They must be former and current leaders. They swiftly fade into the background as I'm once again drawn to the windows.

Crystal-clear glass lines the frame from floor to ceiling, like an open gateway to the entire Territory. I devour every inch of nature's scenery in the distance. Based on our studies, Eastates' landscape ranges from mountains emerging along the countryside to valleys dipping into the low-lying lands. This region is overwhelmingly flat. The view stretches beyond the horizon. Leafy vegetation forms perfectly parallel rows within patches of black dirt. *Are those crops? It all looks so healthy from here.*

Instinctively my elbow jerks to the right, nudging the person within its range. I can't take my eyes off the small plots of emerald blooms so stark in contrast to the barren land at home. Stretching my neck, I lean toward my fellow delegate, nodding toward the window. "You see those out there? They're rows of plants, aren't they?" I turn, awaiting a response to my hushed question.

But Hayes isn't beside me. Instead, cool blue irises rake over me as a hint of pine drifts to my nose. I nervously scan the handsome stranger as my heart surges. Tufts of dark hair and strong features frame those narrowing eyes. His thin lips part to answer the question I forgot I asked.

"You into plants or something?" He grins, rendering my mind incapable of intelligent thought and my vocal cords useless. I hitch my shoulders up awkwardly, the only response I can manage. The smile fades and his eyebrows jump as he awaits an actual answer. When I verbally fumble, he mutters, "I thought they were only picking smart people."

What. A. Jerk. Irritation wakes my brain.

"Well, that theory should have been blown out of the water when you were selected." Poison laces my words, but every bit is justified.

"Whoa." He raises his hands innocently. "Just trying to lighten the mood a bit . . . guess that didn't really work."

Where is Josli when I need her? Hayes doesn't seem to need me in this sea of delegates, but without him, I'm completely alone.

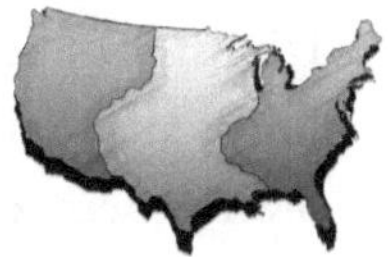

CHAPTER 19

UPPER DIVISION, CENTRESTATES

Within a few minutes, Kiera sweeps through the door again, this time with Lisum and Wynter in tow. She clutches a shiny silver platter while the others follow with stacks of rectangular books. They make a beeline for a wooden podium I hadn't noticed before. Kiera shuffles through some papers while her assistants organize the tray and books on a nearby table. Kiera scans the room and clears her throat.

"If you'll all take a seat, we will officially call the delegation to order." Kiera waves a hand toward the empty chairs lining the tables. We all descend upon them. I don't end up next to Hayes, but the girl from Centrestates who sat beside me at lunch slides into a seat beside mine.

"A few of our colleagues from the information broadcast have joined us." She points toward the back of the room. Sure enough, the two people who took our photos at the train station stand against a wall. When all eyes turn toward them, one nods while the other throws a hand in the air to wave. Each wears a boxy camera slung around the neck, ready to capture this historical event.

"I promise they won't be offended if you pretend they aren't even here. That's how they do their best work." She flashes a toothy smile at the photographers, who take advantage of the moment by snapping her picture. She smooths her golden hair back and places both palms on the podium, returning her focus to us.

"Now, before we dive into your duties while you're here, I'd like to first acknowledge the sacrifice you have all made," Kiera starts. I glance around the room. Most of the others watch her with wide eyes. Like a kid on his birthday, about to receive his annual sweet treat in his rations, Hayes wears a giddy smile. I chuckle to myself. Of course he does.

"Some of you have traveled very far today, and all of you have left behind your family, friends and everyday lives. We thank you for that, and for the work you're about to do. We will spend plenty of time talking about how the Territories can better work together and what we are hoping to accomplish through this delegation, but today is for you to get acclimated with Centrestates and to know how much we value your time and input. So, in appreciation of your willingness and dedication to making the Divided States a stronger country for many years to come, the Societal Order has a few gifts to bestow upon you." Kiera pauses, weaving a stray lock of hair behind her ear before she continues.

"As I announce your name, please come up to the podium. This exercise should also help you learn each other's names and divisions, so I encourage you to listen intently. Consider this a head start on becoming a team."

Her gaze sweeps across the room. Even the brief flash of attention makes me feel like a fish in a tiny clear bowl. Though she wears a smile, her cheeks properly perked and her stance welcoming, I sense she's gauging our reactions. Watching for cracks in the polished surfaces. But why? *Does she want to understand us to make us stronger, or would she rather detect any potential weaknesses?*

One by one she summons each delegate to the front of the room. I struggle to match faces with names. There's a Prisha, Ryland, Chander and what feels like so many others. At least Vanen is easy to remember after our little confrontation with the old man outside.

Besides that, I'm too nervous about my own introduction to truly focus on the others. *What if I stumble and crash right into the podium, knocking Kiera and her silver tray of gifts into oblivion?*

Inhaling a deep breath, I glance toward Hayes. He sits up straight with his shoulders back. Some of the other delegates adopt the same attentive posture, while others shift uncomfortably in their seats. I make an effort to raise my chin and pretend that I'm confident. As my eyes bounce from one delegate to the next, the dark-haired boy from Westates catches my attention. The one who's already managed to annoy me in the short time since we arrived. He slightly slouches in his seat, as if this whole scenario bores him. A few random wrinkles snake along his green pants and shirt.

As if sensing the visual inspection, he faces me, tilting his chin in slight interest. Challenging blue eyes meet mine. *Josli would be memorizing every feature of his perfect face.* I blink several times but can't force myself to look away. Fire flushes my cheeks. Considering the sudden smirk tugging at the stranger's lips, I'm guessing my mortification is on full display.

***

"And from the upper division of the Eastates, we welcome Everly Scott." My head snaps to Kiera, whose broad smile encourages me to rise on shaky legs.

My breathing hitches as my eyes shift around the room. The opulent space suddenly contracts as if the walls are closing in around me. *This was a mistake. I don't belong here. It hasn't even been one full day and I'm already cracking.* I concentrate on blocking the chastising thoughts blooming in my mind.

Slowly inhaling a deep breath, I remind myself that this day has thrust many firsts upon me: leaving the only people and places that have been constants in my life; hurtling over land, balancing between the train's smooth speed and my body's instinct to pace its own movement; and tempering my reactions as I absorb a new world so different from my own. The added pressure of perceived scrutiny of my every blink and breath doesn't help.

My feet carry me forward at a snail's pace. Each step is calculated and careful. The others will all stare at me anyway, but at least I'm less likely to stumble or misstep this way.

As I approach the deep red wooden podium, Kiera raises her eyebrows expectantly. I cringe inwardly. *Why wasn't I watching what the other delegates did when they approached her?* I force a smile big enough to crinkle the corners of my eyes and bow my head slightly. That seems to appease her. She nods and reaches toward the polished silver tray, producing a golden lapel pin.

Its round edges form a wave of cresting curves that elegantly frame a raised eagle figure. Smooth ribbon-like swooshes cradle curvy letters that spell "Divided" crowning the eagle's head and "States" cupping its outstretched talons. It's frivolous, but beautiful. And instantly becomes the most valuable thing I own.

Invading my personal space, Kiera slips my shirt collar between two fingers and pokes a hole in the fabric, securing the ornate accessory. *I wonder if I'll be allowed to wear this back home?* We aren't supposed to alter our clothing in any way. But if the leaders of Centrestates gifted an item meant to be pinned on my shirt, it would be allowed, right? My drifting thoughts return to the present.

Smoothing my shirt collar back in place, Kiera slides her hands to my shoulders and gently squeezes. Hesitation sweeps through me. The gesture feels too intimate. Goose bumps erupt along my arms. I fight the urge to rub them away.

"Everly Scott, of Eastates, please accept this token in appreciation for your service and sacrifice. Wear it always, as a constant reminder of the important role you played in bettering this great country, for all citizens and for many years to come." Although she's clearly speaking for everyone in the room to hear, her eyes never leave mine as she officially welcomes me to the delegation.

"Thank you," I reply as heat flares in my cheeks once again. Kiera turns back toward the table and clutches what I thought was a book. Close up, it's clearly much more than that.

"And I also present to you this personal computing device, which will support you in completing the pivotal work you will be doing here. May it assist you in all your contributions to the Divided States, throughout this delegation and beyond."

"Th-thank you," I stutter, grasping the handheld electronic with shaky hands. *She just gave me a computer. And said I get to keep it! Wait until Dad sees this. And Easton. And Josli.* We've all used computers before, but none of us owns one.

When Kiera reaches toward me, I reciprocate and we shake hands. A moment later, she pulls back, releasing her grip. She effectively dismisses me back to my seat with a quick nod and pivots toward the podium to summon the next delegate, Hayes.

He practically jumps out of his seat as I turn on my heel and attempt to slow an instinctual beeline for my chair. As we pass each other, he raises his eyebrows and opens his palm for a low "high five." I follow through with the gesture, tapping his hand in passing. Once I'm back at the table, I can breathe again. I run my hand over the device's thick tan cover, eager to take a closer look. Now isn't the time though.

Soon enough, I'll glide my fingertips over the keys as words burst onto the screen. I'd love to just let my thoughts pour out through the keyboard, but there's never been time for that. Now, with my own computer, I could write stories. Like the ones I used to make up to distract Easton. I never thought I'd be able to use a computing device for whatever I wanted.

Some occupations in Eastates require the use of computers, and we have them in school, but they stay in the classrooms and sometimes we have to share. They aren't exactly mass produced. Yet here, they have enough to hand out to visiting teenagers? This trip has been nearly unbelievable already, and we just got here.

Once the pinning ceremony concludes, Lisum and Wynter flank Kiera at the podium. She explains that the computers they gave us will stay here for tonight so that everyone gets theirs properly set up at the same time – tomorrow morning. Disappointment flickers through me, but it's quickly replaced with interest. Our next stop is to see our living quarters. All delegates will be housed in a smaller building tucked away behind Centrel Hall. It's walking distance and we will each have our own room, complete with a bathroom.

The girls will be assigned one floor and the boys another. That means Hayes and I will be separated. Not that I expected to stay in a room with him. That wouldn't be appropriate, but my nerves tingle as I anticipate the tour of our temporary home. I'm used to a small living space, and I'm thankful for the privacy we'll be afforded not having to share bathrooms like at school. I just wish the only person here that I know would be more accessible after our daily duties.

I have no intentions of wandering around the boys' floor, looking for him, and I'm sure Hayes will be just fine socializing with nearly half a dozen strangers. I, on the other hand, would prefer a larger group. That way I could blend into the background, throwing an occasional nod or smile as a minimal means of contributing to conversations. Even in school, where everyone's known each other since our first year, and I often exceeded the educators' expectations, I somehow managed to avoid the spotlight. Until this delegation was announced.

Trying to shake my mind free of anxiety, I numbly follow the others as we file through the building. Our hosts point out areas of interest along the way – restrooms, a small alcove with supplies like paper, the closed door leading to Kiera's office. Although we're encouraged to stop in any time, the invitation to visit her within those walls doesn't feel sincere. I can't imagine I'd ever need to talk to her privately anyway. *At least I hope not.*

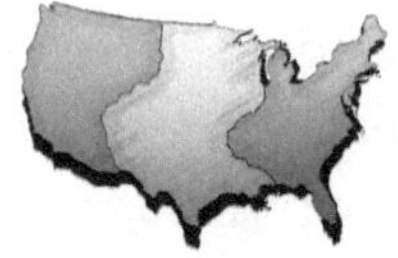

CHAPTER 20

UPPER DIVISION, CENTRESTATES

A few workers weave through our clustered group as we continue up one hallway and down the next. I pay little attention to those around me though. Instead, I'd rather take in every intricate detail of this place. Natural light touches every corner of the space, spilling in through floor-to-ceiling windows that alternate with walls. Enormous painted images adorn the flat surfaces – eagles with their wings spread in flight, flags bearing white stars and red bars, and a rusted bell with a thick crack splitting one curved side.

Strings of soft white lights climb the walls in linear patterns. They cast a perfect glow across the artwork, but I'm not sure what other purpose they serve. Rounded bulbs hang from varying lengths from the ceiling. They dangle well out of reach over our heads. Surely they provide more than enough light to illuminate this space even on the darkest of days.

We follow the winding stairway back to the first floor and breeze past the cafeteria. It's empty now, other than a few workers who wipe tables and sweep the floor. Once again we pass through the entrance doors; they slide open as the first of our group nears them. It feels like we just got here, yet so much has already happened. It's nearly unimaginable to think I was in my home just this morning.

I purposely gravitate toward Hayes. I'm a little disappointed that he's adjusting to being here so easily. It doesn't matter who he ends up sitting or standing beside; words and conversation flow easily for him. For once, he seems quiet. He must be turning something over in his mind. Probably that handheld computer he had to leave behind. If I'm eager to get my hands on it, he must be obsessed.

When the footsteps behind us grow louder, I glance over my shoulder. It's the other two delegates from our Territory. I jab Hayes in the side.

"The night dwellers from Eastates are right behind us," I whisper. "I met Vanen already, but have you talked to the girl he came with yet?"

"No, but now's as good a time as any." He throws them a side-eye and runs a hand through his curly hair before turning toward them.

"So, Vanen, this must be your counterpart from the lower division."

"Obviously." The girl shakes her head as if Hayes just said the dumbest thing she's ever heard. She sighs and crosses her arms. All that's left is an epic eye roll. *Ooooookay. Not planning to make an effort being her friend.*

Vanen rushes to offer a civil response. "Don't mind her. She's not used to being awake around this time." He turns toward her, muttering under his breath. "You could try to be just a little friendly."

Huffing out a sigh, the girl exudes complete disinterest. Completely oblivious, or aware but uncaring, Hayes animatedly gestures between us.

"It's okay. I'm Hayes and this is Everly." It feels a little contrived considering we've both met Vanen already. Still, we both flash a smile but mine fades as my gaze shifts to the girl. She thrusts a palm over her mouth, stifling a yawn. *Maybe she is just tired.* She falls a few steps behind, apparently content to avoid any unnecessary human interaction.

"Sorry about that," Vanen says. "That's Prisha and she's actually nice . . . when she isn't completely exhausted." His honey brown eyes radiate honesty.

"It must be hard, changing your schedule like that," I mutter. Hayes flashes me an encouraging smile, a silent acknowledgment of my attempt at extroversion.

"Yeah," Vanen agrees. "They gave us some pills to help us sleep at night and then another set of pills to help us wake up in the morning." He tilts his head toward Prisha. "The medication works, but it kinda messes with your head. It'll just take some time for us to adjust. This all happened pretty fast." He slides a palm across the back of his neck.

I cringe inwardly, suddenly thankful to be a day dweller. This is stressful enough without being compromised by chemicals just to stay awake. *I wonder who gave them that – was it before they left home or did they get more medication after they got here? It's none of my business to ask though.*

"It was so fast for us too," I add. "They told us about it two days ago. We barely had time to say goodbye to everyone."

The memory sours the conversation. I imagine we all feel the same way. Even Hayes, who was beyond excited to leave home, suddenly seems a bit withdrawn.

We continue in silence, following a long sidewalk that winds around Centrel Hall. When we turn a corner toward the back of the building, the concrete melds into a softer pathway lined with grass. Narrow strips of turf separate each individual rectangular stone. Wrought-iron benches practically invite us to sit and enjoy the lush foliage. Beds of flowers and clusters of shrubs dominate the lawn that stretches between where we'll work and where we'll sleep. It's a short hike from one to the other.

Even though the city streets are just a few minutes' walk from here, this area feels isolated. Only one building sits back here and it looks like a smaller version of the capitol building. They definitely favor windows here. The tan exterior is mostly glass. *At least that means we should have a good view from our rooms.*

An enormous sign sits atop the roof, declaring this Centrel Quarters. While a door awaits on either side of the entrance, Kiera leads us through the main focal point – a revolving door positioned between the others. I can't help but smile as I follow the others through the giant cylinder of swirling, spinning walls of glass. The feeling is surreal as air swooshes through the short passageway with me. *I wish Josli could see this. Actually, I wish she was here with me.*

"You know," Vanen starts, "it's all worth it. To be staying here." He points toward our home for the next two weeks. *I hope he's right.*

***

The inside is even more elegant than Centrel Hall. Whereas that was made for business, this was made for comfort. Puffy couches and comfy-looking chairs are grouped together in clusters of three and four. Thick carpet, tan with flecks of gold in ornate black swirls, sprawls across the floor. Gold-framed paintings adorn the tan walls. Each one features imagery of Centrestates' agricultural and electrical industries – grain mills, greenhouses and the power grid.

After our initial visual sweep of the interior, we all stand before Kiera, Lisum and Wynter, eagerly awaiting our next instruction. Fully anticipating the attention, Kiera throws her arms in the air and drops her chin, shooting us a sly smile.

"You are about to stay in the very accommodations where visiting leaders stay." She raises an eyebrow as jaws drop and whispers fall silent. "That's right, Eastates Societal Order Leader Tage Ault has stayed here numerous times, just as Westates Leader Shane Huntsman has. Now, let's get your room assignments so you can get settled."

Lisum and Wynter scurry behind the biggest desk I've ever seen and rummage through the drawers, retrieving a small stack of cards. Above their heads, words and images float across a flat screen embedded in the wall. *It must be their information broadcast.* I'm mesmerized by the visual motion. It's so different from the faceless audio that feeds into each home in Eastates. But here, they have actual video of people talking, sharing announcements.

My jaw drops when I recognize faces on the screen. Pride and fascination wash over me. It's us, the delegates. Video from everyone's arrival, then when we all huddled around Kiera inside the train station and yet again when we received our pins and computers. *I wonder if any of this is being shared with the other*

Territories? Dad would love to know what's been happening here so far, even if he could only hear it and not actually see it.

The space falls silent as everyone watches the screen, mesmerized.

"I see you've all noticed the information broadcast," Kiera states, raising an eyebrow. "You all have viewing devices in your rooms, so you can enjoy watching yourselves! Now, let's get you to your rooms. The young ladies will follow Lisum to floor three and the young men will follow Wynter to floor four. Your belongings are already waiting for you inside your rooms. Take some time to unpack, freshen up and make yourself comfortable."

Surprised gasps trickle through the group, my own included. *We can watch the information broadcast in our rooms and we get free time already?*

"After that, you'll all meet right here. Lisum and Wynter will be back to escort you to dinner. After dinner, I encourage you to make this an early night." She casts a wistful eye around the room, as if she's concerned for our well-being. Somehow it feels forced.

"You must be exhausted from your travels today, and tomorrow we will really start to dig into our work, so you will need plenty of rest. Have a good evening. I will see you all in the morning."

With Kiera gone, we divide up by gender and follow our designated escorts. The girls are dismissed first. Hayes is too busy chatting with Vanen to even notice us file down the hallway. A twinge of disappointment tugs at me, but I will it away, instead anticipating what my private space will look like.

Lisum leads us beyond the couches and chairs to a small alcove where two identical sets of shiny gold doors await. When she pushes a button on the wall, one set of doors slides open. She waves us all inside the large box. An elevator. We read about them in our studies of the Industrial Revolution, but I've never been in one before.

"Going up!" she says as she crosses the threshold and presses another button inside. The air rushes from my lungs as we glide just a few floors into the air. *Josli would love this. She'd probably want to ride in this thing all evening.*

I can't help but smile as this box defies gravity, launching us all skyward. It reminds me of the train, except this ride is much shorter and vertical instead of horizontal. But for both, the machine does all the work of getting me from one place to another.

We reach the third floor in no time. As the elevator doors part, they reveal carpets and wall decor that perfectly match the main area we just left. Sparkling gold swirls stretch across the cream-colored carpet. Bold streaks of deep green and purple dominate the tan walls. They arc in semicircles, the dried paint widest and thickest in the middle of the curve.

Lisum shepherds us to one end of the hallway. Before she begins to assign our rooms, she requests assistance from one delegate.

"Saya." She nods toward the girl I sat beside at lunch. I knew she was from Centrestates but I wasn't sure if she was from the upper or lower division.

Saya steps forward, twirling a lock of hair nervously. "Yes?"

"As our resident delegate, could you make sure everyone is gathered in the reception area on the first floor for dinner?" She smiles and taps on her watch. "You've got one hour. Just enough time to unpack and take a breather."

"Sure," Saya affirms. Her eyes shift around the group anxiously. When she notices me, I flash a subtle smile and nod. She smiles back before returning her attention to our host.

"Thank you," Lisum says. "Now, let's get on with it! I'd like you to all come along, even after I point out your room, so you can see which rooms your peers are staying in." She holds up one of the cards she collected from the desk on the first floor and explains that the cards are actually keys. She demonstrates how to use one on Saya's room. *It looks easy enough.*

We follow Lisum down the hallway. She stops at every third or fourth door, raising one of the cards and calling out a name. It feels like the person she announces has won a prize. By the time we reach the other end of the hallway, it's finally my turn.

Before I press my key against the small black box affixed to the wall beside the door, I face Saya.

"If you need any help gathering the others, just let me know."

A look of relief and gratitude washes over her features. "Thanks, I will."

"Why, Everly, that's very kind of you," Lisum adds. "That's the sort of model citizen behavior we like to see."

I nod, unsure what else to say. After a moment, Lisum bids us goodbye and heads toward the elevator. Saya meanders back the way we came, in the direction of her room. With that, I swipe my card over the keypad and push through the door.

CHAPTER 21

UPPER DIVISION, CENTRESTATES

The bed is the first thing I notice. It's enormous – probably three times as wide as my mattress at home and it could probably swallow me whole. Josli, Easton and I could all sleep in it at the same time comfortably. *But it's all mine.*

Beyond the bed lies a giant window that overlooks Centrel Hall and the city it's tucked within. I plan to spend a lot of time watching this new world, but it will have to wait for the moment.

Everything in here – from the plush carpet to the sheer curtains to the thick blanket covering the bed – is tan with swirls of gold, green and purple. Dark wooden furniture lines the walls. As my eyes trail the desk, I notice that my luggage sits on the bench beside it. *It made it here, all the way from home. That's a relief.*

My attention drifts back to the bed. I untie my shoes and slip them off before climbing on it. My whole body sinks into the foamy mattress. *It's so soft!* As I stretch, my muscles instantly relax. *I wish Josli could see this.* Propping myself up on my elbows, I take in the rest of the room.

A gold clock hangs on the wall just above the desk. It's unlike anything I've ever seen – metal rods bloom outward, like flower petals, from the clock's round face. Some are longer, some are shorter, but they're all bent in a slight wave to create a fluid design. A single round crystal is threaded through each rod. It looks like someone's captured the sun, or its essence. I allow myself another minute to admire it before studying the rest of my temporary home.

Just as Kiera said, a large black screen sits on a long, narrow table across from the bed. This must be what televisions looked like. They were in every home and offered way too many options for people to squander time. Just another frivolous invention that the Societal Order has found a way to make useful, purposeful.

I have a feeling I'll be watching the information broadcast here whenever I get free time. It makes me wish that our version back home had video and not just sound. After a careful inspection of the device, I locate the power button, tearing myself away from the constant stream of information only to unpack my bags, wash my face and tame my hair. Before long, it's time to face the other delegates again.

***

A few minutes before 6:00, I slip outside my door. In that moment, realization strikes me. The last thing I'd be doing at home right now is leaving. Since this is the upper division of Centrestates, everyone here – as day dwellers – should remain in their homes from six p.m. to six a.m. But if that was the case, the cafeteria would be closed before we got there. And no one would be there to prepare food or clean up.

As I stand in the hallway contemplating how this is possible, a slight creak echoes through the corridor. Another person emerges from her room and starts down the hall toward me. As she draws nearer, a smile washes over me. I recognize the long, wavy reddish-brown hair. It's her most prominent feature, nearly overwhelming Saya's pale complexion and thin frame.

"You came out early to help me round everyone up?" she asks, eyebrows raised.

"I did."

"Great!" She points toward the opposite end of the hall. "I'll start knocking on those doors. You start at this end and we'll meet in the middle."

"Sounds good."

It doesn't take very long, considering there's only six of us total. Within a few minutes, we climb into the elevator as a group for the short ride down. The other two girls at Saya's end of the hallway don't appear to appreciate our reminder. I overhear one of them mutter to the other about how they're capable of following simple instructions on their own. I don't even remember their names, but it wouldn't matter anyway. They just dropped to the bottom of the list of people I'd make an effort to get to know better.

We reach the first floor to find the guys already there. Our groups merge together seamlessly as dialogue sparks, most of us eager to compare rooms. Everyone seems much more relaxed than when we first arrived. They wear genuine smiles in place of their earlier tight lips and wide eyes.

Well, all but one. I have a feeling this one enjoys being different from the crowd. The cute guy from Westates wears a disinterested scowl. He crosses his arms and narrows his eyes, distrust oozing from his every breath and blink. And he's not wearing his pin. My eyes bounce from delegate to delegate, taking a visual inventory. Yep, everyone else is still wearing theirs – just where Kiera affixed it to their collar.

The doors swoosh open as Lisum and Wynter charge through them.

"Oh, it's wonderful to see you all socializing! You'll have plenty of time for work while you're here. Enjoy your free time when you have it. Now, let's go get you some dinner. Our culinary experts at Centrel Hall have prepared a special meal just for our delegates." Wynter folds her hands together before spinning around. Lisum motions for us to follow her.

Like a flowing river, we meander between the buildings, following the sidewalk. The pale blue sky yields to an orange haze peeking out from the horizon. It's all that's left of the day. The sun has started its descent. And it feels so wrong to be outside during a time that's reserved for night dwellers. I wonder what Hayes thinks. He must be overanalyzing this right now.

Just as I decide to seek him out to ask him about it, someone taps my shoulder.

"Thanks for your help back there." Saya runs a hand through her hair and smiles shyly.

"Oh, sure. I kind of felt bad that Lisum put you on the spot," I say. "You know, expecting you to sort of be in charge of everyone coming downstairs on time."

She pushes a stray lock of hair behind her ear. "My parents told me that might happen. That Callan and I might be expected to do more because we live here. I mean I guess we do have a clearer understanding of how Centrestates works, but . . . " Her voice trails off as she takes another approach. "Can I tell you something?" She giggles nervously.

"Of course."

"I don't feel any different from anyone else here. Like, I don't feel like I know what's going on. At all. And I'm certainly nothing like Callan." She shoots me a side-eye, as if she's just waiting for me to ask how so.

"What do you mean? What's up with him?" If Josli was here, she'd grill this poor girl for every last detail.

"He's just . . ." she starts, twisting her head from side to side, gauging if anyone else is paying attention to our conversation. "I guess *arrogant* is the best word to describe him. His dad is part of the security forces. Pretty high up in the chain of command. It kind of makes him think he can do whatever he wants."

That reminds me, right now I'm doing something I could never do at home. It feels strange to walk around freely, with somewhere to go, at a time when a day dweller would normally be inside. I wonder if Saya is thinking the same thing. I open my mouth to ask her, but reconsider as we all merge together again to funnel into Centrel Hall.

The air rushes from my lungs as we cross the entranceway. Once again it's like being transported to another world. I notice details I missed earlier today, like the ceiling's intricate mosaic of glass, pearl and gemstones. And the mighty columns that run from this floor to the next. *Will this flutter in my stomach ever go away when I walk in here? Do the people who work here even notice the sheer beauty of this building?*

"All right," Lisum announces. "We'll head straight to the cafeteria and sit at the same tables we used at lunch today. Go ahead and start a line to choose your dinner. The options are rather limited, but I believe you'll enjoy what's there." She steps aside and watches us all pass. Other than a few workers, we're the only ones in the room.

I slide through the food line quickly, eagerly reading the little tented signs announcing what each item is. I choose a beef filet slathered in a brown sauce, a scoop of multicolored rice, a mountain of plump green peas and a perfectly square piece of chocolate cake with fluffy white frosting.

By the time I reach an empty seat at our table, right next to Saya, my stomach growls in anticipation. Without pause, I dig into the meal.

As I shovel a forkful of rice into my mouth, the table slightly shifts as someone takes the other seat beside me. I can guess who it is before even looking. Somehow, with all the amazing aromas in the air, I sense the subtle hint of pine.

I turn toward Saya, eager to talk about something. Anything. But she's distracted by who just sat down. Glancing past me, she whispers, "Westates hottie on your left!" I can't help but giggle.

"What was his name again?" she asks softly. I shrug. "Well, I think it's time we found out."

"Ummmm . . ." I stutter, not exactly volunteering to strike up a conversation with him. She stretches forward, pivoting toward him.

"Hey, I'm Saya and this is Everly." She raises her hand in a slight wave before motioning toward me. His gaze shifts between the two of us. He looks utterly unimpressed.

"Beckett." He hesitates just a moment before turning back to his plate.

"Well, Beckett, it's very nice to meet you." He nods but that's the extent of his willingness to interact with us.

Saya raises her shoulders and tilts her head as if to say, "Oh well, I tried."

While eating and chatting with Saya, my eyes drift to the windows. I'm not used to having such an expansive view of the evening sky. A few stars dot the growing darkness, but they're mostly outshined by the city lights just a few blocks away. It makes me wonder if they're conserving power at all here. *Maybe I can ask Saya about it when we're not surrounded by the others.*

After dinner, Lisum and Wynter corral us together for the walk back to Centrel Quarters. They take turns explaining some rules, although they prefer not to use that word.

"So we have just a few *guidelines*," Wynter explains, "for all delegates to follow. Most of your time will be spent in either Centrel Hall or Centrel Quarters. After dinner most evenings, you will have free time, but we expect you to stay on the campus. While the city is nearby, almost all of you are unfamiliar with it. And we don't want any lost delegates wandering around."

"Plus," Lisum adds, "we just might have a few events planned where you will get to explore some off-campus locations. But we'll all do that together. We'll put in some work and then get to have some fun. Educational fun."

Yeah, like those two words go together.

"Tomorrow morning you should all report for breakfast in Centrel Hall at eight a.m. From there, we'll escort you to the conference room and return your computing devices so you can take notes throughout the day. Does anyone have any questions?" Lisum asks. I sense she doesn't really expect any – she doesn't slow her pace or even scan us for a raised hand. But sure enough, that doesn't stop one person.

"Are we able to come over earlier if we're ready?" Hayes asks, sliding his glasses up the bridge of his nose. "Because I wouldn't mind putting in extra time, kind of like extra credit."

Eyebrows raised, Wynter and Lisum share a glance.

"Perhaps a little later this week," Wynter answers. "But for tomorrow, let's stick to eight a.m. You've all had a very busy day and we want to see you fully rested for our first full meeting day. Now, back up to your rooms."

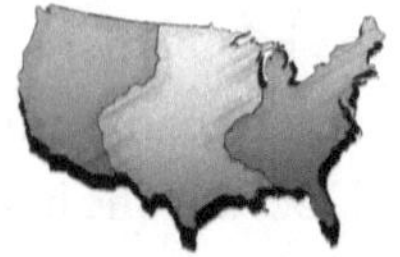

CHAPTER 22

UPPER DIVISION, CENTRESTATES

The delegates shuffle through the Centrel Quarters entrance and file onto the elevator in clusters. Saya and I are in the first group while Hayes hangs back with Vanen in the second group. As the doors slide closed, he calls out good night.

The privacy of my room is a welcome sight. With a full stomach and our first official day complete, I ready for sleep and crawl into bed, finally letting exhaustion reign.

***

Breakfast is quiet the next morning. Everyone's probably tired or nervous about the day ahead. Myself included. Lisum greets us in the cafeteria and leads us upstairs after everyone has finished eating.

We follow her through the winding hallways, passing one closed door after another. Having moved past the initial shock of being here, I notice small details I completely missed yesterday. Each entranceway bears a gold plate with formal black letters. We pass the Liberty Room, the Allegiance Room and the Freedom Room before stopping outside the Unity Room. *Appropriate, I guess, since we're supposed to renew a plan to promote peace among the Territories.*

"I trust everyone got a good night's rest and is ready to dig into your assignment," Kiera greets us animatedly as we cross the threshold and spill into the room. Most delegates acknowledge her with an overly enthusiastic, "Good morning," but a few choose to focus on claiming a chair. Narrow tables link together, carving a hollow square in the center of their boxy formation.

She pulls the door closed and strolls to the waist-high podium. Rustling some papers, she taps them on the smooth surface and slides a narrow pair of glasses along the bridge of her nose. While the act should be unremarkable, my eyes are drawn to the bright red frames. In the Eastates, citizens deemed to require corrective lenses to fulfill their education or perform their job are rationed a pair of glasses. But they're cobbled together with scraps from previous generations. Hayes' round frames are almost comically too big for his face. Yet Kiera's look . . . sophisticated. In a world where the shade of your Territory's fabric is as fashionable as it gets, stylish glasses are rare. Or at least I thought they were.

Once we're all seated, with our attention properly aimed at our host, she continues.

"Each day you will report to this meeting room. I will provide you with a topic and discussion points." She tosses her hair back. "So, I'll get you started and check in on you throughout the day, but you'll largely be left to discuss ideas and debate proposals independently. Lisum and Wynter will remain with you, but their role is to serve as facilitators. That just means they will distribute your computing devices and make sure you stay on task. You should all use your devices to take notes and ensure that concepts are captured for further contemplation."

"I have a question," Hayes cuts in, raising his hand.

"Yes, Mr. Crimshaw." She dips her chin and zeroes in on him.

"Can we take our computing devices to our rooms in the evening? That would give us time to add in any other thoughts, like supporting arguments." His eyes widen with hope and expectation, but she purses her lips. I can sense he isn't going to like her answer.

"Unfortunately, Mr. Crimshaw, we prefer to capture your organic conclusions. So while I'm certain your individual input will be valuable, the notes you take will conclude with what comes out of the full delegation discussions."

"Okay." He nods disappointedly.

"Think of it this way." She spreads her arms wide. "Together, you make up one body. And at the end of each day, that body has to agree on one suggested course of action. You'll consider and blend various opinions for a result that defines recommendations and the reasoning behind them. Does that make sense?"

"Yes," he answers. With that, Kiera narrows her eyes as they search the room.

"I hope that you all take pride in your service to the Territories." She wraps a palm around the edge of the podium. "One way to express that is by wearing the pin you received yesterday. That's all I'll say about that."

I'm thankful I remembered to affix the pin on my collar this morning. When I scan the other delegates, only one person isn't wearing his pin. Beckett.

Kiera clears her throat and waves her hands in the air, as if resetting herself.

"Before you can discuss ways the Territories can work together, you have to understand how each individual slice of the country functions. Rather than educate you on the economics and trade relations as they exist today, I would rather glean your perspectives and perceptions from your own experiences."

Sidestepping the podium, she paces around the room. Her hands are folded together in front of her as she circles the tables, sharing glances with those she passes.

"So, today is for you to acclimate yourselves with each other and your Territories. You'll need that base knowledge to explore the questions I'll pose to you over the coming days." She returns to the podium and straightens the papers on it.

"For now, I'll bid you farewell. If you need anything at all, just let either of these ladies know. You are in good hands." She winks at her assistants. "I'll check on you in a few hours."

Lisum and Wynter scurry around the room, delivering computing devices to each delegate. Some eagerly inspect the object while others turn it in their hands curiously. We start with a lesson on powering them on and creating a space to type our notes. Once everyone's settled with their device ready to go, Kiera's assistants waste no time getting started.

"Now, before you get too distracted, we're going to give you a question to discuss as a group. You are welcome to take notes but please stick to the subject at hand." Lisum shoots us a stern look as if she's an educator scolding the class for not paying attention.

Wynter cuts in. "Our first question is . . . what is the most important thing for others to know about your Territory?"

Most of the answers are boring like the girl from Westates who believes that they have the biggest population, greater than Eastates or Centrestates. Or a night dweller from Centrestates who claims their educators are the most qualified.

Hayes shoots me a disgusted look when I admit that the upper division of Eastates has been trying to grow crops, but hasn't had much success at it yet. I'm sure he thinks I shouldn't have said anything that would show weakness, but I think it's important for the others to know, because based on how little output we have, they would probably think we don't even try. *And isn't that worse?*

The only answer that catches my attention is Callan's. He runs a hand through his short blond hair as he announces, "Our military power is stronger than the other two Territories combined. We're like a powerhouse, in fact we–"

Wynter interrupts and motions toward the girl sitting beside Callan.

"Good, good. All right, next person, let's let you have a turn. Wynter and I will be right back! Take notes!"

"That was weird," Saya whispers to me as they slip outside the door. She twists an auburn curl around her finger as her green eyes narrow.

The girl beside Callan starts nervously rambling about how her division allows those graduating from final school to narrow down their interests to three career paths. The educators try to match students up with a career they are interested in, and would presumably be good at, based on their skills and test results. Before she can explain any more, Callan raises a hand in a "stop" gesture and interrupts her.

"So, we cooooouuuuld keep going," Callan says, rubbing his palms together. "Or, maybe we could talk about what we all want to know." He glances around the room, eyebrows quirked in question or challenge. When no one responds, he answers himself. "This assignment is boring as anything. Maybe we should be starting with a little . . . icebreaker . . . instead of this crap."

Um, probably not the smartest move considering anyone can come back and check on us at any time. Although nerves taint my enthusiasm, I am curious to know what it's like to live in the other Territories. I wouldn't mind just listening to what the others have to say. And so far our first discussion question has been a real snoozefest.

"Yes!" a girl from Westates chirps. Soon enough, a few others agree, their responses ranging from eager nods to cautious shoulder shrugs.

"Why don't I keep typing notes," Hayes suggests. *Did I hear him right?* "I'm a pretty good multitasker. I can listen and come up with some ideas at the same time."

"Good man!" Callan points to him before facing the group again. "So, where do we begin?" He wiggles his eyebrows and singles in on a girl from Westates.

Before anyone can respond, Lisum and Wynter sweep back into the room. They must notice how backs straighten and postures stiffen at their approach. The whole room seems to exhale a disappointed breath.

"All right, what did we miss?" Wynter asks, looking around the room.

Looks like we don't get to gossip after all.

***

The rest of the discussion fades into boredom as we all talk about our neighborhoods, schooling and expected career paths. Callan is slated to follow in his father's footsteps and become a government official. The girl from the upper division of Westates plans to work in forest management. Beckett expects to spend his life in a hard goods mill, which he admits almost begrudgingly. Of everyone, he's definitely the least happy to be here. And he doesn't bother to hide it.

After our lunch break, Kiera returns to the Unity Room and drones on and on about each Territory's Societal Order governing style. If my brain wasn't completely worn out, I might find it interesting. The two people from the information broadcast slink into the room and observe for a while. They scurry around, attempting to fade into the corners, capturing moments from our day in photos and film.

Thankfully they don't take much interest in me. Probably because I observe more than I speak. At least typing notes on my computing device affords me the chance to avoid eye contact with anyone, making it less likely I'll be called on.

By dinner time, I'm more tired than hungry, but it's our last chance to eat before bed. And it's our last stop before we can retire to our living quarters for the day. After shuffling through the cafeteria line, I'm surprised when Hayes slides into the seat beside me. I offer him a smile but the one he reciprocates looks forced.

He leans toward me and whispers, "You shouldn't say that we're incapable of growing our own food. It makes the whole Territory look bad. Besides, look at the kind of food they're used to here.

Compare that to what we have at home. I don't want anyone to know what we're used to eating."

"I was just being honest," I counter. "Besides, do you think anyone even cares? Most of them were probably zoned out."

"Just be careful, Everly," he warns. "I'm getting the sense that we just stumbled into some sort of superiority competition, and we don't want to present ourselves as a burden on the whole system."

I nod and fork a square piece of pink meat, swallowing it down, along with my annoyance. I spend the rest of dinner interjecting a few words into the others' small talk now and then. But ultimately, by the time the meal is over, I'm ready for the alone time my room affords.

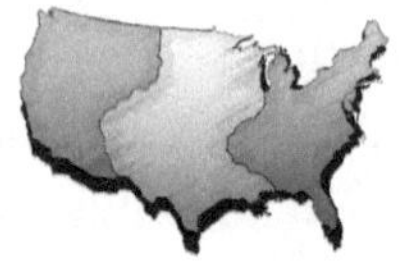

CHAPTER 23

UPPER DIVISION, CENTRESTATES

Morning arrives before I know it. I vaguely remember crawling into bed and resting my head on the pillow before slipping into a vivid dream about home.

I'm sitting in our living room with Dad, Easton and Josli. We're talking and laughing when a sharp knock at the door interrupts us. Before anyone else can make a move, Easton jumps up, darts to the door and yanks it open. Waiting on the other side is Beckett.

Not the mysterious, brooding guy with striking blue eyes, but a broken version of him. Blood and dirt streak his face. His dark hair is slicked back, plastered to his head. His clothes are torn. He reaches toward my brother, but Easton stumbles back, mouth and eyes wide open in horror. My dad lunges for Beckett, knocking him to the ground. Josli screams and clenches my arm. Against all instincts, I brush her off and spring to my feet.

"Everly! I need to see Everly!" Beckett grunts as he struggles with my dad. My feet cooperate and catapult me toward them. Just as I yell "Stop!" and wrap my arms around my dad to pull him away, the alarm yanks me from the unsettling dream.

My heart races and my senses slowly return as I sit up in bed. Rubbing my eyes, I attempt to banish the images that just flashed through my mind. Beckett's not my favorite person, but seeing him in such a vulnerable state, calling for me . . . leaves me feeling somehow responsible for his pain. And the fleeting reminder of everyone I'm missing is like having a bandage ripped off an open wound.

Trudging to the bathroom, I pause only to power on the information broadcast. It's a perfect distraction while I shower, brush my teeth and dress for the day. The major focus this morning is a meeting of the three Societal Order leaders. Their images materialize on the screen – Westates Leader Shane Huntsman, Centrestates Leader Kirill Imperant and Eastates Leader Tage Ault.

The focus quickly shifts to the delegation, and how unusual that a group of citizens from each Territory is gathering today as well. That leads into footage from our meetings yesterday. I cringe whenever I see myself among the group. Worse, though, is seeing Beckett. I turn away when the camera zooms in on his face. I have a feeling last night's dream will linger long after the delegation is over.

***

Hayes plops down beside me at breakfast. He casts me a cautious gaze, which instantly reminds me of his warning at dinner last night – not to portray Eastates in a poor light. Luckily, when Vanen chooses the seat beside him, the two of them dissolve into deep discussions only meant for their ears.

Every now and then Hayes peeks over at me, but he doesn't say anything. I keep my head down and avoid conversation. I'm not in the mood to socialize.

Callan seems to be making friends. He's the loudest one at the table, as if each sentence he utters is meant for an audience. Maybe it is. About half the delegates appear to listen intently, laughing when they should or interjecting encouragement to continue here and there. When breakfast finally ends, Lisum and Wynter arrive to escort us to the Unity Room. Kiera's already there waiting for us.

"So," she starts as her slender finger traces the edge of the podium, "today's discussion points should focus on these questions." She squeezes a black fob in her hand and words appear on the wall-length white screen behind her. I didn't even notice it until now. The technology here surpasses what I'm used to by far. Although my only comparison is school, where we have smaller but similar screens. Educators draw formulas and stanzas on them with erasable markers, wiping away each lesson in preparation for the next.

I squelch the jealousy threatening to poison my thoughts. This building is meant for high-ranking leaders. Of course it's saturated with impressive technology and exquisite architectural features. Maybe our own capital building in the Eastates is comparable, or even fancier. Kiera steps to the side to provide an unobstructed view of the digital black letters.

1. What are the greatest threats to peace among the Territories?

2. How can those threats be neutralized or eliminated?

3. How can your Territory form closer relations with the other Territories?

When eyes shift back to her, she nods toward Lisum and Wynter. They rise and join her at the podium.

"Once again, my assistants will serve as your moderators as you discuss these questions. They will record key points and proposed solutions for my review while you break for lunch. Please continue to make notes on your individual computing devices as well. All of the information we gather over this time will be analyzed and used."

Clasping her hands together, she asks if we have any questions about our morning assignment. Hayes shoots an arm into the air. He must be the most acute overachiever in this room. *I wonder if there will be an award for that in the end?* Maybe they'll have a farewell ceremony to recognize those who shared the most brain power.

"Do we need to agree on answers, by a majority vote? Or do you want to see all of our thoughts?" Hayes watches Kiera expectantly. A wry smile curls her lips. She's clearly pleased someone's brave enough to address her. Or at the very least, hang on her every word.

"Excellent question, Mr. Crimshaw. At this point I'd like to see all your thoughts. Your morning sessions will inform the afternoon discussions. That is why I will evaluate the group's initial thoughts and draw out the areas I'd like you to focus on to create recommendations. I think you'll find that these meetings will ease into an efficient process."

So Kiera's going to review our work before deciding what we'll do next. My stomach flutters as I wonder if we can meet her expectations. I hope Lisum and Wynter don't single anyone out in their note-taking. At this point, I'd rather stay under Kiera's radar in case she doesn't like what we come up with. Maybe that will change the more I understand our role, what she's hoping to see from us and how I might be able to leverage this experience to boost my future.

Hayes nods a quick thank you before Kiera scans the room in one last implicit offer to answer any lingering questions. A charged silence races through the air.

"One last thing, today our friends from the information broadcast will be joining you early. They'd like to start developing segments about each of you that they can share with our citizens, as well as those in the other Territories. Lisum and Wynter will coordinate that, but please be ready."

She barely takes a breath before bidding us farewell. "When you finish discussing this morning's questions, my colleagues will escort you to lunch before delivering their notes to me. Then I'll be back to talk with you this afternoon. Have a productive morning!"

With that, she sidesteps to the podium, snatches the papers and disappears through the door.

The light, fruity pastry that made my mouth water less than an hour ago now threatens to make a return appearance. My stomach flutters as Kiera's words sink in. The last thing I want is to be the focus of anything for an audience. *Why can't we all just blend in together? There's no need to single anyone out.* Either way, I don't have much time to agonize over it.

Soon after we start talking about this morning's discussion points, the information broadcast representatives quietly slink into the back of the room. Lisum and Wynter instruct us to continue discussions while they excuse themselves and disappear into the hallway with our visitors in tow. Less than ten minutes later, they return and explain that half of us will be interviewed today and the other half tomorrow. *If I have to do it, I just want it over with.*

"We don't want any one Territory completely absent from discussions, so those from the lower divisions will go first. And as long as we can keep on schedule, those from the upper divisions will be interviewed tomorrow. Not to worry, you'll all get your turn." Wynter promises.

Great. So now I have to worry about this all day and tonight.

"Think of these profiles, or introductions, as a way for those watching on the information broadcast to get to *meet* you," Lisum adds.

These two are masters at tag-teaming. *I wonder if they finish each other's sentences on a daily basis.*

"Now, Lisum and I will help get everything set up in the smaller conference room right next door," Wynter says, tilting her head toward it. As if on cue, something heavy screeches as if it's being dragged on the other side of the wall. The information broadcast people must be in there already rearranging the space, positioning tables and chairs at just the right angle for the cameras.

Wynter pauses, searching the room, seemingly for someone to take charge in their absence. "Callan, Saya, can we entrust you with guiding the group until one of us gets back?"

"Yes, ma'am," Callan answers, a bit too quickly, as if he's been waiting for the invitation. Saya smiles politely and nods her head in agreement.

"Thank you. We'll start with the Centrestates lower division delegates. Please follow me, we will leave the rest of you to get to it. Don't forget to take notes!" As the chosen delegates push out of their chairs, Lisum rushes them toward the door.

Callan jumps up and races to the podium, eagerly taking his place behind it. He throws the departing group a wave and a sickly sweet smile as they leave. As soon as the door closes behind them, his demeanor shifts. He points to Hayes.

"You. Yesterday you said you'd take notes as if we were actually talking about this boring crap. You good to do that now?"

"Okay . . . I guess," Hayes stammers, adjusting his glasses. I know he's fully capable, but even I'm put off by what sounds more like a demand than a question.

With his own computing device on his lap and his fingers poised to type, Vanen rolls his chair toward Hayes. *Looks like we've got two people making up the conversation for us.* I think I'd rather be talking to them than listening to Callan.

"Soooooo." Callan swings his arms forward, clasping his hands together when they meet near his waist. I don't envy him, being expected to lead a group of strangers. He and Saya may be citizens of this Territory, but the experience is new to them too. They're staying in the living quarters just like the rest of us. Although, Callan seems to love being in charge.

"Where should we start?" Callan asks. "We got Easty over here doing our work. So what do we actually *want* to talk about?"

At the very least, he could learn Hayes' name. Or at least not refer to him by some stupid nickname. Hayes doesn't even notice though; he and Vanen chatter while feverishly typing on the keyboard.

"Do you really think we should be doing this?" Saya's voice is nearly a squeak. She twists a lock of hair and chews on her bottom lip. I open my mouth to agree but Callan beats me to it.

"How about anyone who wants to do the stupid assignment sits with Easty and anyone who wants to actually learn something interesting stays put?" He glares at Saya, who seems to wither under his scrutiny. She purses her lips as her cheeks flush crimson. Tension punctuates every second as silence swallows the room.

After a moment, Hayes and Vanen return to their chatter and typing. It must awaken the others.

"So, what don't we know about Centrestates?" a boy from Westates asks, his deep voice oozing curiosity. "Something you can't find in a textbook." He flashes a crooked smile as his thick eyebrows arch toward the sky.

"Weeeelllll," Callan starts, crossing his arms, "there are rumors that blackouts are coming. If the power grid can't support us all, then we'll all have to go without it."

Beckett smirks and tilts his chin defiantly. "Some of us already do go without it. Half a day every day."

Callan shrugs. "Well yeah . . . we do too . . . I mean more than that."

My eyes dart to Saya, but she appears to be fascinated with her fingernails. *Is she avoiding eye contact because she knows something about possible blackouts or because Centrestates doesn't really go without power?*

CHAPTER 24

UPPER DIVISION, CENTRESTATES

"What else?" Beckett says, suddenly interjecting himself into the conversation. "Someone must know *something* interesting."

"You got something to share, Westy?" Callan counters, his eyes narrowing on Beckett. "You haven't exactly been forthcoming with anything since you got here."

The girl named Kinsley jumps up and raises her hands. "I know, I heard that night dwellers sleep in coffins because it keeps the sunlight out. Is that true?"

Her blue eyes widen with curiosity. The girl beside her, I think her name is Nyra, rolls her eyes and scrunches her face. She's the one who came with Beckett, so she's a night dweller.

Beckett shifts in his chair and huffs out a sigh, exuding annoyance and possibly boredom. "Anyone else hear rumors about underground tunnels that connect the Territories?"

Chatter erupts, a blend of questions and speculation. After a few untamed minutes, Beckett slams his palm on the table, commanding the room's attention. "Look, this isn't helping. Does anyone actually know anything?"

As I scan the others, one person captures my attention. For what feels like the first time, Callan has nothing to say. *If he knows anything, he surely isn't about to share it with us.*

One voice responds, yet completely ignores Beckett's question.

"I've heard that day dwellers live longer than night dwellers," Prisha says quietly. Her admission is surprising both because I've barely heard her speak since we arrived, and because she's a night dweller. She and Vanen are our counterparts in the Eastates. If her statement is true, I certainly have no hand in it, yet guilt blossoms within me. An uncomfortable silence urges her to continue.

"The sun and the moon are supposed to give our bodies cues for when to sleep and rise. It's going against our natural rhythm to fight it." Her eyes drift to the floor. "But that's exactly what we do."

In school we're taught that the other Territories are just like ours, following the upper and lower division patterns to ensure that there are enough resources to go around. While one division works, the other conserves. Even though we live separately, we still benefit from each other's contributions. Never mind that we'd typically never meet, or truly know what each other does and when they do it.

Every citizen is supposed to be equal. But even before we officially arrived – like when we stepped on board that fancy train – doubt has tickled my mind. It's like a wave lapping the shore, washing away remnants of set beliefs I've held for so long.

"Did you know that the active hours in the Eastates used to be based on moonrise and moonset?" Vanen interjects, tugging my wandering mind back to the present. No one answers, so he explains. "Yeah, years and years ago. But it was too confusing to keep adjusting the timing when seasons changed. Darkness fell earlier and the sun rose later. It was easier to just set active hours that never change, no matter what time of the year it is. That's where the six a.m. and six p.m. came from."

I didn't know that. And based on Hayes' slack jaw and unblinking eyes, he's never heard that either.

Before Hayes can unleash the dozen questions that must be zipping through his mind, the door swings open. Lisum and Wynter charge into the room, trailed by Ryland and Chander, the first two who were interviewed. Ryland practically prances back to her seat, clearly pleased with her performance next door. Chander leisurely strolls behind her.

"Everything coming along in here?" Lisum asks, glancing around our small cluster.

"Let's just say that if we keep going at this pace, all of our work will be done days ahead of time." Callan crosses his arms and tilts his head smugly before motioning toward Hayes and Vanen. "And we have designated note takers to record the main points of our discussion."

The lies slide off his tongue so easily. I'd be grasping for a believable response if anyone asked me that question right now.

"Excellent!" Wynter chirps, pressing her palms together. "Then we'll just collect our next two delegates and assist with their interviews. Prisha and Vanen, you're up."

Prisha rises from her chair as Vanen sets his computing device on the table. They share a quick glance before advancing toward Lisum and Wynter, who lead the way, practically bouncing through the doorway. It makes me wonder what they do on a normal workday. They're spending so much time babysitting us. But they seem to enjoy it.

Perfecting his phony leadership role, Callan taps on the podium until all eyes land on him. After a dramatic pause, probably so he can be sure Lisum and Wynter notice, he reads one of the discussion questions out loud and shares his thoughts on the matter. But as soon as the door clicks closed, he returns to his alternate agenda.

"So let's get back to it. Ryland and Chander, we're not wasting our time on mindless crap. We'd all much rather talk about what we really want to know about each other's Territories." Callan raises his eyebrows as if he's awaiting some great revelation from them. Considering they're from Centrestates like him, they probably know more than the rest of us, but I doubt they know more than Callan since his dad is some big hotshot around here.

Maybe he knows his turn is next for the interviews, snuffing out the time that's left to speak freely, or maybe his patience has cracked, but Beckett grinds out through gritted teeth, "So are there tunnels beneath Centrestates or what?"

Chander shifts in his chair before volunteering, "My dad works in inter-Territory transport. He helps schedule shipments across the borders." He pauses, scratching his chin. Hesitation sweeps over his features.

"And..." Beckett prompts, twisting his wrist in an impatient roll.

"And . . . yes . . . he's told me stories about tunnels that connect the Territories. They're completely off limits except for certain transport workers. It's not something that's meant to be common knowledge."

"What's the big deal? So what if they exist and people know about them?" Ryland asks.

Chander relaxes enough to explain, "They could be used illegally. People might try to cross borders or start trying to smuggle things back and forth that aren't allowed. Like seafood. Seafood isn't allowed in Centrestates. If people knew there was a way to get it here though, they might try to create an illegal market."

"Wait, that's not illegal. We send seafood to the other Territories," I state, looking to Hayes for reassurance. It's one of the only fresh foods our Territory produces, even if we don't have very much to share.

"Well, maybe it's not banned yet, but it will be soon." Chander scratches his chin as if he's casually discussing the color of the carpet. "It's a health risk. If a train breaks down or is delayed, it could spoil. And we all know how contaminated the seas are. Who really wants to eat something living in that water? Filtering it through their gills. They can't be healthy." He cringes with disgust.

"How do you know it's about to be banned?" Hayes asks, his eyes darting around the room until they focus on each Centrestates delegate. "Did they announce it somewhere?"

"I told you, my dad works in transport." Chander runs a hand through his thick black hair. "Look, he didn't tell me specifically, but I overhear bits of his conversations. And based on some stuff he said . . . let's just say, I would bet on it."

He crosses his arms and leans back in his chair as the room dissolves into chaos. Voices blend together in a cluster of accusations and questions.

"What else will they ban?" "Who decided that?" "They probably banned other stuff that we don't even know we're missing out on!" "Yeah, this can't be the first time!"

When the door swings open, silence descends. All heads turn in that direction. With a smug smile, Kiera marches in.

"I hope I didn't interrupt. I just wanted to check in and see what you're all working on."

~ Kiera ~

I should have come down here sooner. Why would Lisum and Wynter think they both need to oversee the information broadcast interviews? The delegates can't be expected to facilitate their own discussion – not yet at least. This will not happen again.

"You can take your seat, Callan. Thank you for leading the group." I effectively take over, steering them back to delving into perceived threats and how the Territories could counteract them. Once they get talking, my earlier anger returns.

How dare Chander share confidential transport information. The question about the tunnels could have been laughed off as some useless myth, but now they're talking about that too. And the seafood ban. No one should know about that, and they certainly shouldn't be sharing it. They're planting seeds of curiosity in each other. That's not what they're here for.

Of course it was the lower division Westates boy trying to stir things up with the tunnels. Beckett. He's the only one not wearing his pin today. I already know who needs to be watched more closely than the others. Of them all, he looks the least worthy of being here. Besides the permanent scowl he walks around with, his posture clearly demonstrates his distrust and unwillingness to participate. *He will not waste my time. No matter what it takes, I will glean the information we need from every last one of them. He is no exception.*

Wynter peeks inside the room when the two lower division delegates from Eastates return from their interviews. She startles when she notices me at the podium. I hold her gaze just long enough to convey my disappointment in her. She sidles over to me and whispers, "Want me to take over so you can go?"

I tilt my chin and lean closer, keeping my voice low. "I've got it under control. You finish up the interviews. We'll talk later about protocol for leaving the delegates unattended."

She steps back as if I've struck her. It almost makes me feel guilty. I had planned on spending some time this afternoon with them anyway and this is my "pet project," but my trusted assistants should know better than to be so careless. It will be addressed. After she leaves, I remind them to take notes on their computing devices and steer the conversation toward what I really want to know – what are their Territories' biggest weaknesses. Granted, this is from a teenager's perspective, but they may know something an official sitting in a capitol building would never consider.

Even as they share their thoughts, this morning's conversation with Leader Imperant drifts to the forefront of my mind.

"I expect you'll keep them under control." His tone, low and smooth, is clear. It's a warning. But it's unnecessary. I don't fail and neither will this project.

"Of course, sir." It's the only correct answer. He raises his eyebrows, but I hold his gaze and await whatever else he feels the need to say.

"Is anyone checking on them at night to make sure they aren't doing anything . . . extracurricular?"

As if I didn't consider that. Before they arrived, I figured they would be too far out of their element to defy our prescribed rules. But now that they're here, I sense that a few of them would ignore our requirements – especially some of the Westates delegates. But that's why I've taken precautions.

"No." I allow a smirk to play across my lips. "They don't have that much down time and besides, I know everything they're doing." He doesn't need to know every last detail of my plan just yet. I'd rather reveal pieces of it on a continual basis. It's not like he's going to object to any of it, so I might as well keep some ammunition in my arsenal for the exact moment that I need it.

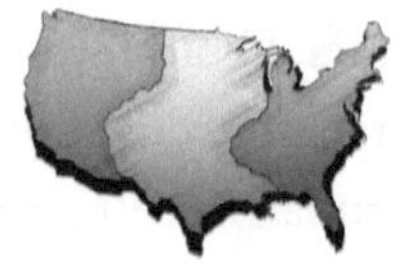

CHAPTER 25

UPPER DIVISION, CENTRESTATES

The mood completely shifted when Kiera showed up. I'm not sure exactly what I expected would happen here, but this isn't it. We're not writing a peace treaty or even talking about one. It makes sense that we have to understand some basic information first, but this all feels like a useless exercise. *Waste of time.* But at least it's not Callan trying to boss us around anymore. If Kiera knew how little we accomplish with him left in charge . . . hopefully we'll never find out what she would do.

After lunch, Lisum escorts Beckett and Nyra to their interviews – the last ones for today. This time Wynter stays with us. Saya takes the seat next to mine, nudging my arm whenever everyone's attention is focused on the other side of the room. She quietly cracks jokes. Mostly about Callan. It helps pass the time.

And it distracts me from the nagging annoyance that flares when I think of what Chander said about banning seafood from Eastates. *Refusing another Territory's contribution to the Divided States doesn't sound very peaceful to me. What else happens that we don't know about?*

After what feels like hours, Beckett and Nyra return. *I wonder how his interview went.* Now that's one I want to watch on the information broadcast. Those interviewers must have worked hard if they actually got him to open up. I quickly banish the thought as my stomach twists into a jumbled knot. Thinking about the interviews reminds me that my turn is coming too.

We take a brief break before Wynter and Lisum announce our next topic: current trade practices between Territories. They want us to explore areas of weakness and ideas we have for improvements in the trade system. They lead the discussions and mostly everyone chimes in with responses, alternately typing notes in their computing devices. Time creeps along at a torturous pace as my mind drifts, tuning out much of the conversation. For the most part, I stare at my screen and type questions that will probably never be answered.

Why does everything taste and look so much better here? Why don't we have food like this in Eastates? What else does Centrestates have that we don't? Why are there so many lights on at night here? Don't they conserve energy like we do back home? Home! Do Hayes and I even have a ride back to Eastates?

The last thought stalls my mind. Worry snuffs out any other questions. Until we know what's going on with the train ride home, I need a distraction. Newly attentive, I focus on the discussion, which quickly reminds me how boring it is. After what feels like forever, we're finally done.

"Well, this was a productive day!" Wynter gushes. "Thank you to Saya and Callan for leading the group in our absence this morning. We'll be sure Kiera knows that you already assumed a leadership role."

"It was truly an honor." Callan bows his head, feigning modesty. *Yeah right, the rest of us know better.*

Saya and I share a side-eye before I squeeze my eyes shut. It's the only way to ensure I don't roll them in annoyance. If Josli were here, she wouldn't hold back. *Maybe that's why she isn't here.* My stomach quivers as I stifle a silent chuckle. It probably looks like a single dry heave. *I hope no one saw that.* When I glance around the room, sure enough Beckett's amused eyes anticipate meeting mine. I break contact, sliding my gaze back to Lisum and Wynter.

"Great job today, everyone. It's been a long day." Wynter presses her hands together and grins from ear to ear. "Please turn in your computing devices and then you are free to go back to your rooms. Remember, you are expected to stay on the grounds. Meet back here at the cafeteria for dinner at six o'clock."

"Vanen and I can help collect devices if you'd like," Hayes volunteers. In such a short amount of time, the two of them have become inseparable. They're definitely good together. It makes me chuckle.

"Thank you both. Yes, that would be a big help." Lisum nods her head and motions to the storage cart. A rush of giddiness washes over Hayes and Vanen. I'm the first one to pack up my device and hand it over to the guys. When Vanen takes it, I step toward Hayes and lean close, catching his eye.

"Hey, I sort of forgot to tell you . . . but when we were on the train coming here . . . I overheard the transport overseers talking and they didn't see our names on the return list to Eastates." I pause for a moment, letting the information seep in. He narrows his eyes and cocks his head. Since he doesn't say anything, I continue. "Look, it was probably nothing but maybe we should ask someone about it . . . just to be sure."

He gulps and nods once. Thankfully he doesn't reprimand me for not telling him sooner.

"How about as soon as I'm done here, I'll stop by Kiera's office and ask her about it," he offers. "I had a few other questions I wouldn't mind asking her anyway."

"That would be great." Of course he would jump at the chance to ask more questions. And if it means I can avoid talking to her, that's fine with me. "Just let me know what she says, okay? At dinner tonight."

He offers me a salute before turning back to the small mob of our peers, eager to turn in their devices so they can go. As I head for the door, Saya catches up to me. We both wave a quick goodbye to our hosts. Just as we're about to slip into the hallway, Wynter's voice reaches my ears.

"Hayes and Vanen, can you connect each device to a docking station? That automatically uploads the day's content to Kiera's computer."

I nearly trip on my own feet as alarm courses through me. That means Kiera's going to read my questions. I cringe inwardly. There's nothing I can do about it now. Mine was the first computer the guys took. I'm sure it's already snapped into place and my notes are probably on their way to Kiera at this moment. *Maybe she'll tire of reviewing so many notes and skip over mine? Or maybe some of the others typed more interesting stuff and she'll focus on that?*

Saya and I keep pace down the stairs and all the way to the exit doors. As soon as we clear the building and reach the sidewalk, she breaks the silence.

"So today was...anything but interesting, huh?" She raises her eyebrows, awaiting my response.

"It was pretty rough," I agree.

"We need to decompress! Wanna hang out in my room for a little before dinner?" she suggests.

"Okay. I'll just stop by my room for a minute and then come down." It's not like I've got anything else to do. And there's no one else to hang out with. I'm sure Hayes isn't leaving Vanen's side anytime soon.

***

I take just a few minutes to run a brush through my hair and wipe my face with a damp washcloth. I reach Saya's door as the others on our floor spill out of the elevator and return to their own rooms.

As soon as I plop onto her bed, she hops on the other side, facing me.

"I had an idea! What if I invited the other girls to come to my room and we all hang out together? Like tomorrow night?"

Inwardly I cringe, but the smile spreading across her cheeks is so hopeful. Eyebrows raised, she nods quickly, as if trying to coax a response from me.

"Yeah, that's a great idea," I lie. Hanging out with Saya is becoming comfortable. But hanging out with all the other girls makes me a little anxious. In group settings, I tend to fade into the background and quietly observe, hoping that I don't say something stupid or seem awkward.

"Oh good! I thought so but I wanted your opinion. You know, Callan has too much power but if we all band together, that would change the whole group dynamic."

Oh great. So it's even worse than a let's-all-get-to-know-each-other gathering. It's a choose-my-side sort of function. I nod and pretend to listen as she evaluates each delegate and his or her potential allegiance to Callan. He gets on my nerves too, but I'd rather just pretend he isn't here and avoid him altogether when it's possible.

Not too soon, it's time for dinner. We all gather on the first floor and walk to Centrel Hall together. I approach Hayes, even though he's practically glued to Vanen's side.

"So?" I ask anxiously.

"So what?" He pushes his glasses up the bridge of his nose innocently.

"The train? Our ride home?"

"Oh yeah." He relaxes when he realizes what I'm asking. "No big deal. Kiera said it must have been an oversight. She'll have Lisum and Wynter fix it."

"Oh, good." Relief washes over me. At least that's one less thing to worry about.

When Hayes returns his full attention to Vanen, Saya catches up to me. We chat as we make our food selections and sit beside each other at the table. It's not the same as having Josli here, but it feels good to have made a friend.

I focus on savoring each bite of the crisp green lettuce with juicy tomato slices, saucy noodles and buttery breadsticks. My taste buds are fully aware that this isn't going to last forever. *How am I supposed to go back to eating the mush we get back home?*

After dinner, Saya invites me over again but I force a yawn and claim I'm too tired. Besides, I'm sure I'll be back in her room tomorrow evening for the gathering she's planning.

***

When I'm finally alone, I sprawl across the bed and watch the information broadcast. The smiling host talks about Societal Order Leader Imperant returning from his meeting with the other leaders earlier today. They show him stepping off the train – the same one Hayes and I rode to come here. As the camera zooms in, he offers a curt nod and wave before stalking into the station.

The woman speaking speculates about what the leaders probably discussed, which includes the delegation. And that leads into a segment on us. Music and swirling lights bombard my senses, practically jumping off the screen. Ryland's picture bursts onto it, surrounded by her name in big block letters.

As the picture fades, images from her interview flash across the display while a man's voice summarizes her life history. She's got an older brother and younger sister at home, along with her parents. She hopes to become an educator when she graduates. While I wouldn't have guessed that about her, from the little bit I've observed, I believe she'd excel at bossing kids around.

Next they show an extended clip from her interview. She rattles on about how important it is that the Territories each focus on their strengths so that we can offer the best of what we have to each other.

She then proceeds to list all the ways that Centrestates provides for the other Territories. I can't help but roll my eyes and yawn.

Are there other options? Something else to watch? Standing, I press the button that made this video come to life. It just scrolls through black screens until it circles back to this one channel. I flop back onto the bed and settle in.

My interest dwindles as the interview seems to go on and on. I know I should be paying attention so I'm better prepared for when it's my turn, but when my eyes flutter closed, I surrender to the rest my body craves. Ryland's voice fades to a distant murmur as my senses retreat.

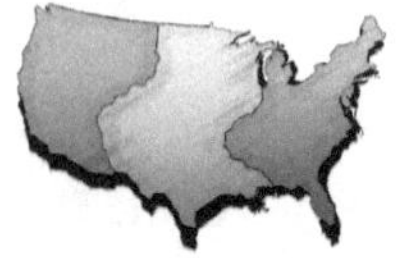

CHAPTER 26

UPPER DIVISION, CENTRESTATES

At breakfast the next morning, the chatter seems to revolve around last night's information broadcast. I must be the only one who completely missed Chander's interview and part of Ryland's. Snippets drift around the table – about how Ryland seemed to just repeat herself, but Chander sounded thoughtful yet sharp.

When Beckett takes the seat beside me, my posture automatically stiffens. He's ranked pretty high on the least-friendly list around here.

"You watch that crap last night?" he mutters, digging his spoon into a bowl of plump dark berries.

I glance over, meeting his piercing blue eyes before they drop to my birthmark. *Why is he looking at it again?* I raise my left elbow and rest it on the table, sliding my palm over the stupid heart-shaped defect. I usually forget about it until someone notices it.

"Um, no, I started to but kind of fell asleep."

"Can't say I blame you." He smiles, seemingly pleased with my answer.

"So you didn't watch it?"

He blows out a sigh as if I'm wasting his time by even asking.

"Hell no. It's all for show. Everything here." His words are resentful.

I'm not sure how to respond, so I don't. It sounds like something that old man said outside Centrel Hall when we first arrived. He told Vanen and I not to trust anything we were told here. *Did he talk to Beckett too?* When Hayes and Vanen shuffle over to the table, Beckett nods toward them.

"What's up with them?"

"What do you mean?" I ask. "I think they just really get along. Fast friends, you know?"

"Not that," he grumbles. "What are they carrying around?"

Only then do I notice the brown bag slung over Hayes' left shoulder. As soon as he sits, he slides it down his arm and lets the bag rest on the floor. His eyes flick around the table, gauging if anyone saw. He pauses when he catches me looking and subtly shakes his head "no." As if I know what that means. He shouldn't be taking anything in or out of the conference room. So whatever's going on is clearly a secret.

"I don't know what he's got," I admit. *But I plan to find out.*

***

As we filter into the conference room, Kiera greets us with a genuine smile blooming from ear to ear. Lisum and Wynter take their places at her side. All three of them appear way too excited to be here with us. *I wonder what they have in store for us today?*

As soon as we all sit and face her, Kiera flattens her palms on the podium and speaks.

"I have a very special announcement this morning. Leader Imperant just returned from a very important meeting with Leader Huntsman and Leader Ault. And he has generously agreed to carve time out of his busy schedule to welcome you."

The walls seem to shift closer, boxing us in. I study the other delegates. They squirm in their seats, angling to catch a glimpse of a person we've all heard of but never expected to actually meet. This man is in charge of everything that happens in this Territory. While he has help, and plenty of it considering how many people seem to work in this building, ultimately every decision falls to him.

Steady footfalls echo from the hallway moments before Kirill Imperant strides into the room. The others watch this man with the same fascination that flows through me. He's lean yet muscular. His posture exudes such confidence that his presence swallows the room. His height matches Hayes', but the difference is night and day. Hayes is all gangly limbs and awkward movements, while Imperant is a tower of authority, fluid motion and poise. Although his mouth hasn't yet formed one word, he already commands our full attention.

Kiera's smile practically cracks with adoration. She eagerly watches his approach to the podium. He throws her a disinterested nod, signaling it's time for his official introduction. Clasping her hands together, she centers herself behind the wooden console and straightens her back.

As she speaks, I watch Leader Imperant. I better start thinking of him with the official title since that's how she refers to our guest. His slicked-back hair is dark as midnight. His eyes are only half a shade lighter, more black than brown. They sweep over us with instant evaluation. His strong, sharp facial features paint a mask of emotionless obligation.

The man oozes agitation, thinly veiled by tolerance. It makes me wonder, is he angry or is this just his personality? Is this what it takes to be a leader? Perhaps his meeting with the other leaders didn't go well. Or maybe he has no interest in meeting us.

Either way, this introduction can't end soon enough. He clearly doesn't want to be here. Tension smothers the air, sparking an attentive discomfort among the delegates.

Although he wears the Territory's standard tan attire, it's somehow better fitted than anyone else's. Pleats and creases tug at the material stretched across his broad chest and strong limbs.

A superficial attentiveness precedes his words. Even before he opens his mouth, distrust floods my senses. I have heard our Eastates leader, Tage Ault, speak on our information broadcast, and I've seen his picture in schoolbooks. Somehow he conveys an air of trust and conviction that feels genuine. Maybe I'm just biased toward my own Territory though.

"Greetings, delegates." Leader Imperant pauses to meet our curious gazes for just a moment. Somehow the brief connection injects a sharp tinge of violation, as if he can read my thoughts, the collective suspicions that challenge his intent. Not soon enough, he returns to the script in his mind.

He rests his palms on the podium, splaying his fingers. As he leans forward, settling into a formative posture, he begins again. "Each one of you is here not only to learn firsthand about governance and leadership, but to also actively contribute to the process. The work you do here will be recorded, analyzed and shared with the other Territories. I myself will present to them a list of proposals, both fortifying relations and ultimately improving lives throughout the Divided States.

"You may be asking yourself why you're here. Why you? Why now? After all, you are the future of this great country. By the time this delegation adjourns, you will have formulated recommendations to ensure that we avoid errors of the past. Because unless we continue to question our processes and make improvements, we risk traveling down the very path we have worked so hard to evade."

When he pauses, silence overtakes the room. As uncomfortable as this man makes me feel, I'm riveted by his words. The others must feel the same way. They sit up straighter in their seats, pressing their shoulders back with pride. Well, all but one. Beckett wears clear distrust from his narrowed eyes to his tight lips.

"You will spend some time acclimating to each other and Centrestates before you focus on the Alliance Agreement and your recommendations both to strengthen and modernize it. The agreement was written and adopted in 2050. Much has changed since then. Perhaps not everything for the better . . ." He raises an eyebrow.

"But that is exactly why you are here. You all know that the Territories work together, sharing resources to help each other's citizens not only survive, but thrive. But that's where any overlap ends. And an updated Alliance Agreement could change that." He plunks a finger down on the podium, emphasizing his next words.

"What you do here is for the benefit of every citizen of the Divided States. I want you to think about that – consider how your ideas can benefit, or harm, your neighbors, your educators, your classmates, everyone."

For some reason, an image of the ragged old man who was talking nonsense when we first arrived flashes through my mind. *It didn't look like anyone was worried about him. And he was right outside their door.*

"Now, I have to get back to my work, but I trust that Ms. Saign and her assistants will guide you through each of the seven principles of peace."

The principles of peace. I remember studying them but before I can conjure any to mind, Kiera practically jumps to his side, rushing to join Leader Imperant as he bids us a final farewell.

"I look forward to seeing the results of this fine delegation. Make your families proud by what you do here." He steps aside as Kiera raises her hands in the air as if she's presenting him to us. Again.

"Let's show our appreciation for Leader Imperant." She leads a round of applause, but the broad smile on her face wavers when Hayes' hand shoots into the air.

"Mr. Crimshaw, we don't really have time for—"

"It's okay, let him speak," Leader Imperant interrupts. He rocks on his heels in anticipation. Hayes takes a deep breath and slides his glasses along the bridge of his nose.

"Sir, would it be okay if I shook your hand?" *If Josli was here, she'd be cracking up right now.* Hayes looks like a little kid asking for a special treat. His eyes widen as he awaits a response.

Leader Imperant's stiff facade cracks for a moment. A small smile tugs at his lips. "Of course, son. I'd be happy to shake everyone's hand."

"All right, why don't you all form a line and come up here?" Kiera releases an awkward laugh and waves a hand, motioning for us to join them. Her shoulders visibly relax. Maybe she was worried Leader Imperant wouldn't like what Hayes said.

Almost all the others jump at this chance. Hayes is first of course. I dawdle getting out of my seat, more concerned about casually wiping my sticky palms on my thighs so Leader Imperant doesn't cringe when he touches my clammy skin. When it appears that no one is looking, I swipe my forehead with the back of my palm, brushing away the beads of sweat there.

My delay tactics work and I find myself at the back of the line. The only one behind me is Beckett. *Maybe we have a little more in common than I thought.* Drawing in a deep breath, I smooth out my shirt.

Before long, it's my turn, I force my feet to carry me forward. It's like my body trudges through an invisible barrier. Leader Imperant leans toward me and grasps my hand firmly.

"And you are?" he asks, wearing a rehearsed smile. As I answer, a chill sweeps through me. Maybe it's just the intimidation of meeting someone so powerful, but my instincts scream to retreat.

"Well, Everly, I hope you find your time in Centrestates both productive and enjoyable." Immediate relief washes over me when he releases my hand.

I thank him, as is expected. Before the moment passes, his eyes rake over me. It's only a matter of seconds, but it leaves me feeling vulnerable. As if he already knows everything about me.

***

As soon as Leader Imperant strides out the door, Kiera explains that we are taking a break from the information broadcast interviews today so that we can start discussing the first principle of peace. Relief surges through my veins. *As much as I want to get my interview over with, this delay gives me a speck of hope that someone somewhere will forget about mine.*

Kiera explains that representatives will still come and take photos and videos today, but they will finish up the other segments before they start the next round of interviews.

"You are all on the verge of serving your Territories by entering the workforce." She exhales a deep sigh. "I can't think of anyone better suited for this critical task."

Palming a controller, Kiera summons the wall-length white screen with an exaggerated flick of her wrist. A list appears on it.

"These are the seven principles of peace. You will discuss each one in depth." She pauses as everyone's eyes scan the screen.

1. Citizens' rights

2. Equitable contribution to resources

3. Equitable distribution of resources

4. Community cooperation

5. Consequences for threats to peace

6. Trust in leaders

7. Trust in government

"The first principle we will be discussing is citizens' rights. You'll spend the rest of today coming to an agreement on what common rights citizens should have within each Territory. Keep in mind that each principle must build upon the previous one."

Sure, that sounds easy enough. My stomach flips as I realize how big the task before us truly is.

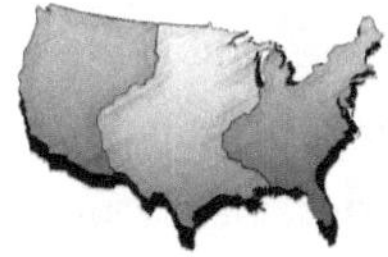

Chapter 27 ~ Kiera

Upper Division, Centrestates

It didn't take long to determine which ones to watch closely. Of course it's no one from Centrestates. Instead, Westates delivered Beckett, who still doesn't wear his pin. Beyond that, he doesn't even try to appear vaguely interested in the presence of Leader Imperant, the most important person he'll ever meet.

I need to study him a bit more before intervening. His intentions and motivations aren't yet clear. And his refusal to wear the pin certainly doesn't help my progress. I'll have to give it another day or two. I won't ask Lisum and Wynter to talk to him about his attitude. I can't even call attention to it. Maybe they'll notice it on their own and address it, but that's highly unlikely.

If everything I'm planning comes to fruition, my assistants have to be just as surprised as the rest of the country by what unfolds here. They follow orders for the most part, but they can't be trusted with full disclosure. Besides, I may need to lean on them for an alibi at some point. The less they know about the ultimate plan, the better.

And then there's Hayes and Vanen. Both from Eastates, yet they've never met before they came here. Those two are intriguing. If they had been born in Centrestates, I'd enlist them to work for me. When they were of age, of course. The notes they take during delegation meetings are thoughtful and comprehensive. They both take their role seriously, but they might be taking it a little too far.

Of course I know what they're shuttling around in that bag. While Hayes dutifully turns in his computing device at the end of the day, Vanen sneaks his out and takes it back to his room. The two of them found the bag in Vanen's room. It was a mere oversight – whoever cleaned the room in preparation for our special guests neglected to find and remove an empty bag left behind by the last occupant. I didn't realize it was there either, but then again that isn't my job. With everything I do, I can't oversee every aspect of every person who reports to me or Leader Imperant. This little misstep will be addressed.

I scan through my files to check their backgrounds a little closer. Vanen's interest in the device makes sense. His father is a computer scientist. He writes programs that regulate information sharing and monitors electronic system security. Sounds like he's quite good at it too. He could have shown the kid some tricks or maybe just piqued his interest.

Still, for how intelligent Hayes and Vanen are, it's surprising they think they can keep this little secret they share. They scurry past everyone as if we can't see the bag they exchange. Not to mention the twitchy nervousness in their facial expressions and posture.

While I should probably be annoyed that they are so willing to defy a rule, the gold lining is that they inspired another layer of this project. The old saying was to look for the silver lining in a rain cloud. But why would I bother with silver when I can have gold?

What started as a single-focused goal of verifying the absence or presence of brain implants that were supposed to be injected at birth has grown into much more. I don't want to just see an X-ray of their brains, I want to climb inside them. I want to understand what motivates them to maintain Societal Order values and also what deters them from it.

Knowledge is power, and I'll learn everything I can if it helps us achieve our goal of uniting the Territories under one leader. Each day brings us a little closer to that reality, and this delegation is helping us build ammunition. We're going to watch this hypothesis play out. Let's see what they do with that computing device.

At least it's much more interesting than the Eastates girl, Everly, who just types random questions in her notes. She's caught up in the food and how much better it is here. Of course it is, we are superior after all. This girl's notes are just proof that what we're doing is so important. Everyone wishes they could live like us in Centrestates. And when we're in charge of the whole Divided States, citizens will get that and so much more.

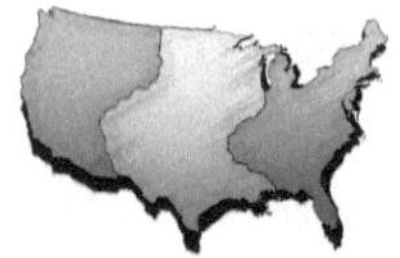

CHAPTER 28

UPPER DIVISION, CENTRESTATES

By lunchtime, my temples pound and my ears ring. I haven't contributed much to the discussion, but just listening to the debates makes my brain feel like it's been syphoned through a strainer. While I crave the solitary sanctuary of my room, I know the afternoon still stands between me and it.

As soon as I sit, ready to enjoy my own personal feast, Saya nudges my arm.

"I'm going to let the other girls know about our little gathering in my room tonight," she whispers. "One at a time." She dips her chin and levels me with an intense gaze.

Since when did this become our *gathering?* While I had nothing to do with it, I'm in no mood to argue so I just nod. *Tell them or don't tell them. I'd much rather tune you all out and curl up under my covers right now.*

"We should all wear our sleep clothes! It'll be fun!" She pauses, chewing on her thumbnail. "You know, it's not that I want to keep it a secret from the guys, but they might try to copy it if they know."

There it is. She's afraid Callan will do the same thing and somehow one-up her. I don't think he has a care in the world, or that he's capable of harboring self-doubt or concern over anything anyone else thinks of him. *Maybe he's on to something there.*

"Sure, good idea," I say. She's obviously searching for confirmation and the sooner I offer it, the sooner I can eat in peace.

She smiles and nods, obviously pleased with my response. She turns to Nyra, who sits on her other side. I guess it's time to invite the first official guest.

***

By mid-afternoon, I sense that Kiera's grown bored with us. It's the most time she's spent with us since we arrived. When the conversation reaches a natural lull, she praises the depth of our deliberations. She even claims to be impressed by all of us, but then promptly excuses herself, leaving Lisum and Wynter behind to facilitate. The room's intensity seems to drop a few notches within minutes of her exit.

Hayes and Vanen quietly descend into their own world – eyeing each other's screens, probably typing notes to each other on them. Whenever Wynter questions them, one always has a thorough answer, so she leaves them be.

197

The other delegates sit at attention, typing notes as they listen to each other talk. I'm not sure why Kiera, or anyone else, would want to read through whatever everyone's typing, but I guess it's somehow useful.

Saya uses the relaxed atmosphere to her advantage – strategically repositioning herself around the room. She mumbles something about needing to stretch her legs before pivoting toward those she doesn't usually talk to – Ryland and Kinsley. After a brief whispering session, which I'm sure focused on *our* get-together this evening, she settles into a chair beside Prisha. Her last target.

By the end of the day, the dialogue subsides. Wynter and Lisum must recognize that mental fatigue has spread through the room. They announce that we've completed today's assignment. Before they can remind us about turning in our computers, Hayes and Vanen practically vault out of their seats, volunteering to collect devices and put them away. Wynter and Lisum gladly accept their assistance.

"Hey, stranger," I say as I tap Hayes' arm and hold out my device. The contact sends him backward a step, obviously caught off guard. "Sorry, I didn't mean to startle you." *Since when is he so jumpy?*

"It's not you, Everly. We'll talk later, okay?" He dips his chin and stares into my eyes briefly as if to pass information between us silently.

I nod slowly, watching him, and say, "Okay."

I'm not sure what he's trying to tell me, but we'll have the whole train ride home to talk if it's just some random observation he's made. *He can fill me in on all his latest theories then.* That is, if we have a ride home. Maybe we should ask about that again, just to make sure Lisum and Wynter got it all sorted out.

***

The highlight of dinner is catching Saya and the other girls share knowing glances every few minutes. As if we have some enormous secret. We aren't even breaking any rules. The guys could be hanging out together every night and we'd never know. *Maybe if Hayes could tear himself away from Vanen for a moment, I could ask him.*

By the time the meal is over, Saya's practically busting at the seams with energy. She giggles and calls good night to the guys before we descend upon the elevator as a group. As soon as the thick doors slide closed, she clasps her hands together and bounces on her toes.

"So, you're all coming?" Saya asks, eyebrows raised. The enthusiasm she projects promises it will be more interesting than retreating to our rooms alone. Either succumbing to the building excitement or unwilling to be excluded, everyone agrees.

"Okay." She bobs her head and gestures with her hands, unable to contain her excitement. "Give me ten minutes and then I'll see you there! Room 314."

We all retreat to our rooms. I gawk at my reflection as I splash cold water on my face and run a brush through my hair. Dark shadows trace my eyes and my lips curve to a near-frown. *Am I really that tired? That solemn?*

In that moment I choose to brush aside any homesickness lurking beneath the surface. It won't get me home any faster and my situation could be much worse. To be honest, the food around here is the best I've ever had. *And I deserve a little fun, so why not sit back and enjoy whatever this evening brings?* The alternative is sitting here by myself watching the information broadcast. Considering it puts me to sleep, I'm not worried about missing too much. *I did want to see Beckett's interview, but who knows when it will even be on?*

It's good Saya suggested this. It's exactly what I need. I never would have initiated spending more time with these girls, but the prospect is definitely better than staring at four walls for the next couple of hours until it's time for bed. Besides, I've never been to something like this before. Bedrooms are considered private back home and this get-together is basically going to be in Saya's bedroom, which is of course all we really have here.

Smoothing my hair back and inhaling a deep breath, I feel sufficiently ready to socialize. I swallow any lingering nerves, grab my key and push myself out the door.

The others emerge from their rooms and head toward our shared destination. An air of anticipation sweeps through the hallway. Perhaps sensing it's time for her guests to arrive, Saya throws the door open and bounces past the threshold. "Let's party, girls!"

We file past her into the room, which she's transformed into an inviting nook. Puffy white pillows form a small teepee atop each bed's blankets. The desk chair and a footrest cluster the narrow space between the beds, offering plenty of seating for six girls. Once we're all inside, she closes the door and plops on the footrest.

"So, first thing's first. What's the scoop on the boys from your Territories?"

Unlike my counterpart, Beckett repeatedly rises to the topic of our chatter. The girls pepper his classmate from the Westates with questions, but Nyra either doesn't know much or isn't willing to share it.

"Does he have a girlfriend?" Ryland purrs, crawling onto the bed between Nyra and Kinsley.

"No idea," Nyra huffs, shifting toward the headboard in what looks like an effort to restore some personal space. "Can't we talk about someone else?"

"But we want to hear about Beckett," Saya whines in a singsong voice. "You must know *something* about him."

"I mean, I don't even know what classes he has at school. He's not in any of mine." Before I even consider if I should say it, questions spill from my lips. "But how can that be? Didn't they take the top achievers in your school? I mean, that's how they picked me and Hayes." *Or at least that's what they told us.*

"I think . . . Beckett's smart, but not in an academic way." Nyra twists a lock of long, dark hair around her finger. Her eyes drift to the ceiling. "Like, if you wanted to break into a locked building, yeah, he's your guy. But literature and math, not so much." She smirks before painting an innocent look across her face. "I mean, not that I really know him, but that's my impression."

"Well, you know him better than any of us," Kinsley prods, stretching her long legs to take up even more real estate on the bed.

"Although I wouldn't mind getting to know him," Saya giggles, batting her eyelashes and wrapping her arms around a pillow. Her silliness seems to relax Nyra a little. I sense her walls drop when she raises her hands in a playful surrender and smirks.

"Look, he's super moody and barely talks. He must be smart or he wouldn't be here, but he's not exactly a good representative of our division. It's like he's got this invisible force field around him that screams, 'Back off!' to anyone who even looks his way." She shakes her head before adding, "He didn't even talk to me on the train to come here. He sat alone."

The room dissolves into laughter. Ryland rolls on her back, dramatically throwing her legs in the air, which knocks Kinsley off the bed. She lands with a thud and an "oooouuuuch," setting off a fresh wave of giggles. When we finally settle down, Saya clears her throat.

"So he's a mystery. One I'd like to solve." She wiggles her eyebrows and we share one last round of banter. Josli would fit in perfectly here. *I wish I could talk to her.*

The next three hours pass quickly, packed with gossip, laughter and secrets. I spend more time listening than talking, but that's okay. Saya shares some unflattering stories about Callan while Prisha admits to wondering if Hayes and Vanen have a crush on each other. We've all noticed how well they get along, and how much time they spend together. Other than that little speculation, no one's interested in details about Hayes. I make a point to say that he's a good person and really smart, even though any mention of the gangly, curly-haired brainiac seems to naturally direct the conversation back to any of the other guys.

When I ask if the others have underground shelters beneath their homes, I'm met with side-eyes and crinkled noses. Apparently only Eastates has those. A few times Kiera's name bubbles to the top of our banter. Kinsley and Ryland think she has a crush on Leader Imperant. They role-play, with Kinsley prancing around the room barking out orders until Ryland, slicking back her short dark hair and imitating Leader Imperant's cool tone, approaches and commands her to keep all her delegates away from him.

We all crumple into heaps of laughter. I glance at Saya, afraid she might be offended by us mocking the leaders of her Territory, but she giggles along with everyone else.

Too soon, yawns and stretches replace the gossip and laughter. We say our good nights and return to our own rooms. I slip into bed for the first time here with a genuine smile. *Maybe this delegate thing really isn't so bad.*

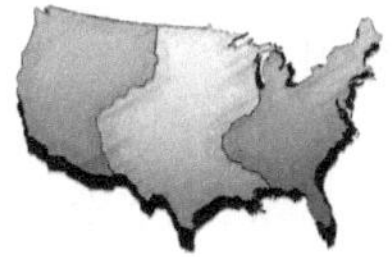

CHAPTER 29

UPPER DIVISION, CENTRESTATES

At breakfast the next morning, I share a few knowing smirks with the other girls as last night's stories flutter through my mind. Like the time Callan jumped ahead a few steps during a chemistry lesson and mixed the wrong chemicals. The result was explosive. Although the damage was pretty minor, he failed the assignment and earned a meeting with the principal.

In the Eastates, specialized courses are offered to test students. Those who demonstrate strengths in specific areas take advanced courses in those subjects. By graduation, they're likely to be offered a career path that meets a Societal Order need while maximizing the individual's skills. I'm guessing Callan won't spend his life formulating engineered food options. Or be allowed near any sort of chemical experimentation.

Although I wonder if they even have that here. Do they normally get rations like us? Neither Callan or Saya seemed surprised by the food we've been offered, but this is a very special situation. So maybe they just have a break from the usual slop like Hayes and I do.

After collecting my breakfast, I choose a seat with an empty one beside it. When Saya emerges from the food line with a tray in hand, I motion her over. But instead of taking the seat beside me, she nods her head toward the other end of the table. I'm not receiving whatever signal she's sending. I watch in confusion as she whisks past me and prowls toward Beckett with her tray.

As if accepting an unspoken challenge, she tosses a knowing glance over her shoulder and paints a perfect smile on her face before turning her full attention to him. After a few words, she plants herself in the seat beside him, clearly proud of her accomplishment. A twinge of jealousy sparks in my gut, which is stupid. *I can't even stand him, let alone like him. Or am I jealous that she'd rather sit with him than me?*

Nevertheless, curiosity draws my attention to their end of the table. I breathe a slight sigh of relief when I notice how disinterested he looks. His eyes drift from the windows to the room's other occupants as she talks, gestures and pauses expectantly now and then, awaiting Beckett's reaction or response to a question.

Maybe it's because he can sense me observing their every interaction, but Beckett's eyes meet mine several times throughout the meal. Each time, my cheeks radiate heat as I shift my gaze around the room. But each time it's a few seconds too late and he knows it. A satisfied smile curves his lips when he catches me. As much as

I'd like to forget he even exists, I know that's an impossibility at the moment.

***

As we meander to the Unity Room in a loose line, I notice Vanen shouldering the bag Hayes had yesterday. He keeps one hand clenched around the strap tightly. When he chooses a seat, he slides the bag to the floor smoothly, peering around the room as if to check if anyone is watching. When our eyes meet, his eyebrows jump in surprise before he recovers and smiles shyly. *What is he up to?*

I plant myself in the open seat beside Hayes.

"What are you two doing?" I ask, raising my eyebrows,

He scrunches his features as if he's confused, but we don't have much time before Kiera or her minions show up, so I ask a more direct question. "What's with the bag?" I nod my chin toward Vanen's feet.

"It's just . . . um . . . one of our . . . computing devices," he stammers, avoiding my eyes. "We've just been . . . using it at night."

"Using it for what?" As soon as the words leave my mouth, Kiera charges into the room and takes her place behind the podium, resting a red notebook on its smooth surface as she gathers everyone's attention. That officially douses any more questions I had for Hayes.

"Good morning, delegates! I hope you're ready to serve these glorious Divided States once again today." She pauses. But other than Hayes' awkward "good morning," she's greeted by silence. It's not like she asked a question. Stepping around the podium, she takes another approach.

"Did everyone take some time last night to watch the information broadcast?"

A few heads nod while others drop in an effort to avoid eye contact. I force my features into a neutral mask. None of the girls watched it last night, unless they switched it on after our little party ended, but I doubt that. By the time we dragged ourselves back to our rooms, everyone was yawning.

"Well, if you missed it, I'm certain you'll be able to watch a playback." Kiera purses her lips in disapproval. "But I highly recommend you turn it on each night after dinner. It will help you be better informed for this work, better able to understand the reasoning behind decisions that are truly best for all."

She skirts behind the podium once more.

"Now, as we continue to discuss the principles of peace, we will also resume interviews. Today we will start with our upper division Westates delegates – Kinsley and Arjun. If you two could please follow Lisum and Wynter, they will escort you to another conference room."

After the four of them shuffle out of the room, Kiera motions toward the cart where the computing devices are stored. *Well, all but one.*

"I'll pull up today's principle for discussion while you all collect your devices."

"Um, Kiera," Hayes interrupts. "Vanen and I have been sort of in charge of handing out and collecting everyone's devices. Do you want us to distribute them?"

Her cool gaze narrows on him. "If that's working for everyone, then that's fine." He quickly nods and rushes to the cart, Vanen one step behind. Kiera palms the screen's fob and pushes a few buttons, glancing at the guys as they buzz around the room making their deliveries.

***

Butterflies flutter through my stomach as my thoughts drift to the impending interview. *It may not be my turn just yet, but it's coming soon. Too soon.* Other than the occasional heated outburst, it's nearly impossible to focus on the topic – equitable contribution to resources. As soon as we start, the conversation turns competitive as each speaker apparently feels the need to justify how much his or her Territory does to support the others. Even Hayes surprises me with his fervor in responding.

It reminds me of lessons we were taught years ago. Every citizen is expected to have a hand in helping the Societal Order thrive. Although the Territories are no longer one united body, we must provide for each other because that strengthens us all. And we can take great satisfaction in knowing that our actions today will create a better tomorrow for future generations.

My wandering thoughts snap back to the scene before me when Kinsley and Arjun slip through the door and march back to their seats. Dread promptly flares in my core. Lisum motions to Kiera from the back of the room.

"Everly and Hayes, I believe they're ready for you."

My legs fill with lead and breakfast churns in my gut, but I push out of my chair. Hayes must sense my hesitation. He pauses beside me so we can walk out together.

"Hey, I can go first if you want," he offers.

"Sure, that would be great!"

Gratitude floods me and, intensified by rising anxiety about the interview, threatens to spill out.

"Hey," Hayes nudges me. When I face him, he continues. "Don't look like you're about to cry, Everly. You'll make us look weak."

Squeezing my eyes shut, I swallow a reply and paint a strained smile across my face. Just like that, Hayes' words have helped me again – he squelched the building emotion and replaced it with annoyance. Stepping into the hallway, I trail Lisum to the Independence Room where our interviewers await.

***

"You kids mind if we grab a coffee?" the tall, balding man asks. His counterpart, a rosy-cheeked redhead, eyes us curiously. When Hayes waves it off as no problem, they both smile graciously and head for the door.

"Well, I guess we could all use a little break," Wynter says. "Some steaming hot coffee does sound good. Why don't we all take just ten minutes and then meet right back here?"

"Sure." Hayes nods. The last thing I want is to spill a drink or choke on it, courtesy of my frazzled nerves.

"I'll just wait here," I add, settling into a chair along the side of the room. Somehow I want to delay this as long as possible and get it over with at the same time.

When the adults all leave, Hayes turns toward me.

"Everly, I have to tell you something." He glances toward the door.

"What?"

"Can we talk alone . . . later?"

"Later when? We're never alone here. Besides, you're always with Vanen," I mutter, expecting some sort of retort. *He probably has some crazy theory about something.*

"Look, Vanen and I . . ." He glances at the doorway again. "We've found some . . . information . . . that we probably . . . shouldn't know about."

His eyes dart from the door and back to me. I've never seen Hayes so nervous. Even though we aren't close, he's the only part of home I have here. And he's clearly worried about something.

"What is it? Why are you acting so weird?" My heart races as I try to decipher his cryptic words.

"It's, what we found, is about the delegation, about all of us and it's not good—"

Whatever he was about to say dies on his lips as Lisum, Wynter and the two information broadcast representatives stride through the door. They laugh and joke, steaming drinks cupped in their hands, as I attempt to hide the sudden alarm racing through my veins.

Hayes shakes his head subtly before shifting focus to the others. I have to block the questions smoldering in my thoughts. This isn't the time to talk, let alone think, about whatever he has to tell me.

"I'll go first if that's okay," he volunteers, pushing out of his seat.

"Well, we have been inviting the ladies to go first." Wynter dips her chin and raises her eyebrows as if she's taken aback by this breach of etiquette. "But if that's what you both prefer . . ."

"It is," I blurt before she can change her mind. After a momentary pause, she motions over her shoulder.

"All right, Hayes, come with me." Wynter directs him to a corner of the room sectioned off by temporary walls. The area is flanked by two boxy lamps that stand taller than me. Their tripod legs stretch toward two high-back cushioned chairs that face each other. I recognize the setup from the brief part of Ryland's interview I watched.

"We have a mirror set up if you'd like to check your hair." I turn toward Lisum's voice. "Or I could brush a little powder on your chin and forehead to help hide any shine the cameras and lights like to find," she offers quietly, standing before me with her hands folded. Her whole demeanor is soothing. *Maybe she senses my anxiety?*

"Yes, thank you." A distraction sounds great right about now. She leads me to the corner opposite from Hayes, where a table is pushed against the wall. Brushes, combs, powders and tubes are scattered across its surface. A rectangular mirror wrapped in an ornate silver frame sits in the middle, like a centerpiece. She angles it toward my face.

"Would you like any help?" she asks. When I shake my head no, she nods and steps closer to the table. She picks up a white tube, twists the cap and squeezes a few drops onto her finger before swiping it under her eyes.

Unsure what to do, I glance toward the voices drifting from the other end of the room. Hayes is perched on the edge of his seat, nearly bumping knees with his interviewer. He's intently focused as he answers a question, probably elaborating much more than necessary. His posture is confident yet comfortable, as though he's enjoying the attention.

Turning back to the table, I notice Lisum dab what looks like a mini paintbrush into a silver tin of tan powder. She dusts her cheeks with it. Selecting a comb, I pull it through my long brown locks, smoothing out any tangles. It's about the only thing on this table that I know how to use.

I watch Lisum out of the corner of my eye. When she finishes with the powder, she unscrews a clear round case that contains a pink gel. Retrieving a thin white stick with one flat end, she dips it into the gel and glides it over her lips. Returning everything to the table, she winks at me before excusing herself to check on Hayes.

She's not going to be on camera at all. She must have done that just so I would know how to use it.

CHAPTER 30

UPPER DIVISION, CENTRESTATES

My stomach lurches with panic when Hayes shakes the interviewer's hand and extracts himself from the makeshift set. He brushes past Wynter and Lisum, who congratulate him on a job well done, and rests a hand on my shoulder.

"You're up, Everly." He eyes me as if I might bolt out the door and never return. "You'll be great. It really wasn't a big deal."

Easy for him to say. He'll share his theories with anyone who will listen. Still, I thank him for the encouragement, inhale a deep breath and force my feet to carry me to my fate.

As I drop into the cozy chair, the female interviewer welcomes me and explains where to look when I speak. She tells me to focus on her when the cameras are recording, that this is just a conversation between the two of us. *Maybe I can pretend I'm talking to Josli.* Now that would be easy.

After introducing me to the camera, she asks what I think of Centrestates.

"It's amazing," I answer honestly, which makes her chuckle. "I just can't believe I'm really here. The buildings, the people, the whole experience, has been amazing. It's like being in a living history lesson."

She acknowledges my answer before asking what I bring to the delegation.

"I'm not as outgoing as some of the other delegates, but it doesn't mean I'm not as interested as them. I just like to think over what we talk about and share my thoughts after I've had time to really process it."

My answers aren't long, but she accepts them and moves to the next question fluidly. As we develop a comfortable pattern, I forget about the camera and ease into a sense of calm. Other than the intrusive bright lights, it feels like an educator is quizzing me on a pretty easy subject – myself.

She asks about my life back home, which feels underwhelming compared to everything that's happening here. Her final question is what I hope will be the outcome of the delegation.

"I think we all want to help make the Divided States a better place for everyone. I never really thought about it before I came here, but everyone brings a different perspective and it's really important to consider each one. Together, maybe we can find the perfect blend of partnership across Territories that will benefit all citizens."

She thanks me and ends the interview. Somehow I survive, only stumbling over a few words here and there. I'm hoping they will edit out anything that isn't flattering, but either way, I don't ever want to see my interview on the information broadcast.

As soon as I climb out of the chair, Hayes greets me with a high five.

"I knew you'd be great!"

"Thanks, what a relief that's done," I sigh, finally allowing myself to truly breathe.

"So I guess we should head back to the Unity Room, right?" Hayes asks Lisum and Wynter. "Do you want us to send the next two over?"

"Well, that would be very helpful, Thank you, Hayes," Lisum answers.

"Oh wait." I stop in my tracks, amazed I actually remembered the question I've been meaning to ask them. "Is everything okay with our train ride home?"

"Oh yeah," Hayes adds. "Kiera said you two were going to check into it."

They look at each other, faces scrunched in confusion. Both slowly shake their heads.

"No, she didn't mention anything like that to me."

"Me neither."

A pit forms in my stomach as Wynter and Lisum turn from us, rushing to clean up for the next delegates. They gather empty coffee cups and organize the makeup and brushes scattered around the mirror without a hint of concern.

***

As soon as we reach the privacy of the hallway, I turn to Hayes.

"How could they not know anything about us getting home? Didn't Kiera specifically tell you she would have them fix it?"

"She did. Maybe she wanted to do it herself?" He scratches his head nervously. Even he doesn't believe that. "Don't worry, Everly, I'll ask Kiera about it again."

"Okay." Maybe she just forgot and if Hayes reminds her, she'll make sure it happens. As we head back to the Unity Room, Hayes glances around to ensure we're alone.

"We need to talk in private." He slows his pace and drops his voice lower. "After dinner. But we can't meet in either of our rooms. I'll figure out a place."

"Okay, but what's going on? Like, not having a ride home is enough to worry about."

"It's about the delegation. I think there's a lot more going on than what they told us."

"If it's about everyone, shouldn't we tell everyone? In private, I mean." Maybe last night's get-together in Saya's room left me feeling more connected to the other girls. If Hayes truly knows that something's wrong, then they deserve to know too. And maybe someone would have an explanation for whatever it is he thinks he's discovered.

I'm certain he disagrees when his eyeballs nearly pop out of his head and he fists a handful of his red curls. "Tell who? We can't trust anyone here," he says. We've come to a full stop now, dangerously close to the Unity Room but unable to end this discussion.

"You said you and Vanen discovered this, whatever it is, right?" I pause for him to nod and he does. "So obviously you trusted each other. Is that only because you're from the same Territory? Because the whole reason we're here is to build better relationships with the other Territories. If we can't do that, then you're right, this delegation isn't what it was supposed to be."

I cross my arms. *How can he argue with that?* His cheeks flush crimson as he clenches his teeth. *Is he frustrated because he knows I'm right?*

"Everly, how do you tell someone from Centrestates that you don't trust them?" He throws his hands in the air. "And that the last thing whoever thought up this delegation wants is peace."

My mouth opens and closes in an attempt to form words but none come. It makes no difference because the conversation is over. Hayes brushes past me and charges into the Unity Room. I follow him numbly, avoiding eye contact with anyone who turns my way.

"Kiera." Hayes takes advantage of the momentary distraction our entrance created. "They're ready for the next group."

"Thank you, would you mind showing them where to go?" she asks after scanning the door we just passed through, likely figuring out that neither Lisum or Wynter escorted us back.

"Of course."

I settle into my seat as Hayes pivots and heads back out into the hallway. I swallow the sharp tang of guilt as he avoids making eye contact with me.

＊＊＊

When lunch finally rolls around, my stomach's in knots. I'm not sure I can even eat.

As soon as we reach the cafeteria, I beeline to Hayes. He hasn't made the effort to sit near me at lunch even once since we got here, and that's about to change. His constant shadow, Vanen, eyes me suspiciously. I follow them through the line and choose a seat across from Hayes. He can't avoid me. Luckily Saya's busy chatting with Ryland and Kinsley. It's perfect – she can't be anywhere nearby for this conversation.

"Hayes, don't be mad," I plead. "We just need to figure out where we can talk."

He and Vanen share a knowing look.

"Are you sure you really want to know? Because it's fine if you don't." He glances around the cafeteria and drops his voice to just above a whisper. "I get what you're saying, okay, but I'm not ready to tell the world what we found."

"Then just tell me." When they both narrow their eyes like I've just said the dumbest thing, I explain, "Not now, not here."

As the others select their food and claim seats around us, our window of time to speak freely narrows. Vanen leans toward me, resting his elbows on the table.

"Meet us after dinner tonight. We'll walk around in the gardens. Technically we're allowed since it's on campus."

"But, Everly, try to sneak out," Hayes adds. "It would be better if we didn't broadcast that we want to talk in private."

***

That afternoon Saya and Callan are the last to be interviewed. While he struts out of the room, she rushes to keep pace with him.

Possibilities of what Hayes and Vanen think they've found consume my mind. I can't imagine they've somehow outsmarted the adults running Centrestates. But Hayes isn't someone who lets his imagination rule. He analyzes everything and I don't believe he would invent something from nothing. *Or has Vanen influenced him? He seems nice enough, but who knows what they're constantly talking about. Has Vanen initiated it all?*

I'm snapped out of the endless spiral of thoughts each time Kiera calls on me, likely sensing my distraction and disinterest. The topic is still resources, but we've shifted to how each Territory distributes what they produce. It's less competitive than earlier today, but still feels insignificant.

Kiera intently listens when each person speaks, scrawling notes in her red notebook, but I fail to see how any of this is useful. It's just a bunch of teenagers sharing what they know, or think they know. How is that supposed to translate into some agreement that the Societal Order leaders will adopt and follow?

Callan and Saya finally return, rescuing us from the endless monotonous discussion. Kiera immediately perks when her assistants reappear. She instructs us to keep talking while the three of them huddle for a few minutes. Everyone takes advantage of the short break, chatting with those around them.

"How did it go?" I ask Saya. She rolls her eyes.

"Callan is so obnoxious. He wouldn't shut up. They actually had to cut him off." I giggle, which encourages her to continue.

"It was kind of funny. He acted all offended that they ran out of time." She presses a palm to her mouth, stifling a chuckle.

As the day's end nears, Kiera taps the podium with a pen. "You've all been working so hard. We tackled not one but two peace principles today and we've given the information broadcast team everything they need to prepare segments on each of you. Thank you for your hard work. We'll get back to it first thing in the morning."

Hayes' hand shoots into the air. *Don't ask some question that keeps us here longer.*

"Vanen and I can collect computing devices." Before anyone can even agree, they both jump out of their seats and scramble to the cart.

***

I dawdle for a few minutes, slow to turn off my device and slide it into its case.

"You ready to go?" Saya asks, nudging my shoulder.

"You go ahead without me. I'll catch up." When she narrows her eyes and purses her lips, I scramble for a believable reason. "I just want to check on Hayes. He was really nervous for his interview, and I felt bad for him."

I gulp, anticipating a challenge but she must not know Hayes well enough.

"Okay, stop by my room if you want. We can hang out before dinner."

"Sure," I nod. As soon as she turns to leave, I snatch a piece of paper and pen. With a quick glance around the room, I ensure no one's watching and scrawl the urgent request.

Need to talk – meet me at the restroom!

I fold the note and crush it within my grasp. My impromptu plan seems to be working – almost everyone else has left by now. As I pass Hayes my device, I press the note into his palm. His eyebrows shoot into the air, but he quickly recovers and dips his chin in understanding.

With painstakingly slow steps, I meander into the hallway and toward the bathrooms. Taking a long drink from the fountain, I linger. A few minutes later, a flustered Hayes appears.

"What is it?" He raises his shoulders, teeth clenched.

"There's a little bit of time before dinner. Maybe we could talk now? It might be hard for me to sneak out later." Saya's face flashes through my mind. *I can't avoid her all evening.*

"Okay," he mutters. "Vanen wanted to be here too, but I guess you're right."

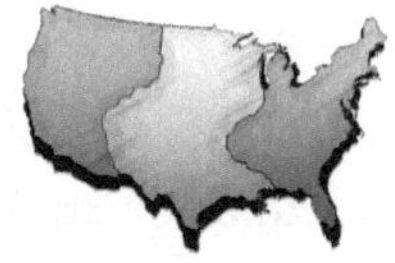

CHAPTER 31

UPPER DIVISION, CENTRESTATES

"**S**o we've kind of been snooping around the network files." Hayes scratches his head.

"What? How? You and Vanen are always taking notes. And anyone could look at your screen at any time. How were you even able to do that?"

He chuckles to himself. "It was actually pretty easy."

"Oh sorry, I forgot we're dealing with geniuses here." I twirl my wrist in a "tell me more" gesture.

"We've been taking a computing device back to the rooms at night. That's when we have time to . . . dig a little and test what we can really do." He slides his glasses up the bridge of his nose as his eyes dart back and forth.

"Anyway, we found lists with our names on them. And they're labeled in different ways. We haven't figured out what they mean, but it feels . . . off." His head bobs as he watches me. It feels like he's imploring me to understand.

"That's it? You found a list of our names? Of course they have a list. They had to decide who was coming from each division."

"No, you're not getting it." He plants a palm on his forehead, gritting his teeth. "There are codes beside our names. And there are other names, of people we know, on the list too. I'm telling you, it's not just a simple list of the delegates. You need to see it, then you'll understand."

"And how do we do that?"

"If you really want to see it, you'll need to sneak out. Make up an excuse." He throws his hands in the air. "Just go back to your room, act normal, and I'll let you know at dinner. Vanen and I can come up with something by then."

I'm not fully convinced that they found anything all that alarming, but curiosity gnaws at my reasoning. They're smart guys. If they think something is wrong, then it is possible. And it's way more interesting than analyzing resource distribution within the Territories.

"Okay, I'll see you at dinner."

***

"So how is Hayes?" Saya's question startles me when I stop by to visit after a quick refresh in my room. I suck in a shallow breath, which buys me more time to answer. She elaborates. "You said he

222

was nervous about the interview. And that's why you were checking on him."

"Oh right, yes." *How could I forget so soon?* This whole lying thing is too much work. Not like I could tell her the truth though. "He's feeling much better now that it's over."

After that little fumble, our conversation soon falls into a comfortable pattern of gossip sprinkled with laughter. At six o'clock, we wander into the hallway and climb on the elevator with the others.

"What does everyone think about another girls' night? My room after dinner?" Saya squeezes her hands together, anticipation buzzing from her every cell.

"Sure."

"Yeah, that was fun."

"Beats sitting in my room staring at the information broadcast."

"Great, then we're all in agreement!" Saya claps her hands together. "Whenever you're ready, you know where to find me."

The doors slide apart and we merge with the guys to form one big group in the lobby. Like a school of fish, we funnel through the exit and follow the path back to Centrel Hall. Vanen and Hayes linger at the back. I slow my pace to match theirs. Falling several steps behind the others, we seize the moment for what it offers – the illusion of privacy.

"So we've been talking about this." Hayes wastes no time, motioning between himself and Vanen. "And it might be a good idea to show what we've found to a few more people."

"We obviously need more brainpower," Vanen adds. "Maybe someone else will see a pattern or code that we're missing." He sighs, shaking his head slowly, like he's disappointed or in disbelief that whatever they found stumped them.

"But not everyone," Hayes cautions. "Just you, Prisha and the Westates delegates. Tonight, after dinner in my room. Don't let anyone see you."

Guilt stabs at my gut as Saya flashes through my mind. I want to trust her. But they're right – if something's going on, we can't trust anyone from Centrestates at the moment. *Wait, Saya's get-together.*

"Saya's having all the girls over in her room after dinner. Kind of a hangout. We did it the other night."

Hayes and Vanen share a concerned look.

"Then no other girls can know. It would be too suspicious," Vanen says. "But it's good that they'll all be together – and distracted – for when you sneak out."

"I already said I'd go too." *How am I going to get out of that? I didn't have plans five minutes ago and now all of a sudden I'm busy tonight?*

The guys go silent for a few steps. Hayes scratches his chin while Vanen taps his fingers together. I can almost feel the intensity of their minds turning over ideas. After a few minutes, they turn toward each other and, lowering their voices, descend into indecipherable banter as they walk. When they finish, Hayes straightens his glasses and focuses on me.

"So here's what you do, start acting like you're feeling sick at dinner," Hayes explains. "Then when you get back to your floor, say you threw up or something and that you're going to bed for the night. Then sneak down the stairway. I'll wait there and watch to make sure the hall is clear."

"Don't tell anyone else about this. We'll tell the guys – the ones we're inviting – and get them to Hayes' room before you." Vanen's words rush out as we near our destination. Once again, our limited time to talk is coming to a close.

"But one more thing. Everly, we know you and Saya are friends. Can you keep this from her?"

They both eye me quizzically. We're almost at Centrel Hall. I don't even have a minute to think, so I say the first thing that pops into my mind.

"Yes, you can trust me. Whether this is real or just a misunderstanding, I won't be the one to tell her about it."

***

"Are you okay?" Saya leans toward me as I concentrate on pushing green peas around the outer edge of my plate. Considering I have no appetite and no ability to look her in the eyes, it's pretty easy to play my agreed-upon role.

"My stomach, it's just . . . a mess," I whisper. "I don't think I can eat." Meanwhile, I suck in my gut in hopes of curbing its rumbles. My body hasn't gotten the message that I am not, in fact, interested in food right now.

"Oh no, I hope you aren't getting sick." Her pained expression only deepens my guilt.

"I'm sure I'll be fine." It's the first honest thing I've said since sitting down. "I kind of just want to go back to my room and crawl in bed."

"Do you want me to tell someone? Maybe I should take you back now so you don't have to sit here until everyone's done?"

Panic flashes through me. If Lisum or Wynter find out that I had to leave dinner early, they might come check on me. Or worse, tell Kiera. That's the last thing I need tonight.

"No, I don't want everyone to know. Then they'll all be talking about me, trying to figure out what's wrong."

She nods in understanding. "Okay." She gently nudges my arm. "But as soon as we get back, you should try to sleep. I'll tell the other girls you're really tired. Maybe I'll say your bed is super lumpy and you can't sleep at night." She giggles, reminding me of Josli. "But really, you should rest. Hopefully tomorrow you'll wake up feeling like a new person."

I don't want to be a new person. I can't tell Saya, but right now I wish I were the old Everly. The one who didn't lie all the time. The one who never left Eastates.

***

Considering we don't have drama classes in school, I think I do a pretty good job of pretending to be sick without drawing too much attention to myself. Saya stays by my side for the walk back to Centrel Quarters. She even makes sure I get to my door before retreating to her own room.

For a few minutes, the floor is quiet. The others are preparing for a few hours of fun. Meanwhile my heart beats wildly at the thought of sneaking out and possibly getting caught. I pace back and forth, wondering how I'll know when it's just the right time to go.

Luckily, it's easy to hear when Ryland and Kinsley head over to Saya's room. They make no attempt to soften their steps or keep their voices low. Their chatter echoes through the hallway. I press my ear to the door, knowing Nyra and Prisha will be much harder to track. Although they still mostly keep to themselves, they seem to have grown more comfortable with smaller groups, like when just the girls hang out.

When silence blankets the hallway once more, I recognize the subtle click of a door latching closed. Within seconds, another mimics the sound. Nyra and Prisha must be on their way to Saya's room. I let another ten minutes pass, agonizingly slow, fully attuned to any other noises. It's quiet. Which means I need to slip out. If I don't do it now, I may lose my nerve.

I slowly crack the door open, freezing in place when it's wide enough that I can see the immediate surroundings. Clear so far. Slipping just past the threshold, I move in slow motion, raising one foot at a time and gently lowering it to avoid making any sound. I twist the handle and gingerly inch it closed, willing it to withhold its telling click.

Knowing my luck could run out at any moment, I barrel toward the stairway. A bead of sweat tickles my forehead as my feet fly over the carpet. Without looking back, I tug the door open and slip through it. Easing it closed, I huff out a deep breath and drop my hands to my knees. *I did it. But I'm not done yet.*

Zipping up two flights of stairs, I pause at the entryway separating me from Hayes' floor. Cracking the door open, I peek through. Even though the view is limited, there's no sound, no movement. *Time to move.*

Pushing through the opening, my dash into the hallway is abruptly blocked. A body appears before me but my reflexes aren't fast enough to react. I crash into someone, practically bouncing off the muscular body. Grunts from the impact echo through the hallway. I can't differentiate his from mine, but a strong woodsy scent rushes my senses.

When our eyes meet, his narrow in annoyance.

"What was that?" Beckett hisses. "Are you trying to get caught?"

"Of course not!" I cross my arms. Justified or not, my words radiate anger. "What are you doing out here anyway? Were you hiding? I looked before I left the stairwell."

"Hayes asked me to come get you because he thought you might not show."

"What? Of course I was coming." That pushes my annoyance to another level. "If I say I'll do something, I do it."

He throws his hands in the air in surrender. "Ooooookay. I'll be sure to let him know."

"So which is his room?" I stomp down the hall impatiently.

When the elevator dings, I stop mid-step. I twist toward Beckett as my mouth drops, along with my stomach. He breaks into a sprint and wraps his arms around me in a gentle tackle. His crisp, fresh scent bombards my nose. Warmth envelops me as he guides us into a small corridor that looks like a closet without a door. We both drop to the floor and he presses a finger to his lips. *As if I need to be told to stay quiet.*

Voices carry toward us. I'm pretty sure one is Callan. The other must be Chander since Hayes didn't want anyone from Centrestates to know about this secret meeting he's called. I hold my body completely still. Other than blinking and breathing, I'm not risking any movement.

When two doors slam shut, Beckett slowly rises and prowls toward the opening. He peeks up and down the hallway, releasing a sigh as his shoulders drop in relief. Without looking my way, he motions with one hand for me to follow him. I stand and shuffle close enough that I can once again feel the heat radiating from his body. My nerves tingle. I don't think it's in anticipation of making it to Hayes' room unnoticed.

With soft, but fast, steps we scurry to room 412. Beckett barely brushes his knuckles over the door, but someone must have been waiting, listening. The door cracks open slightly. When Vanen's serious eyes land on us, he throws the door open and steps out of the way. As soon as we cross the threshold, he gingerly pushes the door closed and twists the lock.

CHAPTER 32 ~ KIERA

UPPER DIVISION, CENTRESTATES

"So what did you think?" It's been two days since he met the delegates. Until now, he's been too busy to carve any time out of his schedule for me. Still, I bite my bottom lip, both anxious and nervous for his opinion. The delegation is a direct reflection on me. He folds his hands, delaying, before blowing out a deep sigh.

"They seem harmless enough. Nothing remarkable. Get what you need and get them out of here." He flips through some papers on his desk, as if this conversation is over. *Far from it.*

"That's something I wanted to talk to you about." He glances up from his paperwork, dejectedly tilting his head as if he'd rather focus on what's in front of him instead of me. His dismissive attitude only spurs me to continue.

"I acknowledge that this project started out with one main goal, but as I spend time with them and review their inner thoughts, I see an opportunity to leverage this toward our ultimate, long-term goal." He opens his mouth to respond but I rush to reclaim control of the conversation.

"We have been planning this for years and it *has* to happen in our lifetime. We have put in all the work, and we deserve the rewards of that effort. Without us, the other Territories would be starving, freezing in the winters and unable to power their factories and homes. If we were in control, every single citizen of the Divided States would benefit. The delegates' notes even confirm that. They're amazed by our food and our technology. We just have to make their leaders see what they see."

"I agreed to this for the sake of checking them for the chip. If we're right and we have evidence, that would seal Ault's fate. He'd be ousted as leader of Eastates. And since we're the ones who discovered it, we'd be primed to take over." His cold stare rakes over me as he speaks. But I don't fear him. He needs me and he needs to hear the truth.

"Sir, we need to overtake them. They'd never hand over power, they'd just find another Ault to take his place." He squares his jaw and grinds his teeth, but he knows I'm right, he just needs a little more convincing.

"Sir, we tried the rolling power outages but that didn't do anything. Eastates just accepted it without any thought of attack, or even threats of one. If we do this right, I can spin a scenario of us being threatened, driven to defend ourselves. And we both know Eastates is too weak to withstand our forces. We would easily defeat them, and all the better if the delegates were the ones who initiated it. Don't you see, we just need a spark to light the match, and the delegation can be that spark."

What I don't tell him is that these "unremarkable kids," as he sees them, are on the verge of knowing our secrets – at least Hayes and Vanen. And once they know too much, I'd bet my life that they would tell the others. Not only that, but they would have proof, if I allow them to continue down their path. I could cut them off now, but I'm learning just as much about them as they are learning about us.

As they continue to uncover information, I want to gauge their reactions to it and monitor what they do with it. I also want to see how far they can go. It's a fine line between studying their capabilities and exposing Centrestates' vulnerabilities. The trick is to prevent anything they discover from reaching Eastates or Westates. And there's only one way to guarantee that.

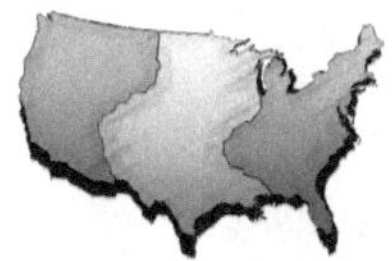

CHAPTER 33

UPPER DIVISION, CENTRESTATES

"What took you so long?" Hayes reprimands me. "Everyone's been waiting for you."

I take in the room. It's a mirror image of mine on the floor below. Hayes sits on the bed, his back flat against the headboard. Vanen slips past me and stands at the foot of the bed while Beckett hovers in the entranceway. But that's it. Apparently to Hayes, *everyone* means him, Vanen and Beckett.

"Well, I'm sorry to keep you *all* waiting." I pull out the desk chair and plop down into it. "It's not like I was just sitting around doing nothing. I had to wait for all of them to go to Saya's room."

"It's all right, Everly. No harm done," Vanen says with a genuine smile. He climbs on the bed beside Hayes, who barely looks up from the computing device on his lap. Vanen nods toward his constant shadow. "He's just anxious."

"Hey, why isn't Arjun here? He's from Westates. Shouldn't he be a part of this?" I cross my arms.

Beckett leans against the closet door and scratches his neck, unwilling to even look in my direction. Vanen opens and closes his mouth a few times but fails to find the right words. Hayes raises his chin as his eyes slowly slide from the screen to me. *They must have talked about this already.*

"Look, we know that Kinsley and Ryland talk. Constantly." Hayes rolls his eyes. "So, what if Arjun told Kinsley something and she told Ryland?"

"We know you wanted to tell more people," Vanen adds. "So we invited Beckett. The two of you are low risk. Hayes can vouch for you and it's not like Beckett's made friends here. He pretty much avoids talking to everyone."

"Thanks, I guess," Beckett mutters, running a hand through his hair impatiently. "So why don't you tell us exactly what you found?"

Wordlessly, Hayes passes the device to Vanen, who immediately taps the keyboard. His eyes sweep across the screen as the glow casts a pale light over his scrunched features. "You should see this."

We crowd around him. Instead of going to the side Hayes is on, Beckett wedges himself behind me, close enough that his warm breath tickles my neck. The room's temperature seems to surge as his arm brushes against mine. Despite the sudden stuffiness, a shiver dances along my spine. Although my nerves tingle, I hold still and try to stay focused.

Vanen's deep timbre returns me from the momentary distraction. "I found a list of names," he says. "Our names." He hovers a pointer finger an inch from the screen, drawing our attention to the information next to the delegate roster. Silence descends as we huddle closer. Hayes and Vanen must have read this list a dozen times. But still, confusion taints their features – scrunched noses, narrowed eyes and slack jaws.

Beside each of our names is the abbreviation "IND" and then another name. In my case, it's Caro Scott. My mother. *She's been gone for years now. Why isn't my father listed?*

"There must be a connection." Vanen taps his chin. Unspoken thoughts choke the air. "Why are these people listed and what does IND mean?"

Beckett answers first. "Mine's my brother." *So it isn't just parents.*

"Mine's a neighbor," Vanen admits. "I kind of forgot about her because it was so long ago. I was pretty young, but she lived next door. There was a fire and . . . she didn't survive."

Pain pierces my heart. There's one commonality – his IND died, just like mine. *Is everyone on that list dead?* Now we know it's not just a list of parents, or even relatives for that matter.

"Mine is my dad's supervisor," Hayes mutters before throwing his hands in the air. "I barely know the guy. Why would he be listed for me?"

They are right to question this. It isn't just a list of delegates or contact names. It's something more.

Beckett takes a step back and starts pacing the room. Thoughts rocket through my mind, but none of them make sense.

"I'll make a new file," Vanen says. "We'll start tracking how each person's IND is related or known to them. We'll list as many details we can think of. If we have it all in front of us on a screen, maybe we can make some connections. If we can crack that code, maybe this mysterious abbreviation will make some sense."

My stomach drops in nervous anticipation. I don't want to admit that my mother is dead. It's an intimate detail of my life. It feels too private to share, but besides that, it's still hard to say. Hayes already knows, but it's not anyone's business. *But what if Vanen's right? What if this is the only way to figure it out?*

Before we can start, Beckett crosses his arms and shakes his head.

"I already told you. Next to mine is my brother's name. That's all you need to know." His tone conveys a finality that does not invite disagreement. I'm relieved his refusal paves the way for me to avoid having to talk about uncomfortable things. *Although how else can we piece together this puzzle? For the moment, I've got to back him up.*

"It's just the four of us anyway. If we're going to figure this out, we need to tell the others. We need to know who their INDs are." Not that I want to share my private life with the whole delegation, but I don't see how we can figure this out without including them somehow. And maybe the four of us can add our information first and then just collect the others' information. Maybe we could still keep the whole list of how people know their IND to just the four of us.

"She's right," Beckett agrees. "Even if everyone isn't willing to share, any information is better than none. We might not need too many details to make a connection."

Hayes grumbles but Vanen raises a hand to silence him. "We don't have to tell them everything, but it would help to know who the names are on the list. It's our best shot at figuring out what the heck IND means."

"Fine, I'm outvoted." Hayes slumps against the headboard, practically sulking.

"So what else did you find?" Beckett asks, ready to move on.

Vanen turns back to the device and runs his fingers over the keys again.

"I'm not sure how significant this is, but the original Alliance Agreement has eight pillars of peace. But Kiera said we're only discussing seven."

"Yeah, that *has* to be intentional," Hayes says. "If you're updating an official government document, you review the whole thing. Or," he scratches his chin, "you acknowledge that one part is being removed as irrelevant or otherwise unnecessary. You don't just skip it and hope that no one notices."

He's got a point. *Why would they just ignore one pillar of peace?*

"So what's the eighth?" I ask. I'm sure we learned this in early school, but that was too long ago to remember.

"A just, equitable, accountable government," Hayes recites from memory.

"Why wouldn't we talk about that too?" I ask, not really expecting a response. Still, Beckett's answer surprises me.

"Maybe because Centrestates doesn't want our advice on what a government should be. Maybe they have no desire to be just, equitable or accountable."

"Maybe they removed that principle since we come from three different governments." Vanen stares into the nonexistent distance as he thinks out loud. "I mean, why ask us about how a government should work when that's the greatest variant in each Territory?"

"Or maybe they're hiding something," Beckett sneers. "Why all of a sudden would we be here? This stuff they have us doing each day, it's a waste of time. They don't really want to hear what we think." His tone is fraught with bitterness. Considering we're really not getting anywhere, I try to diffuse the conversation before it explodes.

"Maybe we're too focused on this one small detail? We only have two weeks here. There's not enough time to talk about everything." I press my fingers to my mouth, covering a yawn. It's been a long day.

"Yeah, Everly's probably right." It's the first time Hayes has ever said I'm right about something. Somehow it feels like he's admitting defeat. "We should probably call it a night." He looks at each of us expectantly. It's his room and he wants us to leave.

"All right." Vanen closes the files on the computing device and powers it off. He slips off the bed and tucks it in the bag I've seen him and Hayes take turns carrying. I head toward the door. It's clearly time to go but this whole thing feels unfinished.

"So tomorrow, we gather everyone, right?" I ask no one in particular.

"I'd say so," Beckett agrees, joining me at the entryway. But it's not his answer to give. He's not the one who found this information. Like me, he was only entrusted with some of it.

"I need to think about this." Hayes rises from the bed, crossing his arms. He shoots Vanen a pointed look. "We have to consider the risks that come with telling everyone."

"Well, sorry we couldn't help more." I'm not sure why I'm apologizing but I don't like seeing Hayes so deflated, so withdrawn. It's like he's a completely different person than the one I arrived with just days ago.

Beckett grabs the door handle and murmurs over his shoulder, "I'll go first and make sure no one's out there."

"Thanks," I say to his back. Cracking the door open, he peers up and down the hallway. After a moment, he raises a hand and motions for me to follow him. I give Hayes and Vanen a quick wave before slipping out the door behind Beckett.

He guides me to the stairway, although I'm not sure why. I made it up here just fine without him. In fact, I was doing better on my own. If he wasn't lurking in the hallway earlier, we wouldn't have crashed into each other.

"Want me to check your floor?" he whispers. That earthy scent invades my senses whenever he gets too close. And this is one of those times.

"No, I'm fine," I say as I sneak into the stairway. "Besides, it would draw even more attention if they saw you on our floor. At least if anyone catches me, I can say I needed to get some fresh air or something."

"Everly, I've got to te—" he starts, but before he can finish, a door slams in the hallway behind him. Heavy footsteps approach.

"Hey, that you, Beckett?" I don't recognize the voice, but it must be one of the other delegates.

Alarm races through me. Beckett holds a steady posture but mutters, "Go now," through clenched teeth. I turn and sprint down the steps. *Just need to get to my room. Just need to get to my room.*

When I reach the third floor, I peek into the hallway. There's no movement, and I'm not willing to linger in case whoever called to Beckett saw that he was talking to someone. I burst through the door and barrel to my room. My shaking hand fumbles for the key card in my pocket, clumsily grasping it and swiping it across the rectangular reader. When it clicks unlocked, I push through and release a sigh. Flopping on the bed, my body melts into a puddle of relief.

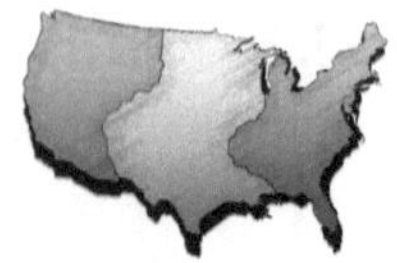

CHAPTER 34

UPPER DIVISION, CENTRESTATES

A series of sharp knocks jolts me from my morning routine. Rinsing away the last remnants of toothpaste, I swipe a towel over my chin and rush to answer the door.

"Good morning. I wanted to come check on you." Saya's forehead crinkles with worry.

"Oh, good morning." I open the door wider. "Want to come inside while I finish getting ready?"

"Sure, if you feel up to it." When I nod, she crosses the threshold and sits on my bed. "I came by to check on you last night, but you didn't answer. I guess you were sleeping?"

"Yes," I agree. "I was pretty out of it, but all that sleep really helped. I feel much better today." *The lies are flowing freely.*

"Good! Because we've got some catching up to do! You missed all kinds of gossip last night!" She practically bounces on the bed, clearly eager to share every last detail with me.

All through breakfast, she whispers snippets of secrets in my ear. It's hard to find interest in Ryland's ranking of the guys from hot to not when all I care about is why my mother's name was on that list last night. *What do they know about her? And what does it matter now? It feels like she's been gone forever.*

I steal glances at Hayes and Vanen, but they mostly keep to themselves. They appear to be in a deep discussion, but that's nothing out of the ordinary for them. Beckett's eyes meet mine a few times, but neither of us dares to let our glances linger.

When breakfast is finally over, I half-listen to Saya's stories on our way to the meeting room. I giggle when I'm supposed to – like when she recounts embarrassing moments the other girls were only too happy to share about their classmates. Even as we take our seats, the words pour out of her. She only stops when Kiera enters the room. When the seat beside mine slides out, I glance over. It's Hayes.

"Morning," he mumbles. Behind those glasses, intensity flares in his green eyes. I'm unable to decipher the hidden meaning reflecting in them. As Kiera shuffles some papers around on the podium's smooth surface, he raises his hand and asks to use the bathroom. Something lightly brushes my pant leg just before he excuses himself.

I peek beneath the table. A perfectly folded one-inch-square piece of paper rests beside my shoe. Before anyone else notices, I lean forward and stretch until my fingers clasp its corner. Slowly and subtly, I palm the paper and open it, smoothing it out along my thigh.

Meet me at the bathrooms. Now!

My hand shoots into the air with no hesitation. Clearly annoyed by a second request so soon, Kiera dismisses me with a sharp nod. I focus on tamping down the adrenaline that begs me to rocket out the door and blast down the hallway.

I practically sprint toward the restrooms, accelerating with each twist and bend in my path, nearly slamming into Hayes as I turn the last corner.

"What's going on?"

"Everly, I'm worried about telling everyone." When I start to respond, he raises a hand to stop me. "I know we want their help, but Vanen and I could get in a lot of trouble if someone decides to tell Kiera that we hacked into her network. What Vanen said last night is true. We trust you, and Beckett clearly hates everything about this place. But the others . . . how do we know they won't report us?" He clenches and releases his fists as he talks.

"You're right, it's definitely a risk. I guess you two need to figure out if it's worth the chance to find out what's going on here."

His eyes drop to the floor. I can't tell him what to do, but I can't blame him for being afraid either. I touch his shoulder.

"Hayes, I wouldn't blame you if you just dropped this whole thing. It's not too late. I don't want to see you guys get in trouble." A need to know what's going on burns deep within me, but I also understand the risk involved. *Would I be brave enough to do what he's considering? How can we get answers without giving away too much?*

Hayes slips his glasses off and presses the heel of his palm to his forehead, releasing a sigh.

"You know, you don't have to tell them everything." It's the only idea I've got, so I share it. "Maybe you just say you saw a piece of paper with that list on it? No one else has to know how you found it. Beckett and I would back you up." *Great, now I'm committing someone else to a lie. Unless . . .* "Or better yet, we'll act like we're hearing it for the first time too." *That would feel like less of a deception.*

"This could get us in a lot of trouble. If someone tells . . . what kind of punishment would there be? This could ruin my whole life." He paces, just a few steps back and forth.

He's right. Societal Order laws are clear and strictly enforced. And while we've never been taught what exactly the sentence would be for breaking into a government computer system, it's definitely not an acceptable act. Vanen and Hayes are both brilliant and probably never thought they'd have this sort of opportunity. I guess it was too tempting to ignore.

"I wish this was easier." I'm not sure what else to say. *I would never be brave enough to admit I had done something like this. But I don't believe I'd ever actually do something like this either.*

He squeezes his eyes shut for a few seconds before blowing out a deep breath and sliding his glasses back on.

"Thanks for listening. I just wanted you to know that I don't think I can go through with it. And I wanted you to know why." He turns toward the hallway we came from. Slowly, we meander back to the Unity Room.

"Let's just forget the whole thing happened, okay? I swear, I won't tell anyone and I bet Beckett will keep quiet too." I chew my lower lip, hoping that's not another lie. *It's a big assumption, given how agitated Beckett was last night.* Hayes nods, but indecision obviously weighs heavily on him.

We enter the room together, taking our seats quietly. Beckett's watchful eyes practically bore a hole in me. The most I can share right now is a sad smile.

"Well, as I was saying." Kiera looks at the two of us pointedly. Our absence must have inconvenienced her. "Everyone should be wearing their pins every day." She smiles brightly, slipping on a more pleasant mask. Although she doesn't single anyone out, we all know who she means. As usual, Beckett isn't wearing his. "Consider it a sign of respect for the Territory hosting your stay," she continues, twirling a hand in the air. The motion punctuates her words. "It shows the officials who work in this building that you value your role and value our token of appreciation."

After a moment of what feels like a silent standoff, she steps around the podium and clasps her hands together. "Now, I do have a special announcement. We're not quite halfway through your time here but you've all been working so hard that I'd like to give you a change of scenery, see if that keeps your debates and discussions going strong. We're taking today's meeting outside, to the garden area. Lisum and Wynter are setting up seating right now." *I didn't even notice they weren't here.*

The room seems to suck in a collective breath. Whispered anticipation charges the air.

Hayes' hand shoots up. "Kiera, what about our devices? Will we take them out with us?"

"Yes, and since you won't have the benefit of the building's technology, you will be expected to take detailed notes. But I'm sure you can handle that." She winks at Hayes. He audibly gulps.

"If there are no other questions, let's gather ourselves and get started on discussing the next principle of peace."

***

Kiera was right. Talking about community cooperation is livelier than the past few days' conversations. Lisum and Wynter stroll back and forth around the makeshift setup, but they seem to grow less attentive each day. They interject direction when there's a lull in the discussion and remind us to type notes in our devices, but other than that, we're largely on our own.

By lunchtime, they seem satisfied with our progress. Kiera shows up to consult with Lisum and Wynter. She announces that, as long as she's satisfied with our progress, we'll jump to the next principle this afternoon.

As a group, we make our way to the cafeteria. I stick with Saya although I can feel Beckett's presence behind me. He lingers close by, but I know he won't dare bring up anything about last night. Not with everyone around.

When we reach the cafeteria line, he inches up behind me, brushing my arm when reaching for a bowl of green beans. Goose bumps erupt from the brief touch. He leans close and mutters, "Anything from Hayes?"

I shake my head "no" just as Saya turns toward us, raising her eyebrows. *If she only knew that we share a secret.*

Giving up on me, and apparently my counterpart, Beckett chooses a seat beside Vanen. Saya nudges me and jerks her chin toward them. "What's up with him? Was he actually talking to you in line?"

After a moment of contemplation, I conjure a response.

"Oh, he thought I was reaching for a bowl of green beans so he offered to get it for me. But I really wasn't . . . I didn't want any." It's one of the dumbest things I've come up with yet, but at least she lets it drop after shooting me a disbelieving side-eye.

Luckily, once we start eating, she joins in the chatter around the table. In just a few days' time, we've gone from complete strangers to comfortable companions. While I still miss Josli, Dad and Easton, being here with my peers isn't really so bad. Even Callan's been more tolerable. Or maybe that's just because I haven't spent much time around him lately.

I can't help but peek at Beckett and Vanen every chance I get. This must be how Beckett felt when Hayes and I took the bathroom break together. He had to know what we were talking about. And now I'm just as curious to know what they whisper about just a few feet away.

I strain to catch even a snippet of what they say, but too many other sounds camouflage their words. Hayes sits on the other side of Vanen, but he appears completely disinterested in anything. He pushes food around on his plate but takes only a few bites. He doesn't even lift his head to glance around the table.

When lunch finally ends, the group merges together and moves toward the exit leading to the garden. Vanen strategically positions himself beside me. He nudges my arm, a silent gesture to match his pace.

"Everly, tonight we're inviting everyone to my room. Can you tell the girls?"

"What!?" Genuine surprise amplifies what comes out as a half-bark. When a few heads turn our way, I lower my voice. "Hayes said he didn't want to go through with it. He changed his mind?"

"No, but as of right now, he's out of it. I take full responsibility and I'll tell everyone that. No one ever has to know that he was in on it."

"Look, no offense, but with the way you two carry on, no one's going to believe that he didn't know anything."

"Okay, so I told him what I found, but he never broke into the network. That was all me." The whispered words rush out of him as frustration builds.

"I'm not challenging you," I say, checking to see if anyone around us may be listening. "And I'll go along with whatever you two want, but it has to be believable."

He releases a deep breath, seeming to relax a little.

"You're right, Everly. I'll explain it better tonight. In a way that leaves no room for Hayes to get into any trouble no matter what happens. Just please, can you tell the girls to all come to my room after dinner? It's 419."

I nod. All I really need to do is tell Saya. She's good at spreading a message quickly.

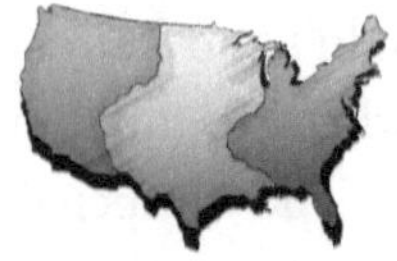

CHAPTER 35

UPPER DIVISION, CENTRESTATES

As I suspected, Saya is thrilled to tell all the girls about Vanen's invitation. Somehow she finds a way to seamlessly spread the word whenever Lisum and Wynter are distracted. Enlisting her was simple, avoiding the questions she fires at me for the rest of the day is exhausting. My only option is to claim to know as little as her.

The afternoon meeting buzzes with anticipation. Maybe being able to sit outside, something we would never be allowed to do in school, cultivates thought and debate. Or maybe the group is more animated than usual, eager for whatever Vanen has planned for them this evening.

For a few of us, the next principle of peace strikes alarm — consequences for threats to peace. Hayes' complexion pales when

Lisum announces it. A cough catches in Vanen's throat. His cheeks flush crimson as he tries to clear it out. A citizen of one Territory breaking into private files of another Territory's government is certainly a threat to peace, which is the very reason we're here. With most of the others so interested in discussing laws and punishments, I'm able to avoid saying much.

When the end of the day nears and the conversation is still lively, Lisum and Wynter promise we can pick up again with the same topic in the morning. They dismiss us and collect our computing devices.

On the walk back to Centrel Quarters, Saya suggests we all meet for dinner early and then go right to Vanen's room. Everyone agrees to meet in half an hour. It's just enough time to mentally unpack the day and freshen up for the evening. As promised, we all make the trek to the cafeteria.

Although the few remaining workers seem a little surprised to see us all before our usual six o'clock mealtime, they wave us through the food line. After a day of serving every worker in this building, a group of twelve probably seems minor.

The evening meal is abnormally fast. Every delegate selects their food, scarfs it down and cleans up in record time. Within less than an hour of arriving at the cafeteria, we're all practically running to Vanen's room. After everyone crams inside – wedged on the bed, pressed into a corner or leaning against a wall – he begins.

"Thanks for coming, everyone. I wanted to tell you about something that I believe impacts all of us. I'm not sure what it means though, and I was hoping we could all talk through it and maybe figure it out together."

That garners a few nods and muttered affirmations. I glance at Beckett. We need to act like we don't already know this.

"Before I share anything though, I need to know that anything we discuss in this room stays secret. That means you promise not to tell Kiera, Lisum, Wynter or anyone else here. Is anyone uncomfortable with that?"

No one speaks up. Instead, they look around the room, seeking out anyone who might admit to being a snitch. I gulp, wondering if all these people can be trusted. There's no way I'd tell, and I know Beckett wouldn't either, but what about the others?

"Okay, then we're all in this together," Vanen starts. "I'm going to show you what I found." Just as he did the night before, he slides a computing device from his bag. That yields a few gasps. We all know those aren't supposed to leave Centrel Hall.

Hayes rises from the desk chair and motions for Vanen to sit in it. When he does, everyone gathers around him, bumping into each other as their eyes never leave the screen. He pulls up the list of delegates and scrolls through each name, explaining that he wants to figure out who each IND is. Once everyone acknowledges they recognize their IND, he opens the file he started to track the connections.

For a few excruciating seconds, my heart hammers in my chest and sweat tickles my forehead.

Last night Beckett and I told Vanen who our INDs were. But we're supposed to be hearing about this for the first time right now just like everyone else. How are we going to explain it if he added any notes about our INDs last night and they show up in the file he's opening?

Goose bumps erupt when a hand brushes my arm. His clean, crisp scent wafts around me, offering an unexpected sense of comfort. Beckett's forehead crinkles and his lips press into a thin line. *He's just as worried as I am.*

When the file appears on screen and Vanen scrolls through it, the only cell with information in it is the one next to his IND. I release the breath I was holding and Beckett runs a hand through his hair. We share a brief but relieved smile. Thankfully Vanen thought to delete the answers Hayes, Beckett and I gave last night.

One by one, we share details about whose name is listed beside our own. Once again, Beckett reveals that his IND is his brother, but that's all he'll say. Most delegates provide only basic details, but some overshare, rattling on about the last time they saw that person listed. They're all people we know, but some are mere acquaintances while others are cherished loved ones. It's a stark reminder of those we had to leave behind. As we work our way through the list, there's no single commonality among the INDs. Some are no longer alive and others were last spoken to days ago.

Vanen huffs out a frustrated breath. "Okay, this is the complete list. We need to figure out what it means. How are all of these people connected to the delegation? What's the pattern?" Then, more to himself, he mumbles, "I'll see if I can find anything else in here."

His eyes affix to the screen as he types commands, pausing every few minutes to review whatever he's found. The rest of us talk. We recycle theories that lead to dead ends. Some suggest outlandish ideas like maybe our INDs all somehow know each other, but that can't be it. My temples ache from the rampant, yet fruitless, ideas attempting to claw their way into clarity.

When a hush descends over the room, Vanen raises his voice louder than necessary. "I found something else. And it's just as weird as the IND thing."

Everyone turns to him but his eyes never leave the screen. "It's another list. This time, there's a code beside each of our names, either C-O-N or S-U-B."

Once again we crowd around Vanen, seeking out our own names even though the letters beside them are meaningless. There's one of each for every division. According to whoever made this list, I'm the "SUB" and Hayes is the "CON" for the upper Eastates division.

"Hey, why am I the CON?" Nyra utters as if she's appalled. "They've got this wrong! Why wouldn't Beckett be the CON? It couldn't be me."

Before I can stifle it, a chuckle escapes, earning me a death glare from Beckett.

"I don't think it means convict or criminal," Hayes interjects. *It's a relief to see him back to sharing his theories, like the Hayes I came here with.* He's been quiet for too long.

"Then what is it?" Kinsley asks, her voice rising in pitch with each word. "I'm a SUB, what the heck is that?"

Callan and Chander question if it has to do with who was chosen first from each division. *But why would that matter?*

"Well, my IND is my dad and I'm a SUB." Saya wrings her hands together. "But what does that mean? Why would they track anything about us?"

"I'm sure it's nothing," Callan huffs, raising both hands in the air. "It must be some classification system. Just to keep us organized. Like a grading scale or something."

"I don't know, but we'll figure it out." Hayes shoots Vanen a knowing look. "We should stick to the first puzzle we have to solve. Then we'll tackle this new one, okay?"

Those two have really hit it off. I'm glad he found a friend, but it's not surprising. Back home, Hayes would talk to anyone willing to hold a conversation. I think it's always been easy for him to connect with peers and even adults. Where he could walk into a classroom and make a dozen new friends, I'd fade into the corners, too shy to approach anyone I didn't know.

"Hayes is right. One thing at a time. Let's make a list of words that start with I-N-D." Vanen's authoritative tone quiets the chatter, smothering everyone's random guesses. His fingers fly over the keys as people call out random words.

"Index." "Induction." "Induce." "Indistinct." "Indicate."

"That's it!" Hayes announces as he raises one finger in the air. "Maybe IND stands for indicator, like someone in our lives who might indicate how each of us might react to . . . something."

"Something? How is that helpful?" Beckett asks, crossing his arms as his tapping foot reverberates impatient boredom.

Hayes blows out a deep breath. His eyes dart around the room. I sense he's holding back. It's not like him to have half a theory. With all eyes on him, the rest of his thoughts spill out in a rush of words.

"What if it's like a red flag to predict our behavior? Or at least to *try* to predict our future behavior?" He scrunches his curly red hair, awaiting our reaction.

"What about our behavior?" Kinsley throws her hands in the air. "What would they want to know?"

"All the Societal Order cares about is controlling us," Beckett says bitterly. "Every last one of us."

Callan shakes his head and laughs. "You really believe that, Westy?"

"Wait." Hayes raises a hand, deflecting the rising tension. "Maybe they want to avoid conflict. Or be able to predict conflict before it happens. That would align with the peace treaty."

"Yes!" Vanen pounds his fist on the desk. "What if we're each associated with someone who did something to threaten peace? Or maybe someone who acted . . . not in the government's best interest.

Maybe that would suggest one of us could act in a similar manner. Like an act of sedition."

"Act of sedition?" Ryland snaps. "I don't know about your Territory, but things like that don't happen in Centrestates." I push back the smirk threatening to crack as I wait for her to toss perfectly coiled golden ringlets over her shoulder and indignantly raise her nose in the air. She doesn't. Instead, she holds every gaze that lands on her, silently challenging any disbelievers.

Hayes adjusts his glasses. He's not intimidated, and he's not done yet. I don't think he's one to shy away from a debate. Not that this is a debate exactly, but it's probably close enough to make him feel all warm and fuzzy inside.

"Anti-government acts could happen anywhere." He licks his lips and continues, "It could be someone breaking a rule or speaking out against a leader. The Territories could handle it differently too. Some may broadcast a punishment to make an example out of an offender. Another may hide it so others don't get the same idea."

As the implications of his suggestion wash over me, defensiveness curdles in my stomach. *That can't be right.* My mother never would have been part of anything anti-government. The memories of her I carry are happy. Foggy wisps of her smiling face. A subtle breeze chasing her warm, inviting hugs. A flash of pride when she offered compliments on an assignment I completed. I don't ever recall overhearing her plot to dismantle the government or otherwise sabotage our way of life. My father would never break a rule or even question one. There's no way she would have.

"Okay, we need to know more about each person's indicator," Vanen says. "We'll just call it that for now, until we know for sure. Who wants to go first?"

I gulp, attempting to swallow the dread rising in my throat. *How am I right back to where I started?*

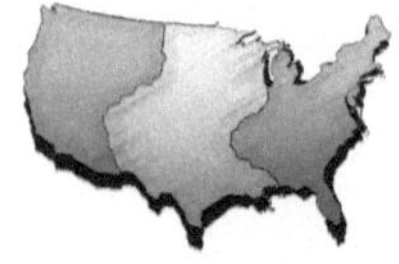

CHAPTER 36

UPPER DIVISION, CENTRESTATES

"What about Everly?" Beckett suggests. Nice of him to call me out, considering he's stated a few times that he's not sharing anything about his brother. My cheeks flush with embarrassment. Although I want to shoot him a look that screams, "Why would you do that?" it wouldn't matter anyway. His eyes slide directly to the birthmark below my left ear. I swish some hair in front of my shoulder, blocking his view.

With the scrutiny of almost a dozen sets of eyes on me, I have no choice but to respond. "So mine is my mother but the whole anti-government theory doesn't really fit. My family follows every rule. My dad makes sure of it. So it just doesn't make sense. In my case at least."

"You know, that actually might make sense for me." Prisha admits quietly. Thankfully, all focus shifts to her. She taps a finger against her lower lip as if it helps trigger memories. "There was a family that lived on my street. The little girl would get sick a lot. Sometimes I'd watch her so that the parents could collect their rations or if they got a maintenance infraction and had to fix something on their property. Sometimes they just needed a break."

Her eyes water. She squeezes them shut, no doubt consumed by flashbacks. Saya approaches, laying a gentle palm on Prisha's back. The show of unspoken support prompts her to continue.

"The name beside mine on that list was the mother in that family." Prisha's lips twitch as she struggles to say the next part. "They disappeared. One day they were just gone. I never really found out what happened to them. We weren't supposed to talk about it."

Saya gently rubs her back and leans toward her ear, whispering something. Prisha sniffles and nods. She blows out a deep breath. "After they were gone for a while, rumors started. People said they were organizing secret meetings in their underground shelter. I never saw or heard anything, but who knows."

My mind searches for a connection between her indicator and mine, but other than them both being mothers, I'm coming up blank. And even that commonality doesn't mean anything because some of the names on the list were men.

"The name next to mine . . . it's one of my dad's coworkers." Hayes gulps as his mind wanders to the past, evidenced by the faraway trance in his green eyes. "He was trying to figure out how to divert more power to his house, and he asked my dad to help him."

Shaking the memories from his mind, Hayes pauses before glancing toward me. Shock must be evident on my face. How did

I not know about this? And what else happens that no one hears about?

"My dad told him no way, so he asked someone else at work. Said he needed two sets of hands or something. So this other guy was all set to go and help, but the Enforcers found out somehow. The other guy showed up to see his friend being arrested. We never saw him again – he seemed to just . . . disappear. Nothing ever happened to the guy who was gonna help. I guess they never knew about him."

Someone trying to cheat the power grid? I never knew that happened. Where did the guy end up? Years and years ago there were trials to decide if someone was guilty of a crime and what their punishment should be. Some were sent to prisons. There aren't enough resources to house those kinds of people now. Instead they are punished by losing rations or being assigned extra community duties. If that was the case, the guy would have been sentenced, not erased from existence.

A few others share stories but still, none of it fits together. Frustration reigns as discussions die.

"Obviously the lists mean nothing," Callan's voice cuts through the silence. "You're trying to make something out of nothing. I've wasted enough time here."

"Well, whatever it is, I think we're done for tonight," Vanen announces, stretching his arms and twisting his back. As much as I was hoping to find some answers, he's right. We've all been debating this for hours and all we have to show for it is aching muscles and exhausted minds.

"Maybe tomorrow night we can all meet again?" Hayes suggests. "We can brainstorm about the other list – try to figure out what SUB and CON mean."

"One more thing." Beckett's voice slices through the chorus of answers – about half in agreement to meet again tomorrow night. "If anyone tells Kiera or anyone else what we found, we all go down. Because you can bet that if one person tries to sell us out, the rest of us can come up with a story pretty fast to shift the blame."

"And they think I'm the CON," Nyra mutters. This time I don't laugh. Beckett's right. We've reached a delicate level of trust. The information had to be shared if we're going to figure out what it means, but if anyone here betrays us, we could all be punished.

"So everyone stays quiet and we don't talk about this again until after dinner tomorrow." Vanen raises his eyebrows expectantly, searching everyone's faces for agreement.

"Yeah, maybe," Callan says. He doesn't even wait for anyone else, he just waves a hand in the air before yanking open the door and striding down the hallway.

"I guess he's lost interest in us," Saya mutters.

"He doesn't believe that it's any big deal," Ryland counters, shrugging. "Everything else around here is pretty boring though, so it's probably just some classification thing to keep straight who's who."

"I don't know, it feels like a mystery to solve, but I'm too tired to think anymore." Kinsley stands and motions to Ryland. "You wanna walk back together?"

After a quick nod, they slip out the door with the remaining delegates trailing behind them. Saya waits and asks if I'm ready to go.

"You go on without me," I say quietly. "I want to ask Hayes how he's doing before I leave. I'll see you in the morning."

"Okay." She hesitates but slowly makes her way to the door. When it clicks closed, I turn to the only others left – Beckett, Hayes and Vanen.

In hushed voices, Hayes and Vanen rehash the evening's discussion. But it's nothing new. We're no closer to solving this puzzle than we were yesterday at this time.

"I'm tired, guys, I'm going back to my room." Before I reach the door, Beckett catches up to me.

"Yeah, I'm going too. See you tomorrow."

I head toward the stairwell, expecting he'll go the opposite way, to his room. Instead he darts past me, blocking the way.

"That mark . . . on your neck . . . has it . . ." He rubs his chin nervously. "Has it always been there?"

"Yes, it's a birthmark, okay?" Once again I brush some hair forward to cover it. *What is with him?* "I hate it and I wish I didn't have it."

"Hey, I didn't mean to upset you." He gently squeezes my shoulder. "Everly, I have to tell you something. Maybe we should go in the stairwell. It feels more private."

I cross my arms and narrow my eyes. "Fine, if it gets me closer to my room, let's go."

He rushes forward and props the door open, motioning for me to go first. I brush past him and charge down both flights of stairs. When I reach the third floor, I stop and face him. He hovers just inches from me, his scent and warmth invading my senses. His lip trembles. *Is he nervous?*

"Everly, I know your indicator, or whatever IND means. I met her."

The air rushes out of me with the force of a hurricane. My mouth goes dry as I squeak out the first thing that comes to mind.

"That's not funny, Beckett." Tears sting my eyes but fury refuses to let them fall. "My indicator is dead."

He shakes his head, but I don't care what else he has to say. I scurry around him and run to my door, choking back a sob. My trembling hand slides the key over the entry pad and I bolt inside, locking the door behind me. Closing my eyes, I rest my back against the flat surface and slide down until my butt lands on the floor.

Sure enough, a few seconds later, a soft knock echoes from the other side. I don't move. *Maybe he'll just go away.*

"Everly, I know you're there," he pleads quietly. "Just open the door before anyone sees me out here."

Crud. The others. If any of them sees him knocking on my door after everyone supposedly called it quits for the night, they will *interrogate me until the sun rises.* It's just enough time for my brain to wake from its temporary stupor.

I yank the door open. "Come inside. Now."

Eyes wide and fist midair in anticipation of knocking, he shuffles into the room. *Who would have thought Beckett would ever do something I'd ask, let alone demand of him?* The simple act of compliance emboldens me. I slide the door closed, turn the lock and face him. Pointing a finger at him, I demand answers. "How? How could you know my mother?"

Hooking his thumbs into the sagging waistband on his pants, he hesitates. Although he's a master at withholding information, I've never seen him nervous about it. Until now. His jaw stiffens and he brushes a palm across it.

"I'll tell you, I promise." Those blue eyes sear right into my heart. They don't hold deception. "But there's something else." His eyes shift to the door, as if an intruder lurks on the other side, about to break it down. Arms crossed, I drop my chin.

"What are you talking about? I don't care about anything else right now!" Anger boils within me as my patience dwindles.

"I know you have questions, but I saw Kiera and Imperant sneaking into Centrel Hall about twenty minutes ago, and I want to know what's so important that they're meeting now."

I didn't notice if he ventured toward the windows in Vanen's room. Of course, there were a lot of bodies crammed into the space. I wasn't exactly watching what everyone was doing.

Annoyance flares. This has nothing to do with him knowing my mother. *Who cares what the leaders do when we aren't there?*

"Beckett, it's *their* building in *their* Territory. They can meet whenever they want and it has nothing to do with us."

"You're right about them meeting whenever they want, but I think it has everything to do with us." He steps forward, resting his palms on my shoulders. Warmth rushes through me, shooting waves of electricity to my limbs. My mind struggles to focus on his words, both what he said in the stairway and what he's trying to tell me now.

"What are you talking about? And you still haven't explained how you know . . . knew . . . my mother." *Did he come here to actually tell me something or just to drag me along to Centrel Hall?*

"There's no reason for you to believe me, but . . ." He runs a hand through his hair, shaking his head. "Everly, I just know something is going on and we need to find out what it is. But we have to go now. I promise we'll have time to talk about your mother after."

"Is that why you came here? So you didn't have to sneak into Centrel Hall yourself?" I cross my arms and narrow my eyes at him.

"I swear, I was planning to tell you what I know, and this just came up. I'm asking you to believe me, even though you have no reason to. Please, we're wasting time here. Let's just go and I'll explain everything."

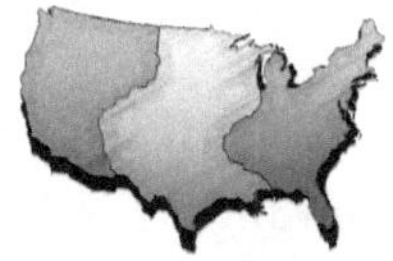

CHAPTER 37 ~ KIERA

UPPER DIVISION, CENTRESTATES

"Okay, we're here. What exactly couldn't wait until morning?" He barges into my office and drops into a chair. I tug the door handle before promptly taking my own seat. It lazily swings toward the jamb but doesn't latch closed. I don't dare delay this one second longer. He's already irritated that I asked him to meet with me this late, and if he senses that I'm not respecting his time, this conversation will not end well. Besides, no one's working at this time of night, so there's no chance anyone will overhear us.

"Sir, it's the delegation. Our progress is off the charts." What I don't say is that two delegates in particular have managed to break into our private servers and subsequently reveal that information to all the others. They're all compromised at this point. They're all a liability. *Now to spin it . . .*

"At this rate, we would be foolish to not take full advantage of the untapped information at our fingertips." I pause, holding his gaze. He doesn't ask how we can do this, but he also doesn't stop me.

"I worked with our analysts to determine one person whose past behavior might influence each delegate's future behavior. This person, who we're calling an indicator, serves as sort of a litmus test. I want to know if the delegates are predisposed to follow actions of those they know who either followed or betrayed the Societal Order."

"And?" His dark eyes fix on me, but they hold no curiosity, no interest. He twists his wrist in the air once, a little too impatiently for my taste. He should be thoroughly impressed at this point.

"If we can test this, we can apply it to the larger population. Our analysts could create a 'citizens to watch' list. It would help us eliminate security threats. It's possible some of the delegates could be direct threats to the Societal Order in the near future."

"What would it involve?" His back straightens and he taps a finger on my desk. *Now I've got his attention.*

"I want to bring them face-to-face with their indicators to see what kind of behavioral response it triggers. We can document each interaction and monitor their actions in the future, for both the delegates and the indicators."

His posture stiffens immediately and I know this battle is lost.

"No. We're not bringing anyone else into this. The more people you bring here, the more likely it is to blow up in our faces." He presses a clenched fist to his chin.

Blow up. *What an interesting word choice.*

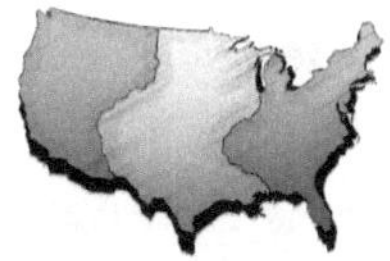

CHAPTER 38

UPPER DIVISION, CENTRESTATES

Impatience smolders within me. Rolling my eyes, I bend in the battle of wills and agree to go with him. Stomping to the door, I don't even check to see if he's following. I don't care what Kiera does when she's not around us, and the less I see of her, the better. She probably perches in her fancy chair, running a manicured fingernail up and down lists of Centrestates citizens' names, randomly stopping on one to fantasize about whose life she can thrust into a state of upheaval.

I shake the rambling thoughts from my head. The last person I want to see right now is Kiera, but I have to know what Beckett claims to know about my mother. How could he possibly know someone a whole Territory away? Maybe that's why he refused to talk about the IND list when we found it. Maybe that's why he's been paying attention to me since we first got here.

My body reacts to the realization faster than I can control. My cheeks flush crimson as comprehension dawns – he was never interested in me, not the way I might have imagined. He didn't feel a magnetic draw to learn every quirky detail about me. He didn't struggle to speak for fear of embarrassing himself by saying something stupid. He just had to get me alone to talk about my mother.

But what are the chances that our paths would cross? Up until a week ago, I joked about night dwellers being vampires. Gossip and childhood imaginings were the closest I'd come to even considering what anyone outside the upper division was like. And my mother. *If she somehow met Beckett, who else did she meet? And how?*

As if sensing the emotional storm brewing, Beckett wraps a hand around my elbow, stopping me mid-step. Hovering his lips beside my ear, he whispers, "Everly, I know this doesn't make any sense right now, but I promise, it will."

I yank my arm free of his grasp. It's completely unwarranted, but a sense of betrayal slinks through me. Somehow, somewhere deep down, I thought, cautiously hoped, that he liked me. And I'm ashamed to admit, even just to myself, that I wanted him to.

"Whatever," I mumble under my breath. "Let's just get this over with."

Once we safely sneak out of the building, we cautiously creep toward Centrel Hall. Each step I take is fueled by anger. My pace slows and my posture stiffens as we near the glass doors. The warm glow of lights in the main lobby illuminates a guard whose narrowed eyes track our every move. Every time we enter and exit this building, it's in a group. We've never been questioned why we were coming or going. It was probably obvious all those times.

The automatic doors we typically pass through don't react when we stand before them. They must get locked at a certain time. Sidestepping to the right, I grasp an ornate bar and heave a heavy door open. Stepping aside, I flourish a hand. "After you."

Beckett holds my gaze a little too long, wielding a narrow-eyed flicker. I flash him a sneer in return. Maybe the guard will send us right back to our rooms. I actually hope he does.

The man rises as we approach the large desk. His broad shoulders and fluid movement exude the authority he clearly possesses. *We shouldn't be here. What if he reports us? Would we be punished?* I focus on the wrinkles stretching from the corners of his eyes to his temples. I search his dark irises for kindness, but only find indifference.

"This building is closed to all visitors after eight p.m."

Beckett tests our status as delegates. From our clothing, the man can clearly see that we aren't from Centrestates, and travel between the Territories is so rare that people our age wouldn't just show up to visit the capitol building some random evening. I don't even know if citizens within the Territory are allowed to be here during the daytime.

"We're part of the inter-Territory Peace Delegation," Beckett starts, not a hint of doubt in his tone. He wags a pointer finger between the two of us. "We were supposed to bring the group's notes back to our rooms and study them. We have to give a presentation in the morning on everything the group discussed today."

I nod dumbly, not exactly bolstering the credibility we're attempting to fabricate.

The guard starts to shake his head but before he can speak, Beckett leans closer, as if he's letting the man in on a big secret. Speaking in a low tone, he injects equal parts urgency and desperation into his next words.

"Look, I heard Leader Imperant is meeting with us tomorrow. If we can't get our notes tonight and study them, we'll make total fools of ourselves. And the whole delegation."

"And the Territories have all made such a big deal about this whole thing." I find my voice, which surprises even Beckett. His wide eyes meet mine, gratitude curving a slight smile in that dimpled cheek. "I bet if everything goes well tomorrow, Leader Imperant will be happy, and he'll never even know that we forgot our notes."

Crossing his arms, the guard tilts his head. He still doesn't believe us, but I sense he wants to get rid of us. Perhaps a reminder of who's in charge of us might sway him to grant our request.

"If we don't get this right, Kiera is going to be so angry," I say, shaking my head as if I can't bear the thought. "I'm afraid she'll take it out on anyone and everyone around here."

"Just five minutes, that's all we need." Beckett raises his hands in a pleading gesture. "We can grab the papers and be out of here before anyone else even sees us."

The guard huffs a deep sigh and jabs a stubby thumb in the air. "Five minutes. Make it fast."

Beckett tugs my hand, rushing past the guard. "Yes, sir, we'll be right back. Thank you."

***

As soon as we reach the relative privacy of the stairwell, I growl, "We have five minutes? What's the point? That's not enough time for anything!"

Beckett raises his palms, stopping my tirade, but it's a futile gesture. He tries words.

"Don't worry, maybe he'll lose track of time and forget about us for a little while."

My eyebrows jump as my chin drops. *He can't really believe that.* I fold my arms across my chest, granting him a moment to conjure a better response. A noncommittal head tilt and shoulder hunch confirm that he doesn't believe those words any more than I do.

I shake my head slowly, rolling my eyes so he can fully absorb my frustration.

"Come on," he whispers, tugging my hand. We prowl over each step, climbing the dim stairway. When we reach the seventh floor, Beckett twists the shiny handle, cringing when it emits a high-pitched squeak. He squeezes my hand, clammy with sweat, and nods. This is taking too long. We've got to hurry if we're going to find whatever he thinks is here.

We inch down the hallway, trying to move quickly yet quietly. I practically cling to the wall as Beckett ducks his head, silently pivoting back and forth on constant alert.

Why did I agree to come here? Why couldn't he just tell me what he knows back at the room? Impatience floods my veins.

"This is such a waste of time!" I hiss. As much as I want to scream in his face, fear chokes my words to an angry whisper.

"We're almost there, just hold on."

"That guard's probably coming to find us right now! We need to just grab some papers and go before we're caught!"

Pressing a finger to his lips, he points down the hallway with his free hand. Kiera's office. Sure enough, dim light spills into the corridor, beckoning us closer.

We tiptoe along the walls, holding our breaths as if the mere effort renders us invisible. Voices drift down the hallway, luring us forward even as caution flares in my mind. Hushed, urgent tones send icy waves of warning to my core. *We aren't supposed to be here. Whatever conversation is happening right now is not meant for our ears.*

Powerless to retreat, we drift onward, carried by careless curiosity. We stop just outside of Kiera's door, crouching to conceal our presence.

"I expressed concerns about this little experiment of yours the first time you presented it. And I was right," Leader Imperant scolds, his tone laced with venom. I imagine that chiseled face twisted with anger and accusation. I'm glad we're not on the receiving end of his words. The realization only heightens my fear of being caught.

"We're making incredible progress," Kiera purrs. "I guarantee we'll glean results that we can apply across the Territories."

"Get this done and send them home. I don't need a mess on my hands." I imagine Leader Imperant pointing an accusatory finger at her, both a threat and a command.

"Of course, sir. We're nearly halfway done and we've already gathered plenty of data that we can extrapolate to predict attitudes and curb future offenses."

"With such a small sample size?" he balks. "We'd have been better off increasing the number of subjects and eliminating the control group altogether."

"Sir, our top scientific staff insists that we have a control group. And keep in mind that we'll continue to collect data even after—" She's cut short by her boss' sharp retort.

"Yes, you've mentioned this. Several times. I want this completed as soon as possible and I want them out of my backyard."

I gulp, knowing that I'm among those he wants gone. Now. Maybe he never wanted us here to begin with. But he's in charge of the whole Territory. This delegation never would have happened without his blessing. Hints of his icy reception spring to my mind. I figured he's a busy man who's rushed from one meeting to another. Greeting us was just another imposition on his schedule.

I nearly jump out of my skin when a screech rents the air. The leg of a chair dragging across the floor, which could mean someone is about to leave the office. As my anxiety spikes, I tug Beckett's arm like a child demanding parental attention. "We should go. Now!"

Before he can respond, electricity-fueled brightness bursts from the ceiling, swallowing the partial illumination of overnight lighting. The echo of clacking shoes bounces along the hallway, headed straight for us. The guard! He was probably tired of waiting for us to report back to him so he could send us on our way.

Beckett's wide eyes meet mine. He turns us around and we barrel toward the stairway. My heart thrashes in my chest. What if there's another guard waiting to catch us sneaking out? I didn't notice if there were others, but I didn't really think about it until now.

"Hey!" a deep voice barks as heavy footfalls slap the polished floor. We burst through the stairwell door and bound down the steps, jumping a few here and there, narrowly avoiding an unbalanced tumble to the bottom. When we reach the main level, we slink through the door, momentarily scanning the large, open lobby. It looks empty.

Beckett sprints toward the reception area as I shadow his every move, nearly tripping us both up in a tangle of legs in motion. A door bangs on its hinges in the direction we just came from, but we don't dare look back.

We're almost at the exit. The guard can't chase us all the way back to Centrel Quarters and leave the building unsecured. He'll stop as soon as he reaches the invisible force field of Centrel Hall. He'll shake a clenched fist in the air at us, hurling insults and threats our way, but we'll disappear into the night before he retreats back to his duties behind the desk. I almost chuckle at the vision. But before we reach the door, the last barrier to our escape, shouting erupts.

"Stop right there . . . your five minutes . . . are up."

We ignore him and push to the finish line. Just a few more steps and we'll clear the exit.

Beckett thrusts his arms forward, reaching for the door. When his palms connect with the smooth metal on glass, he jolts back, crashing into me. Air rushes from my lungs and my forehead slams into his back, rattling my skull. The pain supersedes my brain's attempts to comprehend what's happening. I close my eyes, wishing this was just a nightmare. Warm breath tickles my ear. I don't bother opening my eyes. There's only one person close enough to invade my personal space.

"I'm sorry, Everly. I never meant to get us in trouble."

But you did. I don't say it, even as the words explode in my mind. We're not going anywhere. The doors are locked. And we're caught like fish on a hook.

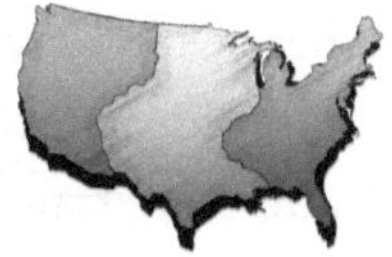

CHAPTER 39

UPPER DIVISION, CENTRESTATES

After a few deep breaths, the guard smooths out his mustache and clasps his hands together. "I'd say you two had ample time to retrieve whatever papers you supposedly came here for. Aaaaaannnddd, seeing no such documents in your possession, along with the fact that you both fled when I attempted to approach you on the seventh floor, I'd say your reasons for being here are not altogether honorable. Would you care to explain yourselves?"

I press my lips together. They disappear into a thin line, projecting my refusal to answer. Nothing I can say will make this better. The only reason I'm here is to get answers from Beckett, but I'm certainly not about to say that.

"Sir, we looked for the notes but they must have been thrown out or maybe one of the other delegates took them by mistake. We couldn't find them, and I guess we spent too long looking."

The uniformed man tilts his chin, training an expectant gaze on us. I've got nothing to add and honestly, Beckett's response was pretty impressive considering he fabricated it so quickly. I don't believe myself capable of inventing a believable explanation for our actions, even if I wasn't under the scrutiny of time and a smug authority figure.

A cheerful ding yanks our attention to the bank of elevators. The thick doors split down the middle, lazily drifting open. As if our situation isn't bad enough, Kiera and Leader Imperant step out of it.

Their eyes land and fixate on us as they steadily approach. While she observes every detail of the scene, distaste drips from his icy gaze. My chest tightens with the pressure of a vise in anticipation of what's to come.

"Everything okay here?" Somehow her question sounds more like a command for the security guard to extinguish whatever they've just walked in on. It's pretty obvious Beckett and I shouldn't be here right now. Her nostrils flare once, the only outward indication of the fury she's attempting to contain. Based on what we just overheard upstairs, this is probably the worst thing for Leader Imperant to see right now – two of her delegates caught trespassing in Centrel Hall hours after being dismissed for the day.

The guard ducks his head respectfully toward each of them, a subtle bow to authority. "Leader Imperant. Miss Saign. I can assure you that everything is under control. I'm just having a word with two of our inter-Territory delegates." He smiles reassuringly. For a moment, a bubble of hope drifts through the charged air. Maybe they'll believe him and walk right past us, eager to get on with whatever evildoing they both have planned for the evening.

"I'm quite surprised to see any delegates here this late in the evening," Leader Imperant says coolly, awaiting an explanation.

"Well, sir, they said they have a presentation to give tomorrow and they needed to gather some notes they left here, from meetings earlier today." I don't dare look at Beckett or Kiera. Instead, I study Imperant's face, searching for any hint of compassion. He slides his hands into his pockets and pivots his hip toward Kiera.

"Is that true?" He doesn't even address us. He looks to his subordinate, the full weight of our lie pressing on her shoulders. Her nostrils flare once more before she answers him.

"Yes, as a matter of fact, I asked them to prepare a summary of the delegation's recommendations thus far, along with a full analysis of both benefits and potential drawbacks of each one."

Pursing her lips together, she pauses for just a moment before solving the impasse. "It looks like they didn't find the notes they were looking for. I'll escort them to the conference room so they can retrieve what they need. Sir," she turns toward Imperant, "there's no need to delay your evening any longer. I'll help them find the information and escort them back to the dormitories."

Scanning our faces, probably for any hint of worry or relief, Leader Imperant gives one sharp nod before striding past us. The guard calls, "Good evening, sir" as Imperant throws a hand in the air in a disinterested wave without looking back.

"Miss Saign, would you like me to escort the delegates upstairs? That way you can get a start on your evening too." *Yes, I'd much rather go with the guard!* At least he might believe we told the truth. And he can't possibly be as intimidating as Kiera.

"Oh no, the delegates are my responsibility. It's my job to keep them in line and make sure they have everything they need to serve their purpose. Thank you for all you've done already but I'll take it from here." She paints an appreciative smile across her face before turning on her heel, making a beeline for the elevators. Beckett and I stumble as we rush to keep up with her.

Pressing her lips together, she shoots us a side-eye as we wait for the telltale ding of the cab's arrival. Beads of sweat dampen my forehead as I avoid our reflection in the mirrored doors. It feels like a march to our execution. And Kiera's only too eager to drop the guillotine.

The shiny doors part and we step into the confining box. We hover in charged silence. I'd rather she just explode and get it over with. We all know it's coming, and the wait only etches more goose bumps into my arm. They rise along with my compounding anxiety. *How bad is this really?* At home we'd lose rations or maybe power for an amount of time depending upon the severity of the infraction. But all we did was sneak into a building. It's not like we damaged or stole anything. And technically we were never told not to come back to Centrel Hall after dinner, so we didn't break any rules. At least none that we know of.

Unable to contain my jittery nerves, I shoot Beckett a sideways glance. As if in tune with my urgency to communicate, he twists his chin, ever so slightly, and raises his eyebrows. *I don't know what that means.* We can't exactly chat freely in front of Kiera, but I need something, any sort of signal, to know what he's thinking. Rolling my eyes, I can only hope he senses that he is completely to blame for this.

The elevator's happy chirp announces our arrival on the seventh floor. Its pleasant tone mocks us as we file from the dangling box that carried us here. We trail behind Kiera. Wrath radiates from her stiff gait and straight posture.

We finally reach her office. She motions to Beckett to close the door behind him and we all slide into chairs. It's unreal to think that minutes ago, Beckett and I were standing on the other side of that door. The adrenaline flowing within me spikes. I slide my palms under my thighs in an attempt to hide my shaking hands.

"So," she says, her eyes sliding back and forth between us. "Who wants to explain what exactly you were doing sneaking around here at night?"

I gulp, the only movement I dare make. Not that I could speak even if I wanted to. Fear strangles my vocal cords.

"Well, we just . . . " Beckett starts. "We wanted to get a head start on tomorrow so we thought maybe we could—"

"Oh don't give me that!" She interrupts him and points an accusatory finger at him. "If you were Callan and Saya, maybe. But not you two."

She nods to Beckett. "You're the only one who refuses to wear your delegate pin. No one else seems to have a problem with it but you . . . you refuse. Even after I've mentioned it. Several times. And you," she turns her fury toward me. "you barely say a word. I don't know if you're daydreaming all day or just mute, but you should be an active participant in this process! Every one of you should be contributing and you should be a touch more appreciative of this amazing experience Centrestates has provided you!"

My fists clench and my feet twitch, not from fear but the anger coursing through me. *I didn't even want to come here and no one ever asked me. I was told I was going, never asked, and she expects me to be grateful?*

"Bu—" Beckett tries. Again, she cuts him off.

"I don't want to hear it. You didn't come here tonight for extra credit." She wags a finger in front of us as if punishing a naughty child. "Now tell me why you were here. Since neither one of you ever seems interested in the delegation's discussions, I know it wasn't that. So what could possibly interest you enough to walk over here and sneak around?"

My stomach drops and my mouth goes dry. Even if I could form a lie right now, I doubt I'd be able to squeak it out. I press my lips together to keep the lower one from trembling.

"We were just bored," Beckett mutters. "We wanted to get out and do something."

"And you thought barging into the capitol building was a good idea?" She plunks a palm down on the desk, shifting her gaze between us. When neither one of us speaks, her cheeks flush red and her nostrils flare.

Nothing we can say will get us out of this. Silence is our safest option. Her frustration mounting, Kiera gives up on waiting for a response.

"You have no business in Centrel Hall other than when you are on official delegation business. I *won't* see you here again after hours." Her crystal blue eyes narrow as they dart between us. If I didn't feel like they could slice right through me, they would be beautiful. But all I see behind them is a hateful fury. Beckett and I meld into our seats, physically withdrawn from this lecture.

"Now, you will both go back to your rooms and neither one of you will tell anyone that you stepped foot inside here this evening. Lucky for you, we are going to pretend that this never happened. Can you both manage that?"

She taps her nails on the desk impatiently. Even though my blood boils with a renewed rage, I'm powerless to express anything other than acceptance. *We've already gone too far. I can't push it any further.*

"Yes," we both agree. She abruptly stands, knocking her chair back a few feet. It skitters along the polished floor, jarring us both into motion.

"I'll escort you back to Centrel Quarters," she announces as she marches past us and swings the door open. Without even a glance back at us, she strides down the hallway to the elevators. We scramble to keep up.

From the moment we step inside the elevator, it feels like time slows. The air in the boxy compartment is humid and suffocating. The walls seem to close in as the car yields to gravity's pull. I stare straight ahead and focus on breathing.

This is all Beckett's fault and I don't plan to ever speak to him again. He's a liar and he's reckless. I'm neither of those things, and I won't allow him to change me. I don't want any part of whatever he's doing to string me along.

We silently trudge behind Kiera, following the windy sidewalk that seems to never end. Beckett lightly tugs on my sleeve, but I jerk my arm away, ignoring him. As soon as we reach the entrance to Centrel Quarters, Kiera abruptly stops and spins to face us.

"There will be no mention of this or the supposed presentation you made up. Ever." She smooths her hair back. "Tomorrow is a new day. I suggest you both use it to make a clean start."

With that, she turns and strides back toward Centrel Hall. Hot tears burn my eyes, but no one will see me cry. I dash into the building and jam the elevator button. When the doors lazily slide open, I slip inside and press the "close door" button until it does its job and puts a firm barrier between me and everyone else.

When I reach the third floor, I beeline for my room and finally escape to the only place I can truly be alone. I lock the door, slip into sleep clothes and crawl under the covers. *I just want to forget this day ever happened.*

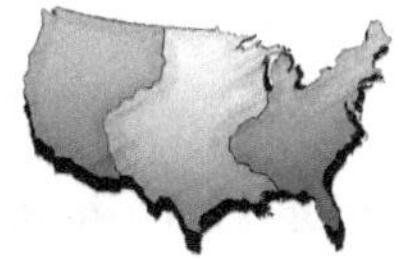

CHAPTER 40

UPPER DIVISION, CENTRESTATES

By morning, I just want to hide under the blankets and pretend I'm too sick to report to Centrel Hall. There's no chance of that happening though. I'm sure Kiera would make a point to check on me herself, which is the last thing I want.

If only Josli was here. She'd say something stupid to make me laugh and then drag me out of bed. Somehow she'd find a way to make me forget about Kiera.

After spending most of last night staring at the ceiling, uselessly chasing sleep, I force myself out of bed. *One day closer to done with this stupid delegation.* The only thing motivating me to move is knowing the day's end will bring me a little closer to going home.

That is, if the train plans on taking me back. It's not like Kiera has bothered to check on that.

I join the others at the elevators, sticking close to Saya. But seeing her reminds me of Kiera's words last night. She knew Beckett and I wouldn't be in Centrel Hall to work ahead. But somehow that might have been believable if we were Saya and Callan. My stomach lurches as the memories flood my mind.

I paint a smile across my cheeks as the group chats, nodding when the conversation warrants, but otherwise I retreat to the depths of my thoughts. *How has my life changed so drastically in such a short time?* At home, I knew exactly what to expect out of each day. And I had a pretty good idea of how my future would play out. But now I'm questioning just about everything I've ever been taught, and I'm taking risks I never would have even dreamt of before.

When we reach the cafeteria, I grab an apple and a piece of toast, taking a seat and avoiding eye contact with the others. If anyone asks, I'll tell them I'm not feeling well. Maybe they'll leave me alone if they think I'm contagious.

Once we get started in the Unity Room, I allow my gaze to fall anywhere but on Beckett or Kiera. Whenever she speaks, I carefully analyze the table, carpet or walls. The only interesting thing she says is that Lisum and Wynter are planning a trip to the power grid for us so that we can see firsthand how Centrestates supports us all with the energy they produce.

We spend the morning dissecting the next principle of peace – trust in leaders. It's starting to seem like each topic comes at the worst possible time. Right about now, I don't have any positive thoughts of Leader Imperant or his henchwoman.

I make a point of talking and sharing ideas anytime I can think of something remotely intelligent to say. Still, all the while, the scrutiny of Kiera's scowl weighs on me. From the moment her icy gaze first sought me out this morning, my every blink and breath were caught in her merciless glare. It takes me right back to last night, to the sinking defeat I felt when we were caught.

Hayes watches me intently each time I speak. He must notice the sharp increase in my participation. *I hope he doesn't ask about it, because I'm tired of lying.*

At noon, we break to eat. Saya waits for me in the hallway so we can walk to lunch together.

"You okay?" she asks.

"Just feeling a little off today." *It's actually the truth.*

"Yeah, you were kind of different in there," she says. When I glance at her questioningly, she adds, "Not in a bad way."

"Just trying harder, I guess." *No need to explain why.*

The rest of our walk is quiet. I've probably made her paranoid to say anything else. When we reach the cafeteria, I slide through the lunch line robotically. I grab a few plates, only noticing what's on them when I balance them on my tray – a leafy salad, vegetable stir-fry and a mound of brown rice. Just as I reach for a drink, a body brushes past me. The hairs along the back of my neck stand on end when the faint scent of pine drifts to my nose. Without looking, I know who it is. I managed to avoid Beckett's penetrating stare all morning, focusing on the mindless discussion and never-ending note-taking instead. Apparently that time is up.

"Everly, we really need to talk. I owe you some answers." Those crystal blue eyes widen with urgency and his eyebrows twitch in expectation. Fiery anger surges at the mere sound of his voice. But just as quickly, curiosity chases the flames. Seething inwardly, I paint a neutral expression across my face and tilt my head to the side as if

I'm considering his request. He nods toward the back of the room, a silent invitation for me to join him there.

"We're not supposed to sit back there. Are you trying to get in even more trouble?"

"No one ever said we *have* to sit at any specific table. We're still having lunch at the same time and in the same room as the delegation," he challenges. "Look, I promised you an explanation and you deserve it. Just sit down for a few minutes and I'll tell you what I know. And then we can go back to the usual table."

Blowing out a sigh, I grasp a cup of water and plunk it onto my tray. The liquid swishes, spilling a tiny stream into my rice. *Figures.* Beckett watches me intently as I mosey toward the small table he's claimed. Before my bottom touches down on the chair, he leans across the table.

"Everly, I'm really sorry about last night. I never thought we'd get caught . . ." He shakes his head but continues when I slide my seat in and stare at him blankly. "Look, I don't know how much time we have, I—"

"What do you mean how much time we have?" The apology I expected, but what else is he trying to say?

"I just think last night went . . . horribly wrong and . . . maybe it pushed Imperant over the edge, you know?"

Narrowing my eyes, I shake my head. *No, I don't know what he's talking about. And I really don't care.*

"Look, that's not the point. I wanted to talk to you about . . . your mother." His eyes sweep across the cafeteria. It gives me the second I need to suck in a ragged breath. I lean forward, thankful the table separates us because otherwise I'd probably be on him like scales on a fish right now. I'm drawn to him, beyond the information he has that I need to know. Even though he completely infuriates me.

"Your mother was sent to my Territory when I was still in early school. I didn't realize that it was a punishment for her. One day she started working at the hard goods mill with my mom. Hey, you better start eating or someone will notice."

I'm so engulfed in his words, everything beyond him fades from my senses – the conversations, the scents, the clanking of silverware on dishes. Nodding dumbly, I grip the fork and shovel rice in my mouth while waiting for him to continue.

"So," he runs a hand through his thick hair, "my mom noticed she was always under supervision. It kind of made her stand out. Anyway, my mom was assigned to train her. They sort of became friends and the closer they got, the more your mom shared. Take another bite." He nods toward my tray, breaking the trance.

"Huh? Oh, yeah." I wrangle a limp piece of lettuce onto the fork before stabbing a tiny but plump tomato. A gob of yellow seeds sprays across my cheek. My face burns from the inside out as I raise a napkin and attempt to swipe the embarrassment away, along with the gooey mess. Beckett's nose crinkles in disgust. I twirl a hand around in a circle, hoping to direct him back to the conversation.

"So, anyway, there was this one day when she stopped by our house after work. My mom was sick and missed her shift. She just slept all night and all day. Your mom came to drop off an extra blanket she said she didn't need. Keep eating. I need to take a bite too."

I raise my cup of water with a shaky hand. I'm fascinated yet sad to think my mother might still be alive somewhere. And that she's spent years away from us, spending her time with other people's families. My foot taps the floor impatiently. I want to know more, but I'm not sure I want to believe any of it.

"So anyway, it was that day. I remember your mom just taking over. She cleaned up the house, got our food rations set up and even made me show her my homework." He chuckles at the memory. "I remember saying, 'You'd be a good mom,' and she told me she already was one."

I shudder. Something inside me bursts, giving way to a flood of emotion. Beckett reaches a hand across the table.

"Everly, are you okay?" When I quickly nod, he adds, "I know this is all a shock."

We both shovel food into our mouths for a few minutes. I'm not hungry but I'm afraid my voice will crack if I speak, and I can't risk having a breakdown here. Now.

"Do you want me to stop? We can talk about this another time if you want." Concern etches his features, but I don't know when we'll be able to talk again. I shake my head, signaling that I'm not ready for this conversation to end.

"Your mom had this made-up background she was supposed to tell if anyone asked—" He shakes his head, clearing away the thought. Glancing at the clock, he rushes through the rest of the story.

According to him, our mothers became friends over time. As they grew closer, mine apparently shared details of her life. Beckett's mom talked about it at home sometimes. Although much of it wasn't meant for Beckett's ears, he overheard things and asked questions.

He summarizes in just a few minutes what he's learned about her over the past several years. Part of me wants to know more, but another part of me wonders how this could really happen. The more he tells me, the harder it is to comprehend. *How could Eastates, the only home I've ever known, tear apart my family?*

"Beckett, this woman could be anyone. And the person you met could have been lying. How can you be so sure she's my mother?"

"The birthmark." His eyes flash to the raised skin I've caught him looking at so many times. "She said her daughter had a heart-shaped birthmark. Just below her left ear. And she said she had a family back in the Eastates and that she got in some trouble." As he speaks, he slowly gathers the utensils he barely touched. I should encourage him to scarf down some food, but all I care about is hearing more.

"I think we should go back to the others, there isn't enough time to explain everything right now." He nods toward our usual table, where nearly every set of eyes is latched on to us. "Looks like we're not exactly keeping this under the radar."

"If you're lying—"

"I'm not, Everly. I swear. Your mom was basically taken from her home in Eastates and smuggled all the way over to Westates. Maybe they were afraid if she was closer, like in Centrestates, she'd try to get back to her family. I don't know, but they told her to forget her old life and she didn't."

Disbelief yields to overwhelming emotion. I'm not sure what to feel. If what he says is true, I've got to find a way to reach my mother. *But what can I really do?*

As soon as Beckett and I rejoin the others, the whispers fade. Saya watches me with wide eyes, grinning. *Great, as soon as she gets me alone, she's going to grill me. Better start thinking of an excuse so the lies roll off my tongue when the time comes.*

Lunch ends soon after we sit. After a quick cleanup, we all head back to the Unity Room. The afternoon discussion is lively as Lisum and Wynter encourage us to share some history of our Territories. Hayes recounts the sayings we repeated each day in early school, meant to foster a sense of community: *Together, we rise, like the tide.*

Help your neighbor today and he'll help you tomorrow. Eventually, they became ingrained in us.

When delegates start talking about their leaders, the conversation devolves into a history lesson – nothing interesting, just restatements of what we learned in school. As each leader ages, he grooms a descendant to succeed him. Technically the leaders ensure that each Territory can fully function independently, but over the years they saw value in exchanging goods that their citizens otherwise wouldn't have.

After a little while, I tune out the discussion to focus on Saya's inevitable interrogation. *Why would Beckett and I sit by ourselves?* No matter how many ideas my mind conjures, only one seems believable. I gulp, because of course it's also what I'd consider the most embarrassing.

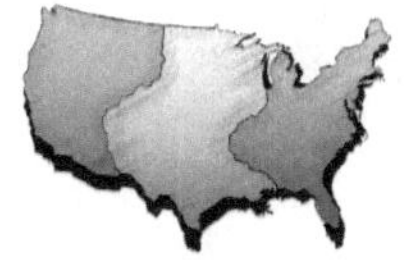

CHAPTER 41

UPPER DIVISION, CENTRESTATES

"S ooo?" Saya nudges my shoulder as we step off the elevator. "Wanna come to my room for a minute?"

"Sure." *Might as well get it over with.*

She links her arm around mine and ushers me to the privacy of her room. Before the door clicks closed, she spins toward me.

"So spill it! What was lunch all about?" She plops on the bed and wraps her arms around a pillow before pulling me down beside her.

"Well, it's just that . . . we . . . wanted to be alone," I practically stutter. "We're sort of . . . seeing each other." I gulp, knowing this can only result in humiliation. *Maybe I can get Beckett to play along. It would make it easier to talk alone.*

"I knew it!" she shrieks. "Tell me everything!"

I jump to my feet, eager to escape before I'm forced to embellish this lie. "I've gotta go! I'm actually supposed to meet Beckett before dinner. We don't have that much more time together, you know?"

She rises, pressing her palms together. "That's so sweet! I totally get it. But promise you'll tell me everything later!"

I nod and throw a hand in the air, tossing her a quick wave as I yank the door open and race through it.

Tiptoeing down the hallway, I go straight to the stairwell and scurry up two flights of steps. When I reach Hayes' door, I knock urgently. Just a few quick taps. He pulls it open, eyes narrowing when they land on me. Without even asking to come in, I push past him into the room.

"What are you doing here, Everly?" He pushes his glasses along the bridge of his nose and lets the door swing closed behind him.

"I needed to talk to you." I rub my temples to ease the building tension behind them.

"Okay." He tugs the desk chair out and sits in it, motioning for me to take the bed. I lower myself onto it and drop my head into my hands.

"Something happened last night, Hayes."

He leans forward and rests a hand on my shoulder. "Are you okay?"

"I'm okay but if I tell you . . . you can't tell anyone, like not even Vanen, okay?" *When did everything here become some top secret spy mission?*

"Okay." He hesitantly agrees, clearly torn by his loyalty to each of us.

"So last night Beckett and I sort of snuck into Centrel Hall."

"What? Why? When?"

"Look, that doesn't matter right now. When we were there, we overheard a conversation, and I think it was important. It was between Kiera and Leader Imperant. I just didn't have a chance to tell you about it until now."

"Forgot about it?" His face scrunches in disbelief. "That's not something you forget about!"

"It was really bad, Hayes. A guard caught us and then Kiera and Leader Imperant showed up. She was pretty angry and she told us not to tell anyone. I 've just been so worried about it, and afraid that we'd be in more trouble today." I take a deep breath and steady myself.

"Well, you're still here so it can't be that bad." He offers me a wry smile and rubs his chin. "So what did you overhear?"

"Imperant sounded angry, like he wanted something to end. Kiera was talking about how great everything is going. She said she's collecting data that they can use across the Territories. About future offenses. And then he said something about just getting it done."

He crosses his arms, clearly not impressed with what I'm telling him. Or maybe not following. I'm even confusing myself, so I try again.

"Ummmm . . . he sounded angry. He said something about a sample size . . . and how she should have more subjects instead of a control group. And then she started talking about data again, but he got even angrier and cut her off."

"Wait." Hayes stands and starts pacing the room. "Say that again."

"What part?" He ignores my question, instead shuffling from one end of the room to another, muttering random words under his breath.

"Sample size . . . subjects . . . control group."

I reach into the corners of my mind for anything else I can remember. He continues to pace, chewing on alternating fingernails. After a few minutes, he stops and his eyes fly open wide.

"Everly, they were talking about us. *We're* an experiment," Hayes announces. "Think about it." His eyes narrow as he slowly shakes his head. "Twelve people is a small sample size. And we found the list of SUBs and CONs. They've labeled some of us subjects and others the control group."

"So I'm a subject and you're in the control group." What have I done to be a subject in this experiment of theirs? And why is Hayes in the control group?

"Everly, I know I promised, but I have to tell Vanen. We need his brain power on this." He gulps, twisting his hands together.

"You think you two can figure out what it all means? Why this is even happening?" It feels like a betrayal. Like Centrestates only wanted us here to use us. We left our families and our friends behind for what – so Kiera could test theories on us?

"I do, and Vanen may have found more stuff on their network by now too." His eyebrows jump with hope that I'll release him from keeping the secret we now share. I have no loyalty to Kiera or Centrestates. But I do have loyalty to Hayes and Eastates.

"Yes, tell him. Maybe you two can make sense of it. I just can't focus on anything right now. It's all too much." We're a bunch of kids being used by adults in another Territory. And we don't even know what for. I don't think I've ever missed my dad or Easton more than at this moment. They're a world away and have no idea what's really happening here. *Although I really don't either.*

With only a little more time until dinner, I leave Hayes and return to my own room. Sinking into the bed, I scan all the luxuries surrounding me – from the framed artwork to the enormous bed to the personal information broadcast screen.

How can a place so perfect on the surface be so flawed in its core?

***

In a daze, I walk to dinner with the others. Saya wears a knowing grin the whole time. She must assume I'm lovestruck. Which leads me to my next problem – convincing Beckett to play along with our supposed relationship.

After I shuffle through the food line and emerge with my tray, Beckett waves me over to a seat beside him. *That's unusual. But definitely helps support the lies I've told about us.*

"Hey." He leans dangerously close, his warm breath tickling my ear. "A few of us are getting together after dinner. You should hang out with us." He watches me, silently awaiting my answer. A spark of excitement sizzles through me, temporarily distracting me from the questions and possibilities running rampant in my mind. *He wants me there?*

Not that it matters. We need to talk and this is the perfect opportunity. Those ocean-deep eyes gaze into mine. His pouty lips tug into a lopsided grin. The nervous energy fluttering between us commands me to agree.

"Okay." *Not a great response, but at least I didn't stutter.* He smiles, forcing me to concentrate on pushing down the heat flaring in my cheeks.

"Don't tell anyone though," he adds quietly. "It's only a select group."

Just as he pulls away, Saya plops into the seat on my other side. She raises her eyebrows but makes no comment. For the rest of the meal, Beckett talks to the others around him. In between chitchat with Saya, I try to mentally sort through everything that's happened in the past day.

***

After dinner, we all retreat to our rooms. My stomach flutters as I wonder if the other delegates are already meeting up somewhere and they've completely forgotten about me. My mind is a jumble of conflicting thoughts, alternating between my mother and Kiera's experiment.

I don't have to wait too long for an answer. A soft knock jolts me into hyperawareness. I dash to the door and crack it open. Beckett leans against the frame and whispers, "We're meeting in room 307 in five minutes. Keep quiet in the hallway, okay? We don't want anyone who isn't invited to hear us."

I nod and close the door. *I hope Saya was invited.*

Checking the mirror, I inspect my face. Pinching my cheeks, I inject a little color into my pale complexion. The bright light makes my eyes look darker than usual – the brown so deep it nearly blends in with my black irises. Some of that makeup from the information broadcast interview would be great right about now. Not that it matters since I have no way to get it.

I smooth out my hair and inhale a few deep breaths. *It's just a couple of people hanging out. I could use a distraction and it could be fun.* If Josli was here, she'd have tugged me out the door as soon as Beckett said where to meet. She probably would have pushed right past him and left him in our dust. The vision makes me giggle. And that's exactly what I need right now – a brief moment to just forget everything that's happened.

With a confidence I don't feel, I slip through my door and creep down the hallway.

***

Muffled voices echo through the door to room 307. I don't recognize whose it is. This end of the hall is darker, as if it's somehow forbidden. I lightly knock. When nothing happens, I pause, tempted to just retreat to my room. A second later, the door swings open. Kinsley stands just inside, one hand propped on her hip.

"I told you I heard something!" she mutters to the others before nodding toward me and impatiently waving me inside. I blow out a deep breath and brush past Callan, Ryland and Chander. *Great. Saya's not here. Unless she's on her way and we'll hear another knock . . . anytime now.*

As they shift out of my way, my eyes land on Beckett. He stands away from the others, hovering near the large window. I quietly join him, unsure where else to go. He raises his chin in a silent nod as my stomach twists with uncertainty.

Maybe I can just tell him about the fake relationship thing and leave. The energy in this room is charged with defiance and excitement. The last thing either of us needs is to get into more trouble.

"Sooooooo, looks like we have everyone," Ryland starts, chewing her bottom lip. "In the time we've been here, all we've really seen is our beds, the cafeteria and that room they lock us in all day."

"Can't argue with that," Callan mutters, crossing his arms and tilting his head expectantly. "So what do you suggest we do about it?"

Her lips split in a blazing smile. That was the exact response she wanted.

"If we don't plan our own *field trip*, the most we'll get to see is the power grid." Ryland scrunches her nose in disgust. "And I didn't brag to my friends about coming here just so I can bore them with the secret inner workings of some stupid generators."

"She's right!" Kinsley adds, rolling her eyes. "They made such a big deal about this whole thing, but what is it really? A whole lot of nothing. We might as well be back home, just going to school."

Anticipation rolls through the room. They're all considering it, while I'm practically choking on anxiety.

"Where would we go?" I inwardly cringe as my voice quavers. Kinsley nearly bursts with impatience, yanking their attention back to her.

"We'll just explore! Who cares where we go as long as we get out of here and *do something!*"

"I'm all for exploring," Beckett starts, grazing a palm over his slightly stubbly chin, "but we probably only have one chance at this. We have to make it count."

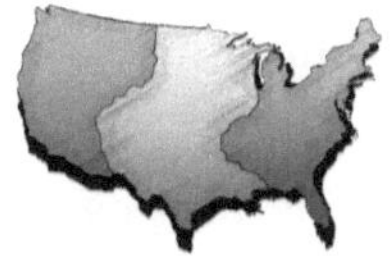

CHAPTER 42

UPPER DIVISION, CENTRESTATES

"Maybe we should ask Saya to come," I practically squeak. Their narrowed eyes blaze with scrutiny as if I just suggested we ask Kiera's permission to sneak out. My fingers twitch as I rush to explain. "She knows what's around here that's worth seeing. How else would we figure that out?"

"No way, she'd tell," Ryland huffs. "Besides, we have Callan."

My annoyance flares. *Why am I even here?* I'd rather hang out with Saya in her room. I trust her more than any of them. But instead someone invited Callan. *If we can't trust Saya, then how can we trust him?* I must not be the only one thinking it. All eyes turn toward him, silently questioning what no one will say out loud.

"Yeah, I'm here and I know where to go." Callan crosses his arms and smirks. "Saya would never come anyway. She's a *good girl.*"

The last two words roll off his tongue with a hint of venom. It occurs to me that each one of us is invisibly tied to the delegate we came here with. It feels like a betrayal to hear Callan talk about Saya. Even though Hayes and I barely knew each other before this, if he comes up in conversation, my instinct would be to defend him, or at least try to deflect any attacks on his character.

I shake my head as my stomach churns with anxiety. This whole thing just doesn't feel right. My only plan was to come here for two weeks, do what was expected of me and return home. I don't need any excitement and it's certainly not worth the risk of getting in trouble. Again.

While the others bombard Callan with questions and details, I retreat to my thoughts, searching for any plausible excuse as to why I should skip their little excursion. *Maybe I could keep the other delegates busy so they don't notice that anyone's missing?* No, I'd never be able to gather a group and entertain them. Somehow I doubt small talk about my Territory's failing gardens and wildlife watching would serve as a worthy distraction.

The brief reminder of home reignites my earlier thoughts. Beckett believes he knows my mother. And that she's alive. In Westates. How could that even be possible?

Suddenly, Ryland slams a fist on the table, yanking me back to the present discussion.

"That's it! We've got a plan!" She thrusts her shoulders back, clearly pleased with whatever they've come up with. I probably should have been paying attention. My gaze passes over the others, searching for an accomplice, someone else who looks even mildly worried. But they all chatter as if we're not about to do something that would put us right in Kiera's line of fire if we're caught.

"Do we need to bring anything like a flashlight?" Chander crosses his arms and looks to Callan.

"Nah, not like we really have anything anyway." Callan shakes his head.

"One more thing, before we go." Beckett's gaze shifts around the room, landing on each of us in turn. "No one outside of this room can find out about tonight. We all have to agree or this doesn't happen."

How can he even consider this after getting caught last night? He acts like this is no big deal, like Kiera isn't just waiting for us to screw up again.

"What do you want, *Beckey*, a blood oath or something?" Callan smirks, cocking his head to the side in challenge. Tension and distrust ignite the charged air. Beckett's nostrils flare. A vein throbs in his neck as his jaw squares. He advances toward Callan as if he's surveying his prey.

"I'm saying if you can't keep your mouth shut, I'll shut it for you." In the blink of an eye, their faces are inches apart, their bodies tensed for confrontation. Ryland jumps to her feet and squeezes herself between them, pressing a palm to each guy's chest, pushing them apart.

"We get it!" she says. "But you guys need to calm down. I'm not missing out on our one chance for some fun because you two have some stupid beef with each other. Just get over it – at least for tonight!" She takes a deep breath and lowers her arms, shifting her eyes from one to the other.

Neither says a word but their stances relax, slightly.

"All right, enough talking. We're wasting time." Callan takes charge. "No one checks on us at night, so that shouldn't be a problem. But sneaking out and then back inside the building . . . that's when we're most likely to be caught."

I wonder if the others can hear my heart crashing into my rib cage. But, like me, they're all intently listening to Callan. He's got the advantage over all of us. And he's loving it. He points to the door. No one seems even remotely nervous about this. Or else they're really good at hiding it. Worry must be written all over my face, because it envelops my entire being.

"We leave in small groups. Take the staircase at the far end of the hall and meet outside. Stay close to the building and try to duck behind the bushes, nearby but out of sight. Or at least blending in with the surroundings." He pauses to face Beckett. "You should know all about sneaking around in the dark, Beckey. I mean, it's just what nocts do."

A grin spreads across Beckett's lips as his jaw tightens. He's a perfect model for lethal amusement. Ryland waggles a finger at Callan. "Fun tonight, that's it! Save the insults for tomorrow!"

"It wasn't an insult, just an observation." Callan raises his hands as if the gesture declares his innocence. She narrows her eyes at him and plants her hands on her hips.

"Enough. Tonight we have fun. There will be no talk about peace treaties or how much we hate each other." The moment hovers for just a moment before Ryland cracks a smile and chuckles. "Who woulda thought two people who can't stand each other would be working on a peace treaty together!"

The rest of us dissolve into laughter. It slices through the tension as we all contemplate the irony and truth of her words. Even Beckett and Callan break into sheepish grins.

***

Just before we slip out of the room, Callan raises a hand to halt us.

"We go in pairs. Stagger your pace so it doesn't look like we're all together." He pauses, as if awaiting protest or questions. When no one responds, he continues. "Ryland, you're with me. We'll go first. Then Kinsley and Chander. Beckey and Everly, you're last." Callan smirks, obviously loving the power he holds over us simply because of where he was born.

Beckett shoots him a sneer but holds his tongue. While I could live without the stupid name calling, it is a good idea to make it look like we're strangers. Which we still kind of are. We'll be less noticeable if we're not all clustered, gawking as if we're on a sightseeing adventure.

"Follow the hallway all the way to the end, where it wraps around the corner. There's an exit door that leads to the stairway. Take that." Serious Callan is back, issuing instructions. "Once you get outside, walk straight ahead toward the main street—"

"The main street!?" Kinsley barks. "We'll get caught for sure!"

Callan's cheek twitches as he narrows his eyes at her. *Big surprise, he doesn't like being challenged.*

"It'll be fine. I was about to say that you'll turn into the alley on the left *before* the main street. We'll regroup there."

"Guys, we can do this!" Ryland says, waving a hand in the air. "Don't worry, before you know it, we'll be far enough away from here and partying!"

"Right," Chander huffs. "Now can we go already?"

Without another word, we slip out the door one by one, practically tiptoeing down the hallway. It's quiet. The others must be settled in their rooms. *Like I should be.*

When we all huddle at the bottom of the shadowy stairwell, Callan reminds us to walk briskly but casually outside – as if there's no reason to question what we're doing or why. I'm sure he and Ryland will easily pull that off. They glance at each other and she nods excitedly, biting her lower lip. *It's time.*

They push through the door and let it slowly swing back toward us. Beckett and I stand there in silence and Chander counts down two minutes. Once he's satisfied they've waited long enough, he motions for Kinsley to join him. They slip through the exit. *We're next.*

I linger for a moment, staring at the closed door, half wondering if I should make a run for it back to the safety of my room. Sure, I wouldn't live it down while I was still here, but the trip's halfway over. After another week, I won't see these people ever again. As I seriously contemplate escaping, hints of pine sweep over my senses. My nerves tingle.

"Do you *really* think this is a good idea?" I whisper. "It's not too late. We can bail on this whole thing and let them risk getting caught."

"This might be our only chance to see what Centrestates is really like." His eyes search mine for understanding. "And besides, we've got a little more catching up to do."

He tilts his head toward the door.

"I think it's time."

So much for my big escape. I nod and gulp down my worry. Forcing one foot in front of the other, I follow in his shadow.

We step onto the sidewalk that snakes around our housing quarters. As the cool breeze rushes over my skin, my instinct is to stay low and move quickly. We hustle in the direction opposite Centrel Hall, leading us to an area we've never been to before. *Or at least I haven't.*

Weaving around the far edge of the gardens, we disappear into the shrubbery separating us from the city proper. Pushing through the prickly leaves and pointy branches, we emerge to a completely different world just a few feet away on the other side.

I'm stunned into a stupor as I realize how vastly different the evening looks here. Lights brighten the whole city. They shine through windows and run along rooftops, illuminating the streets.

"Beckett, all the lights . . . it's so bright out here." I pause to cover my gaping mouth.

"Yeah, so?" He gazes around us before settling on me and scrunching his face.

"This is the upper division, it's supposed to be day dwellers only." Realization dawns on him just moments after it does on me. He's used to being out at night, to seeing his surroundings alight. *Other than being in unfamiliar territory, this is normal for him.*

"You're right, but we better catch up." He nods toward Chander and Kinsley. Every moment we hesitate puts more space between them and us. Which is good so that we don't look like we're together, but we don't want to go too slow and lose them. What if we miss a turn? It's not like Callan told us where he's taking us. But even if he did, we don't know where anything is here, so it wouldn't matter.

We track them in silence for a few minutes. I use the time to admire every crack and crevice revealed by the many beams of electricity sweeping across our field of vision. The world is a different place at night. While my neighborhood stills to a stop every evening, this city glows with life.

Some buildings are boxy squares while others are rectangular columns that climb to the sky. While they're all lit, they alternate in color. Golden light spills from some windows while blues, purples and pinks shine from others. This collection of steel, concrete and glass blends together like a beautiful mosaic. It radiates a stunning calmness.

Sharp spires rise like spikes from a few towers. I wonder what they signify.

My mouth gapes as we pass a stone fountain with three tiers. Water flows from the top to the bottom, swirling in a small pool at the very bottom. *This is nothing like Eastates.*

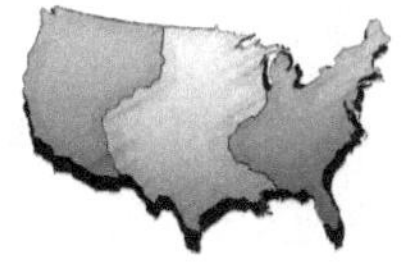

CHAPTER 43

UPPER DIVISION, CENTRESTATES

"Hey, you okay?" Beckett taps my arm. When our eyes meet, I'm momentarily distracted by the concern reflecting in his blue eyes. Still, I'm hesitant to say too much.

"I'm just not used to doing stuff like this," I admit.

"Well, it shows all over your face. I mean, you're even more pale than usual."

My head snaps toward his. Apparently it says more than any witty retort I could come up with. He throws his hands in the air.

"Sorry, that probably wasn't something I should have said out loud." At least he has the decency to sound apologetic. I just shake my head and face forward. The flaring annoyance serves a purpose though, it leads my thoughts back to a subject I'd actually like to talk about right now.

"Beckett, what is my mother like . . . the woman you think is my mother . . . is she . . . nice?"

"She's strong. And smart. And patient."

It's just a handful of words but I'm mesmerized. My memories are of her being kind and caring, but he's seen an entirely different side of her.

"Tell me more."

"She's strong because she could have just kept to herself and lived the life the Societal Order chose for her when they dropped her in Westates. But she never accepted that. She's smart because she did what was expected of her so no one would be suspicious. And she's patient because she never gave up on her family. She knew she would find you again, Everly."

I chew my bottom lip and stifle a sniffle as emotions rush through me. *Don't cry, don't cry.*

"You okay?" Beckett whispers. I nod, looking straight ahead.

"My turn to ask you something," He nudges my arm with his elbow, apparently trying to dissolve the tension. "What's up with that Hayes guy?"

"What do you mean?" I turn toward him, only to turn away when I realize just how little space separates us. My cheeks flush with heat.

"He walks around like he knows everything." He shrugs. Although it's meant to be a slight, the truth in that statement makes me smile.

"Well, he kind of does." I can't help but giggle. *Hayes wouldn't be here if he wasn't smart.* "Some people may keep that hidden, you know? But he puts it all out there. There's no mystery with him.

He's just . . . real." *Even though I'd rather be here with Josli, I could have ended up with a worse travel partner than Hayes.*

"Yeah, I guess," Beckett mutters, stuffing his hands into his pockets. Focusing on the sidewalk ahead, I realize the others are nowhere in sight.

Momentary panic flutters through me. We have no idea where we're going. *If we've lost them . . .*

"I don't see them! Do you see any of them?" My worry crescendos to a hysterical whisper. Callan's words float through my mind. *Brisk but casual.* We don't want to stand out. And right now, that's exactly what I'm doing. Beckett rests a hand on my elbow and slows his pace to a stop.

"Let's stay calm," he breathes. "Just look around, see if you recognize anyone."

I nod, too quickly. Anyone who looks close enough could see I'm one breath away from shattering like glass. *Josli would know in a heartbeat.* I gulp down a deep breath, willing myself to calm down. At least on the outside.

Taking in our surroundings, I notice a flow of people pouring out of a building a couple of blocks down the street. A buzz of excitement swirls in the crisp air. Laughter and chatter rise as the crowd disperses, many of them heading our way.

My mind searches for reasons they would all be out here. We're in the upper division, so everyone here is a day dweller. That means they should be in their homes. Instead, they hold hands and scatter through the streets without a care in the world.

"Hey, we can't just stand here and stare at them." Beckett nudges my shoulder. "Come on, try to look like we belong here."

He takes a hesitant step forward before throwing me an encouraging nod. I square my shoulders and raise my chin before joining him. Together we stride down the sidewalk as if we own it.

I focus on scanning the faces for anyone familiar. *Hopefully not Kiera, or Wynter or Lisum.* The thought leaves my throat dry and my heart racing. *Breathe, stay calm.*

Somehow my feet carry me closer to a brilliant, golden building that seems to shimmer with luxury. As we draw nearer, my jaw nearly drops when the sign comes into view. Twinkling lights reflect the exterior's shiny facade. Large white letters designate the Centrel Theater.

A theater? As in, these people all just watched a show. *How is that possible?* I steal a glance at Beckett, but his features remain blank. If he's at all surprised by this discovery, he doesn't show it. Either way, this isn't the place to discuss it. We've got to get back to our rooms and hope no one even noticed we're gone.

Tan-clothed citizens rush past us, barely noticing our presence in their festive haze. Some of the women wear their hair swept up in elaborate styles. Colorful strips of silky material hug their curves, wrapping around their waists and thighs. Their eyelids and cheeks glisten with hints of color – greens, purples and blues.

I'm completely distracted, mesmerized by the passing faces and fashion, when a hand cradles my side, just above my hips. I nearly jolt a foot in the air as the touch sends a pulse of electricity to my nerve endings.

"Everly, relax. It's just me," Beckett mumbles an inch from my ear. "This is too risky, it's too crowded. Let's go back."

I gulp and nod. The urge to retreat and hide overtakes me. He leads us toward a side street that branches off into smaller alleyways until we're alone.

"Sorry about tonight. I have a feeling Callan left us behind on purpose." He runs a hand through his hair, his demeanor relaxing slightly now that we've escaped the factions of people flooding the streets.

"Why would he do that?" I ask. "If he just wanted to ditch us, why even bother invite us at all?"

"Maybe he wanted us to get caught, maybe he just wanted a good laugh, who knows?"

I narrow my eyes at him but don't argue. Bringing us out here puts Callan and the others at a higher risk of getting caught. *Unless what Saya says is true and Callan believes he's exempt from rules, with no worries about being punished for not following them.*

"Look, I don't trust Callan. I don't trust any of them." He shakes his head. "We're supposed to believe that all of a sudden anyone cares what we think? All they care about is inventing rules and making sure we follow them. All of us. They don't want to hear our suggestions. And it's not worth telling them anything because they'll probably just use it against us somehow."

His anger swells in the air around us. I don't understand his sudden temper. I'm more worried than angry right now.

"Then why did you agree to go with them?" *And, more importantly, why did you invite me to come along?* Of course I don't say that last part.

"I wanted to see this place for myself. You know, beyond whatever pictures they paint for us. Beyond whatever stories they tell us. Because I don't believe what anyone tells me."

"I get it." My words are so soft, I'm not sure if he hears them. *Why is he so distant and distrusting?*

"And think about if I snuck out on my own," he adds. "I wouldn't have any idea where to go, kind of like now. But imagine if Kiera caught just me. She hates me. But if she catches a group and I happen to be part of it, she can't really single me out, you know?"

"You're right, you'd just blend in with everyone and they'd all get the same punishment." Just the mention of punishment makes my stomach churn.

A few minutes of silence weigh heavy in the air. It only serves to rattle my nerves even more. As much as I want to know more about my mother, I fear his answers might send me into an emotional tailspin. We can't afford that kind of attention. Even though we've reached some relative isolation, anyone could be around that next corner, including Kiera or Leader Imperant. I search my mind for a topic that will pass the time without threatening to trigger any tears.

"Why don't you ever wear your pin? The one they gave us?" I throw him a sideways glance.

He meets my gaze, eyes narrowed and features scrunched. Whether it's in disbelief, annoyance or something else, I can't tell.

"Why do you wear it?" he counters.

This guy can be so annoying. I'm just trying to fill the awkwardness between us with simple conversation and he has to make it all weird. I shrug my shoulders and answer honestly.

"It was a gift. I've always been told to show appreciation for gifts by either taking care of them or using them. And this one was clearly meant for us to wear."

"Well, I don't *appreciate* being forced to come here and I don't *appreciate* being told what to wear or what my future should or shouldn't be. So their little gift, they can keep it."

Oooookay. I make a mental note to steer away from anything he might twist into something more than it is. I guess we're back to the one thing he knows the most about.

"So what else do you know about my mother, or the woman you believe is her?"

Huddled together as we wind our way back to the living quarters, he tells me stories of how this woman would join his family for dinners and small celebrations like birthdays since she didn't have a family of her own. At least not in Westates.

As she grew to trust Beckett's family, she told them about her previous home. And how she was ripped from it. One day two Enforcers showed up at the end of her shift at the textile production facility. They escorted her to the medical facility, claiming she needed to be vaccinated against a virus that was spreading on the factory floor. They injected her with something, and the next thing she knew, she woke up groggy, in a similar facility but far from Eastates.

She was given a new identity and told that if she cooperated with this directive, her family in Eastates would be safe. She was permitted to start a new life but would never see her former family again. My eyes sting with unshed tears. Beckett grows quiet, maybe sensing that I can't handle any more information right now.

I remember the other side of that experience – when Dad came home and told us that Mom got sick at work and had to stay at the medical facility for a few days so that we didn't catch anything from her. For the first two days, we believed she was coming home. But that third day, an Enforcer showed up at our door, claiming that the virus overtook her. Her body had to be burned to avoid spreading the illness to anyone else. We never got to say goodbye.

My heart swells with regret when I consider all the time we could have had together, all the happy memories . . . lost. That is, if this woman really is my mother.

CHAPTER 44

UPPER DIVISION, CENTRESTATES

Thankfully we mostly remember the way back to Centrel Quarters. After a few turns that end up being dead ends, we're able to backtrack and find our way. Just as the Centrel Hall entrance comes into view, a voice rings out behind us.

"Hey! What're yeh doin out he'yre?"

My stomach drops as my pulse jolts. *Caught, just the two of us. This really doesn't look good.*

Beckett and I slowly face each other. His Adam's apple bobs as he gulps. If my fluttering nerves are any indication, my complexion is probably a few shades lighter than normal. Together, we turn toward the voice. My heart races and my eyes widen as recognition sharpens my focus. It strikes me faster than a bolt of lightning.

The old man who practically accosted me when we first arrived at Centrel Hall stands before us now. The moonlight illuminates his threadbare clothing and unhealthy pallor. I'd swear he looks even worse than the last time I saw him. A fuzzy nest of uncombed hair sits atop his head, riddled with debris.

"I've seen this guy before!" I whisper. Beckett's eyes narrow on me, disbelief washing over his features.

"Really! It was me and . . . Vanen. It was Vanen. Right before we first walked into Centrel Hall. This guy just showed up out of nowhere and said something creepy. Something about this place not being what we think it is." The memory sends a wave of goose bumps over my arms.

Although I sense his disbelief, Beckett turns his attention back to the stranger. He manages an even tone when he asks, "Is there something you want?"

The old man releases a bark of a laugh. "Oh there's lots I want, but I got no chance o' gettin' it."

"Well, I don't think there's anything we can do about that." Beckett crosses his arms, clearly unwilling to cower or just walk away. Even though that's exactly what my instincts are screaming for us to do.

"Oh, but I thinks ya can." He flashes us a crazed smile. It reminds me of pictures I've seen of carved pumpkins – jack-o'-lanterns. His crooked, yellowed teeth are riddled with hollowed gaps of emptiness.

Beckett tilts his head curiously. "Everly, wait over by the building. I'll be right there."

I shake my head. "No, I'm not leaving you alone. With him."

He gently grasps my hand. "Please, I need to ask him something. It'll just take a minute."

I snatch my hand back and throw it in the air, stomping away. *Of course, why not ask the crazy old man a question. It's not like we have anything else to do right now. Or that any answer he would give would make any sense.*

Overcome with frustration, I stop short after a few steps. I'm tired of Beckett stringing me along, leaving me with more questions than answers. He faces the old man, leaning toward him, and speaks quietly. I can't make out any of their words.

After a few minutes, Beckett twists left and right, scanning our surroundings. He startles when he notices how close I am, but I cross my arms and plant a foot before me. He has enough secrets and I'm not about to let whatever's happening here become the next one he keeps.

He spins back toward the man and rolls his left pant leg up. *What the heck is he doing?* Pivoting his hips, Beckett turns the back of his knee toward the man. In turn, the man bends down and grips Beckett's leg. Squinting his eyes, he kneels and angles his head an inch from the back of Beckett's knee joint.

Releasing Beckett's calf, the man slowly rises. Like an older, rougher mirror image, the man hikes his left pant leg up and straightens his leg. Beckett bends at the waist and inspects the same spot the old man examined on him. After Beckett looks, the old man yanks the tattered cloth back down to his ankle.

They face each other once again, speaking in hushed tones. I take a few steps toward them, more curious than ever. *Why would they expose their skin to each other? And what's there to say about it? It must be important, considering we're still out here.*

The old man spots my movement and shifts his attention to me. "Whad 'bout you? You got it too?"

"Hhh-have what?" I gulp, embarrassed by the slight stutter.

"She doesn't," Beckett quickly dismisses, raising a protective arm between me and the man. It's not necessary. Although his eyes rake over me, he makes no move to come closer.

The echo of stifled giggles and shoes touching down on pavement interrupts the conversation. Both men turn slightly toward the sound. A small group approaches, four figures to be exact. Our already limited time is cut even shorter. The old man leans toward us with urgency.

"War's comin.' Yeh tell who needs tah know," he grits through clenched teeth. Without waiting for a response, he shuffles away, in the opposite direction of our approaching company. I waste no time latching on to Beckett's hand and pulling him toward the bushes lining the building. *We have to hide. Right now.*

The foliage isn't thick, but it is tall. I press a finger to my lips and practically press up against him in hopes the broad leaves will serve as enough camouflage for these people to pass by without noticing us. They're just a few yards away when he grumbles, "I thought you wanted to go back inside. What is this?" He has the nerve to sound annoyed.

"We're not going anywhere just yet!" I whisper. "And what the heck was that back there?"

"I can't even! Are you kidding me?" His gaze is trained on the people rapidly approaching. My confusion yields to anger when I see it's Callan and the others. Before I realize what's happening, Beckett pushes through the light brush and plants himself in the middle of the sidewalk, blocking their way. Unsure what to do, I slip out from our hiding spot and shadow him, hanging back slightly.

Callan takes a surprised step back before a smirk slides across his face. "Well, look who finally decided to show up!"

"Show up? How about catch up? You left us behind on purpose!" Beckett sneers. Callan takes a looming step forward so they're separated by mere inches.

"Maybe you should be thanking me, *Beckey*. I mean, it looks like you two got some alone time together," he winks at me before continuing, ". . . behind the bushes, huh? That's why you came out here tonight, isn't it?"

Beckett launches himself at Callan, knocking him off balance. They hit the ground hard, grunting on impact. In a chaotic eruption, they funnel their urgent rage through flying fists and kicking legs. Beckett rolls on top of Callan, who delivers a swift punch to Beckett's side.

My heart races and my hands tremble. Inside, I want to cheer Beckett on, but fear grips me. Fear that Callan will hurt him and worry that we'll be caught. So much for keeping a low profile out here. I flinch every time one of Callan's strikes connect with Beckett. As they continue to throw hits, my stomach drops, consumed with dread.

When Beckett wraps his hands around Callan's throat, focusing on him with a venomous glare, I glance at the others. They all share matching looks of horror. Chander is the first to act.

"That's enough, guys!" He races over, dodging punches as he tries to separate the two. Consumed with their mutual hatred, they don't seem to notice him. When he takes a swipe to the head, Chander calls out, "A little help!"

Ryland stares, pressing a hand over her gaping mouth. Kinsley and I share a glance before cautiously tiptoeing into the commotion. I'm not too keen on taking a punch because these two can't control their tempers.

"Stop it!" Kinsley hisses as Chander takes a knee to the stomach and rolls over to his side. "Beckett! Callan! Knock it off!"

They ignore her commands, but Ryland finally finds her voice. She's able to cut through their blind rage, as her words have the intended impact.

"You guys, don't look but Kiera is on her way over here and she doesn't look too happy."

The guys release each other, clumsily backing away, seemingly regaining their senses. Using adrenaline-fueled energy, they push off the ground and stand.

Callan flinches when he presses a finger to his bloody lip. Beckett clenches his fist and, with his free hand, rubs his knuckles, which are probably swollen. Both guys brush themselves off while scanning the sidewalk and street.

Nearly frozen in place, my eyes shift from left to right, awaiting our capture and subsequent discipline. *This whole thing was so stupid. What am I even doing here?*

"Where's Kiera?" Kinsley demands as her head swivels left and right. "I don't see her anywhere."

After a frenzied moment of searching, Ryland smirks, planting her hands on her hips.

"So I sort of lied," she explains, raising her chin. "But you should all be thanking me right now. I got these two fools to stop rolling around on the ground together."

Kinsley struts over to Ryland, throws an arm around her shoulder and squeezes. "You are a genius!"

"So let's not waste it," Chander grumbles, massaging his temple. I'm guessing that's where he took one of several hits when he tried to break up the fight. "You can all stay out here and wait to get caught, but I'm going inside."

He brushes past Beckett and Callan, who stand a few feet apart. Callan rubs his chin as Beckett heaves deep breaths.

"Me too!" Ryland chases after him, with Kinsley on her heels.

The night air suddenly feels heavy and constricting. After a charged moment, Callan stomps after the girls, leaving just me and Beckett. When he steps toward me cautiously, I take a moment to study him. He's somehow both vulnerable and strong at the same time. The perfect curve of his cheek is marred by the swollen skin destined to blossom into a blue or purple bruise.

He takes a deep breath and motions for us to go. In silence, we trudge toward Centrel Quarters.

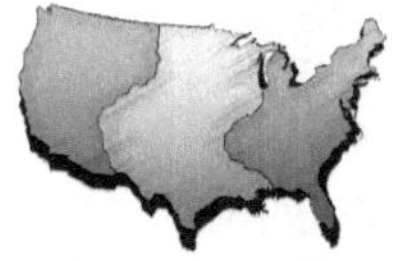

CHAPTER 45

UPPER DIVISION, CENTRESTATES

I nstead of taking the elevator, we sneak into the stairway. At least that won't ding when we reach our floors. We just have to guide the doors closed gently so they don't slam shut.

As we slowly climb the flights of stairs, my mind races with conflicting thoughts. Was Beckett defending me . . . or us? Did Callan's comment about us being in the bushes together burst Beckett's last molecule of self-restraint? Or maybe it was Callan's snide remark about us not keeping up with them. Either way, those two would have just kept pushing each other until one of them exploded. *It was bound to happen and given how the rest of this day has gone, why not tonight?*

I shake my head, wishing we could start this day over. Or better yet, just fast-forward until when we get to go home. That is, if Hayes and I even have a ride home. It's just one more thing to worry about.

When we reach the landing just outside the third floor, I stop.

"I'm tired of feeling like I have no idea what's happening here," I mumble, keeping my eyes trained on the ground.

"What?" Beckett asks, turning toward me, his face scrunched in confusion. Of course he didn't hear me. It was barely audible.

"I need to know what's going on." A fiery pit forms in my stomach. I'm getting the answers I want. Now. My hands shake but not from fear. From rising fury.

"What do you mean?" He leans close and lowers his voice. "I've been telling you all about your mother."

"But what was that out there?" I throw my hands in the air. That whole interaction with the old man on the sidewalk was so strange. It was like they knew each other, only they didn't. And then when the old man questioned me . . . as if he might know me too.

"That was me finally giving that asshat what he deserves." Although the smirk blazing across his face makes my heart thunder, this is no time to be distracted by it.

"No, I mean what you and that old man showed each other!" I stare into his eyes, unwilling to break the connection.

"Huh?" He shifts from one foot to the other.

"Beckett, stop it! Just tell me what's going on. And I don't mean tell me a little bit now and a little bit tomorrow. Just. Tell. Me. That's all I'm asking." I cross my arms and step closer to him, intentionally invading his personal space. The temperature seems to jump at least a dozen degrees in a matter of seconds.

His smirk drops, along with his shoulders. It only fuels my momentum. *I'm not giving up easily.*

"Show me!" I demand. "Show me what that old man was looking for on your leg."

He peers from side to side, apparently scanning for anyone who may be watching us. When his visual search reveals no intruders, he reaches down and tugs his pant leg up. He turns away and stretches his leg toward me. Taking full advantage of this rare opportunity, I bend down and wrap both hands around his shin. He shudders from my touch. At this point, he's probably a walking bruise and even the slightest brush against his skin could make him flinch.

I release him but hover just inches from the back of his knee. There's nothing there. I blow out a frustrated breath.

"I don't see anything," I mutter, shaking my head. If it takes all night, we will stay right here until he tells me what's going on.

"Yes, there is. Look closer." He points to the spot the old man focused on when he looked.

When I check again, only to get the same result, I back away in frustration.

"It's a U shape, about the size of your pinky nail."

I look one more time and actually see something – a faint outline that I'd never notice if I wasn't searching for it. I run a finger over it to make sure it's not just a hair or a squiggle of dirt. After I'm certain it's an intentional mark, I stand and face him.

"Okay, I saw it. So what does it mean?" It's barely visible. How can it be of any importance?

He casts an evaluating stare over me. "It's a tattoo. There's this machine that injects ink into your skin so the mark is permanent." He takes a deep breath and runs a hand through his hair. "The U stands for the Uprising. If you have that mark, it means you're part of it."

"What's the Uprising?"

"It's a group of people who share the same beliefs. People who are tired of the rules and control we all live under."

"An anti-government group!" I take a step back and throw a hand to my mouth to cover the gaping surprise.

"We're people, just like you, Everly. Look, no one should decide that some of us can't leave our homes during the day. Or at night. No one should tell us where to live and decide what food we eat and how much. And our clothes." He tugs on his green shirt. "Everyone in a Territory has to wear the same color. It's like a prison. The Societal Order holds power over everything. They decide who does what and when."

"They have to, Beckett. There isn't enough of everything to go around. They have to ration it so there's enough for everyone." Even as the words leave my mouth, they taste bitter. I've heard the same lies for so long that they're ingrained in my thoughts.

"Really?" He spreads his arms out wide. "Then why doesn't electricity seem to be a problem here? Do they even have day dwellers and night dwellers? And how do they have all this fancy food? Because this isn't like the stuff we have back home."

He's right. All this time, I blindly believed what we were supposed to. It never occurred to me to question anything.

"But everything we saw and did here...you never acted like you cared about any of it." My voice drops as warring thoughts clash in my mind. It feels like I'm standing at the edge of a cliff, unsure whether to jump.

"Of course I didn't. Was I supposed to broadcast what I was thinking?" He pauses before his tone crescendos with growing anger. "Oh wait, I was. We were all supposed to. Because that's exactly what they wanted!"

I shrink at his words. I know they aren't aimed at me, but the ferocity of his accusation stings as if I'm somehow responsible. He must notice my full-body flinch. Dropping his shoulders, he steps toward me and gently brushes the back of my hand with his thumb. The brief contact launches an electrical bolt to my core.

"I was sent here, Everly, for a reason. There are members of the Uprising in all three Territories, and we've infiltrated some pretty high positions."

"So someone here helped make sure you were chosen for the delegation?" *How can this be?* His gaze sharpens on me and he nods slowly, never breaking eye contact. My heart races as I struggle to take a normal breath. As unbelievable as it sounds, I sense he's telling me the truth. And if this is all real, it reminds me of the old man's warning.

"So when that old man said war was coming, is that what he meant? That the Uprising is going to start a war?" Faces of my loved ones flash through my mind – Easton, Dad and Josli. I can't lose them. Tears flood my eyes. Beckett threads his fingers through mine and squeezes my hand.

"It's not about starting a war, Everly. It's about breaking free from the rules. All the rules that we just accept. It doesn't have to be like this, and it shouldn't be this way." He drops his chin, tilting his head closer to mine.

"There's no way I could ever be a part of anything like that." I shake my head and step away from him, releasing my hand from his grip. I instantly miss the warmth of his closeness.

"I was sent here, Everly, to learn everything I could about the Societal Order. And about you. You actually know one of the leaders of the Uprising." He rubs his chin and watches me intently, as if he's memorizing my reaction.

My heart drops and my stomach twists. We both know who he's talking about. That's why he's been talking about her for days. It's why he's shown a strange interest in me from the day we arrived here.

He's trying to recruit me to join the group my mother helps to lead. The Uprising.

Acknowledgements

Thank you to all the readers who devour page afer page, always seeking more. I hope you enjoyed your time with Everly, Beckett, Hayes and all of the other characters. They'll be back for more challenges in *Uprising*. If you enjoyed the story, please take a moment to leave a rating or a review on Goodreads, Amazon and/or whatever retailer you may have purchased this book. Ratings and reviews help both authors and readers.

Publishing a book involves many steps and I couldn't have done it without the following people.

My amazing beta readers – Emily Angeline, Robin Asick, Diane Lesher and Stephanie DosSantos. Thank you for scrutinizing this story and calling out what needed better explanation, what was repetitive and what just didn't make sense. Your feedback made *Upheaval* many times better than it ever could have been without you.

My dedicated advanced reader copy readers – Misty Kevech and Cheryl Lindbeck. Your willingness to review the story and offer input motivated me to make that final push to publish *Upheaval*.

Thank you for taking the time to get to know Everly, Hayes and the rest of the crew. I can't wait to send you *Uprising!*

Scott, Landon and Aidan – thank you for your unwavering support. This author thing takes up a lot of time, but you have encouraged me to follow my dreams and never give up. For that, I am grateful.

A. E. Faulkner was born and raised in Pennsylvania. When she's not lost in a book, she loves spending time with her family, which includes three humans and three rescue cats. One of her biggest fears is the repercussions we will face when nature can no longer tolerate human destruction. As such, she never tires of reading dystopian-themed tales. To learn more about her writing, visit www.authoraefaulkner.com, email authoraefaulkner@gmail.com or connect on social media:

Facebook: @authaefaulkner
Instagram: @authoraefaulkner
TikTok: @authoraefaulkner

ALSO BY A.E. FAULKNER

The Nature's Fury series:

Darkness Falls (Book 1)
Anguish Unfolds (Book 2)
Devastation Erupts (Book 3)
Allegiance Unravels (Book 4)
Hope Emerges (Book 5)
Fate Collides (Short Story)

***

The Spin (Gaia Awakens climate fiction anthology)
Culling Day (Gaia Awakens climate fiction anthology)
Hierarchy of Need (Nature Erupts climate fiction anthology)

9 798991 556507